CASUAL

KOJI A. DAE

COVER ART BY CRISTINA BENCINA
INTERIOR ILLUSTRATIONS BY HELEN WHISTBERRY
EDITED BY ALEX WOODROE

Content warnings are available at the end of this book. Please consult this list for any particular subject matter you may be sensitive to.

TENEBROUS

PRESS

Published by Tenebrous Press.
Visit our website at www.tenebrouspress.com.

First Printing, February 2025.

Print ISBN: 978-1-959790-29-7
eBook ISBN: 978-1-959790-30-3

Cover art by Cristina Bencina.

Interior illustrations by Helen Whistberry.

Edited by Alex Woodroe.

Formatting by Lori Michelle.

All creators in this publication have signed an AI-free agreement. To the best of our knowledge, this publication is free from machine-generated content.

Selected Works from Tenebrous Press:

All Your Friends are Here
stories by M.Shaw

A Spectre is Haunting Greentree
a novel by Carson Winter

From the Belly
a novel by Emmett Nahil

Posthaste Manor
a novel by Jolie Toomajan & Carson Winter

The Black Lord
a novella by Colin Hinckley

Dehiscent
a novella by Ashley Deng

Agony's Lodestone
a novella by Laura Keating

Soft Targets
a novella by Carson Winter

Crom Cruach
a novel-in-verse by Valkyrie Loughcrewe

Lure
a novella by Tim McGregor

One Hand to Hold, One Hand to Carve
a novella by M.Shaw

More titles at www.TenebrousPress.com

VALYA:
MONTH SEVEN

CHAPTER ONE

WOMEN REST THEIR aching backs against the peeling paint of the hospital walls. The cluster gathered around Janice's door isn't a good sign. She must be behind schedule. Again. There are too many people for such a cramped space, and the dim fluorescent lighting doesn't help. At least the air purifiers purr in the belly of the old hospital, so I can slip the elastic of my mask off my ears and tuck the fabric into my purse.

"Is she in?" I ask.

The woman nearest the door looks ready to pop and gives me a disinterested shrug. I spin around and find a sliver of free bench between two not-so-round women. They both glare at me as I wiggle between them, our sweaty arms touching. But I'm just as pregnant as they are, and I'm not about to stand for who-knows-how-long just so they can be a tiny bit more comfortable. My psycher would be proud of me for asserting my needs.

A cork board with a few dozen photos provides the only decoration in the corridor, and my eyes wander over the pictures. They're paper photos, actually printed out, and their edges overlap. On top of the others is a purplish-faced newborn wrapped in a yellow swaddling blanket. One more healthy baby Janice helped deliver. As I stare, the faces of past patients and their newborns blend in an anonymity that makes bile rise in my throat.

My baby can't go up on that wall, pinned between countless bundles. An electronic photo frame would get rid of the clutter and give each baby a few seconds on its own. Generations ago, before the war killed off half of Earth's population, people gave obstetricians gifts after they delivered a healthy baby. I must have read that little detail somewhere, but the knowledge rests in me as if it's part of my identity. I wonder if my mother gave her doctor a gift when I was born. Perhaps a bottle of wine?

The slick button on the side of my phone gives a satisfying pop under the pressure of my thumb, letting me know it's listening.

"Buy photo frame for Janice."

The woman next to me huffs and turns away from my whispering.

The task appears on my to-do list and an assortment of elegant frames fills the screen. My thumb hovers above them, itching to flip through the options, but Janice could walk down the hall at any moment. A present is always better as a surprise.

I lean my elbows on my knees and the dark hair from my loose ponytail falls in front of my face. I pull out my elastic and smooth my hair back up. My face isn't dealing well with the hormones. A row of pimples has popped up along my cheekbones where the top edge of my mask rubs. Pregnancy is supposed to make women glow, but so far, it's turned my face into a festival of bacteria slip-sliding over oils, climbing on angry whiteheads. My fingers make a second pass over my hair, checking for stray strands, but this time they stop behind my ear where a hard bubble—barely bigger than a grain of rice—is lodged beneath my skin.

Childbirth can be unpredictable. If complications arise, hours might pass before Janice returns to her office. The meaty pad of my finger conforms around the bubble, pressing it against my skull.

A warm tingle spreads through my face and the tips of my ears burn. My boredom melts into anticipation.

APPOINTMENT SCHEDULED

My eyes roll at the cream-colored warning flashing in my mind. The system is connected to my phone's GPS. It should know I'm not at risk of being late for the appointment while planted outside Janice's office.

My finger presses longer, overriding the warning.

Two seconds of holding, and another five waiting, before Caz comes into focus. Seven seconds feels like forever when my closed eyes expect to see the inviting glow of my game. It's not like I'm junk for it, but those with a prescription, who actually need Caz, shouldn't have to wait for it.

Not that Orlov would agree.

4

"Valya, you haven't had a panic attack in years, and it's not likely you'll experience them again while using Casual," he would assure me.

Of course I'd argue with him. For the fun of it, not because I seriously believe I'll suffer panic attacks again. I've almost forgotten what they feel like. "But I have anxiety. I could have a panic attack."

"Casual controls your anxiety." He would glance at his tablet, nod, and make the "mmm hmm" sound with his lips pressed together that he always makes when checking my stats. "Your levels look great. Your Casual is working fine."

The imaginary conversation fades from my mind as the music starts. Not exactly music but a loop of horns and light percussion—watered down jazz with none of the harsh accents or diminished chords.

Then I'm in a thick forest of tall, black trees. The whole scene is black and white, not even shades of gray. Fiery red fur, thick and teasing, flashes from behind a distant tree. I grin and sprint after the fox. It darts away, sometimes just out of reach and other times a few trees ahead.

I lean into the slalom of the chase, letting my speed hold me up around curves, reaching out for the black tree trunks in the last moment. I'm weightless. Buoyant. Flying.

As I settle into the game, color seeps into the scenery. The white gains gray, then hints of dripping blues and greens. I'm careful to not look directly at the blossoming color. Keep my attention on the fox, or it will fade away.

A hand curls around my shoulder. My body tenses. The game detects the spike in my stress levels and cuts out. The hallway comes back into view and Janice leans in front of me.

"Your turn, Valya."

A flush creeps into my cheeks. A quick glance at my phone lets me know I've been playing for almost an hour.

After the peeling paint and crumbling concrete of the hallway, the clean sterility of Janice's office is refreshing. The medical equipment might be old, but it's free of dust with the cables coiled neatly on the floor.

"Let's get started." She motions me behind the white partition where two examination tables wrapped with pleather and covered with paper wait for us. Stirrups or an ultrasound, which exam kicks off the seventh month?

Janice senses my hesitation and points to the table with the portable ultrasound machine next to it. "Let's get a picture of your baby, shall we?"

My dirty sneakers slide off easily. My stocking feet curl against the tile floor. The paper crinkles as I mount the table and maneuver onto my back. A quick lift of my flowing tunic and lowering of my waistband reveals my stomach. Round and firm, the bump has expanded since my last visit with Janice. Before, it was amazing to see the tiny squirming fetus on the screen, but now it's believable that there could be a baby in there. In me.

"Twenty-eight weeks, starting the third trimester," Janice murmurs as she squirts cool gel onto my belly. She rubs the gel with the probe and body parts flash on the monitor in grainy black and white. Was that a hand? Maybe it was a foot. Janice speeds through these precious moments. They're probably not special for her. She sees hundreds of soon-to-be-born babies a month.

The machine is as ancient as the building. The monitor isn't even a touchscreen. Janice clicks with a mouse. Click, click—like the snapping of a bar of chocolate. My mouth waters. A circle appears on the monitor, then a line. A final click translates the shapes into a row of numbers. The sequence of shapes and the easy way she manipulates them reminds me of my fox in Caz. My mind relaxes, and my eyelids fall halfway closed.

"Perfect for seven months! Your baby is growing well, Valya. You have nothing to be worried about."

My muscles relax into the exam table, and a smile warms my lips.

"Can I see her face?"

Janice finds my baby's head with the probe. She holds it steady and snaps a picture. Baby-girl's profile takes up the bottom half of the monitor. Janice no longer has to point out the divots of her eyes or her tiny button of a nose. They're clear enough for a layman to see. Or at least for a mother to imagine.

"You know, around now your baby may be opening her eyes for the first time. Getting ready to see the wonderful world you have to show her."

The things I have to show her? A neglected city with crumbling monuments, a war-torn world under the thumb of an emergency global government. No. There are beautiful things too. The lush greenery overtaking the edges of the city. The technology that connects us. Friendship. And what I dream family can be.

Janice moves behind her desk while my soul drinks in the possibility of the life growing in me. She clears her throat, pulling me out of the moment, and I reach for a tissue from the stack next to the monitor. The goop on my belly fills the tissue and oozes onto my fingers. The mess lands in the plastic trashcan next to the table with a sloppy thud, and I wipe the excess on my pants as I reposition them.

"Is that all today?"

She looks at my chart and nods. "Next month you'll need blood tests again, but no lab work this time. I wanted to talk to you about your Casual though."

"My Casual?" I pause, one side of my mask already looped around my ear. I let it dangle, brushing the side of my face.

"Yes. You'll remember I told you months ago you'd have to get it turned off if you plan to register as sole caregiver. I see you still haven't done so. You're still planning on being the sole caregiver, right? No other caregiver to help you?"

Running down my list of trusted loved ones takes exactly zero seconds. "It's just me and soon-to-be baby girl."

That shouldn't be my answer. The baby growing in me should have an excited father waiting to catch her the moment she drops from the safety of my womb. Skylar would have been happy to hear about the baby a year ago. No. Happy isn't the right word. Skylar's emotions run too deep for ordinary happiness. He would have been blissed out.

"Oh, baby. A baby," he would have sung, sweeping me into his arms, swinging me around, covering my face with those fluttery, dry kisses he reserved for his rare moments of chastity.

I would have giggled—a girlish sound to encourage the affection—and snuggled my head into the perfect hollow between his chin and chest. He would have stroked my bare forearm, murmuring into my hair. Told me he loved me and everything had been worth it, hadn't it?

I play the scene out in my head, aching for it. I waited years for that moment of shared bliss. How many negative pregnancy tests did I hide deep in the bathroom trash so he wouldn't have to see them? I cried alone on the toilet, my bright red toenails visible through my tears, anchoring me to reality, reminding me of the blood that would come any day. I had tried to protect him from the pain, only sharing my joy.

Now the joy is wriggling in my stomach and I still can't share it with him. I tell myself I'm wrong. I'm not giving him enough credit. I'll go to him, knock on his door, and he'll see my flourishing belly. The words of our last night together will melt away. We'll get our moment. Our daughter will get her father. But some words can't be taken back.

"My Casual is prescription," I remind Janice.

She purses her lips and squints at me, her brown eyes set like unmoving stones behind their thin frames. She's an efficient woman, no time for pity. "Parents can become engrossed in their Casual environment and fail to take care of their baby. Over the past few years there have been several cases of neglect."

The image of a baby crying in its bassinet pops into my mind. It screams, wanting to be held and fed. The screams become a whimper. Where is its mother? In the next room, lying on the couch, playing her Casual. She doesn't hear her baby crying over the music in her head. It should be an absurd scene, but recent stories on the net prove otherwise. It wouldn't happen to me. Like I said, I'm not junk for it. But I bet all the parents it has happened to also said that.

"I didn't realize it could be so dangerous."

"Unfortunately, few parents realize the risks of the implants. Not just for their own health, but within all aspects of their lives. This time I have to tell you it's not a choice anymore. Two weeks ago they passed a law. The first year, the primary caregiver cannot have Casual."

"Right. That law. I read something about it. They can take away the baby?"

Janice nods. "And they will also stop your basic income to cover the expenses for childcare that year."

"When does it go into effect?" Hiding my shock is impossible. I'd planned to get it turned off eventually, but life sails by without the debilitating bouts of depression or anxiety attacks, and so I never got around to it.

"Not until January. By then your baby will be three months old. It will take time for you to adjust to life without Casual, and you don't want to make those adjustments while you're taking care of a baby." She glances at my file, scanning for something. Her frown of recognition lacks enthusiasm. "Ah, yes. Your psycher is Orlov. Talk to him about other ways to manage your mood during the next year. I wish you had done this when we first talked about it. It would have been easier if you had more time to wean off it."

"Yeah, easier," I mutter, my mouth dry, the words cutting like sandpaper. I shrug off a chill creeping up my spine. "I wanted to talk to you about my mask. Do you think it's okay if I go without?"

She doesn't even look up as she shakes her head. "Nope. Better safe than sorry when it comes to growing a life."

I hadn't worn a mask for years before I got pregnant, except on high pollution days, and it's been hard to get used to the constraints of one again. "But recent pollution levels have been—"

"Valya." She looks me in the eyes. I liked it better when my file distracted her. "I gave you my expert opinion. You're a smart woman who reads the blogs. You need to get used to making these kinds of decisions for your baby."

Outside, my eyes struggle to adjust to the bright orange light of the summer sun filtering through the cloud of smog. I sigh and pull the mask over my nose and mouth. It needs a new filter, and I haven't gotten around to buying one. But Janice is right. While the air is getting better, it's irresponsible to take chances. At least the masks are cute. Today mine has tiny ninja kitties wearing pink headbands. Can't get much cuter than that.

The day is too hot to be out. The few enclosed cafes on the main street are filled with people glued to tablets and phones, watching ads to earn credits. A few people lean back in their chairs, staring into space, probably Cazing out, but most people in the old city still can't afford the implant. I'm lucky. Less than ten percent of users have a medical prescription for Caz. The rest make do with the game on their phones or pay outrageous prices for the tech. My implant is necessary. Prescribed. Most importantly, free.

The only people walking around are Chasers and those of us with places to be. Most of the Chasers wear a few strips of strategically placed fabric, and their exposed skin has the deep red of constant burns. But they still wear their gas masks and combat boots. Dead heat of the day and they put up with the sweat of the rubber hugging their face to achieve their grunge aesthetic. That's dedication. Or insanity.

Two Chasers stand on the corner, scanning the area with minute tilts of their heads. They have that wiry, emaciated look common to Chasers—probably spending all their money on tech instead of food. Something must have spawned nearby. One Chaser finds his target and lifts his hands out in front of him. He twitches his fingers and rotates his wrists in a smooth, practiced motion. The second Chaser, a girl with a high ponytail and dark goggles, follows the motions of the first. Jewels glitter at the base of each of her fingers. She must have rich parents. Or maybe she's a model. Some of the nude ones make enough to keep up with the tech.

As she brings her hands back to her sides a large man in a suit shoulders into her, pushing her off balance. She stumbles, disoriented, but her companion reaches out and catches her arm.

"Hey, man, c'mon," he calls to the large man.

"Get off the streets, you freaks!" The large man's face reddens as he yells. His anger leaves a bad taste in my mouth, but I can't blame him. People who put tech in their brains and implants all over their bodies are freaks. Like me. But not for long. I'm getting mine turned off.

I sit on a bench by the side of the road. The leaves of a tree give me some shade, but they do little against the sweltering heat. A yellow wet-bulb warning flashes on the top left of my phone. I should be inside.

My phone screen displays a choice of articles to read. My finger absently picks out one on the latest tech developments before it reaches behind my ear to engage my Caz. Anyone passing by will have no idea my mind is actually sending imaginary foxes into imaginary holes. Might as well enjoy it while I can.

CHAPTER TWO

"I NEED MY Caz turned off." The statement's out of my mouth before I've closed the door behind me.

Orlov motions to the seat in front of him and refuses to say anything until my butt slides into it. His cardinal rule: sessions don't start until I'm calm and seated. Sometimes he lets me rave for ten minutes until my anger or frustration dissipates. I melt into the leather chair across from Orlov's desk. The familiar fabric cradles me in an earthy, sweet scent.

He takes a deep breath and allows silence to hang between us before starting. "Now, what's this about turning off your Casual?"

"That new law. I plan to be baby-girl's sole caregiver, so I need to turn it off."

He lifts one of his meaty hands to rub the back of his thick neck. "That stupid law. Your Casual is a prescription, and I'm able to monitor your usage. There are extra safeguards programmed into it, and we can add even more to structure your time and make it safe for you and your baby."

"So I don't have to turn it off?" My heart leaps, and I'm not sure whether I dread leaving the device active or am happy I get to keep it. Or maybe baby-girl just did one of her flutters.

"Babies are unpredictable, so scheduling doesn't always work with them. You would have to hire a nanny during your sessions, and you would no longer be able to run your device in response to stressful situations. The usage wouldn't be ideal, but it should be possible."

"Would the government pay for a nanny, since I have a medical reason?"

"Most likely not." The leather squeaks beneath him as he leans back. "Would a nanny be outside your budget?"

I echo his deep lean and try to appear nonchalant. "I think I might be up for syndication with my vlog. I've got a network considering me. They're supposed to call me next week."

"That sounds promising. You're not having success watching advertisements? Even a few a day could help you save enough money to pay for a couple hours of childcare a week."

"I can't watch those things. They make me want to crawl out of my skin." The thought of the advertisements starts my blood racing. I concentrate on the gray-orange clouds outside of the window to calm my nerves. They're probably filled with acid rain, but their familiarity wraps around me and my panic calms.

"I hoped the Casual would stabilize you enough to let you watch, but with your levels of anxiety, it was a long shot." He leans forward with a heavy sigh that's hard to not interpret as disappointment.

"Maybe it's a good thing."

He lifts his right bushy eyebrow, the left one staying low. "Excuse me?"

An image of the near-naked Chaser girl, thin from too much running and too little eating, flashes through my mind. "I only got this to help me get pregnant. It worked, and we should have shut it off then. Maybe I'm too dependent on the game."

Orlov clicks his tongue against his hard palate, the way cocky teens do. "You chose Casual because it was the best method to help you stabilize your moods. Getting pregnant was a great bonus, but not your only goal. Casual has worked brilliantly, and you have come quite far since you started."

The steady, slow rhythm of his voice makes my skin crawl, and I let out a deep groan. Baby-girl does a backflip. The sudden movement startles me and takes away my irritation.

"I'm just saying, I never wanted this in the first place. Maybe turning it off isn't such a big loss."

"But it is. Casual isn't meant to simply distract you, but to heal your neural pathways and allow your brain to develop healthy reactions to stressful stimuli. Ideally, when we wean you off, you will no longer need any medication. But based on your readings, now is not a good time to test your resilience. Not yet. If we turn it off, you'll likely slip into old thought patterns and we'll have to start from scratch in a year."

I itch at the nub on my neck. "But I've had this thing for years. When is it going to be long enough?"

○

Even before I met Skylar, I didn't consider Caz casual. The two-dimensional screen versions were downright gaudy. Most of them had the cachink of gold and jewels sounding in the background with bright flashes of light accompanying each move. People wasted hours playing them. Like any of my peers, I would spin one up while waiting for the bus or between classes, but by the end of a level my jaw ached and my molars were sore from clenching. Skylar told me to forget the game. It was a distraction. "The latest opium of the masses."

Except opium is supposed to be relaxing. "More like the latest meth."

He shrugged and kissed my forehead. "You get the point."

When Orlov suggested a Caz implant to help manage my dexiety—my name meant to make depression and anxiety at least sound cute—a mix of laughter and revulsion filled me.

"No. I've seen those freaks, staring off into space all day, playing games in their heads."

Orlov was standing at his window. He turned his head, and my unfocused eyes zeroed in on the large mole on his left cheek. His dark eyes and brown skin were the same as Olivia's, my best friend since childhood, and they inspired a flicker of the same trust I had in her. "Valya, I'm concerned you may self-harm again. It's time to try something more than therapy."

My three-quarter-sleeve did nothing to hide the thick scars on my forearms. My thumb flitted to my jeans and found the matching lumps on my upper thighs. I jerked my hands away and tightened them into fists.

"A medical Casual differs from the gaming system. It's targeted to meet your specific needs. It could help you concentrate and ease your anxiety. You could vlog more regularly, earn some money. It might even help with your fertility issues."

"We've only been trying for a year. Besides, isn't it addictive?" I didn't mention Skylar was covering my living expenses, so I didn't need to worry about the success of my vlog. Or lack of it in recent months.

Orlov nodded. "There are risks. But we can put in safety features to help prevent addiction. The benefits outweigh the risks at the moment. Besides treating your mood disorders, we can also monitor you in a way we can't without an implant. Our response to an emergency would be much faster."

An emergency? It wasn't as if I was standing on the precipice of suicide. The word echoed through my bones, and I had a sudden sensation of falling. I jolted upright in the chair. "Skylar will hate it. Are you sure there's no other option?"

"No other option is as good. We can try medication again, but I'm hesitant, considering how you responded last time. We can also increase your therapy, but without remote monitoring, I have to recommend you move into a group home where they can monitor you more regularly."

A group home. Away from Skylar.

"I don't even like the games." The complaint was a weak, last-ditch attempt to avoid the implant.

"I've seen the interfaces you've tried so far on your profile, and I'm not surprised you don't like them. They most likely aggravate your anxiety and do little to reduce your depression. You need something more rhythmic and subtle." How long had he been my therapist? Five years or six? My longest adult relationship, he nailed down my concerns with precise insight. "Have you heard of Nature?"

He forwarded the link to my personal profile before wrapping up our session. The first screen shot of the game—a red fox with a sleek coat and its tongue lolling out of its mouth as it chased a rabbit through the snow—reminded me Orlov was usually right about my treatment options. Maybe Nature was actually more natural than the other skins for the game.

Instead of glittery jewels, Nature featured soft, desaturated colors. Lilac, tan, periwinkle, gray—the colors were so neutral, it was almost as if they weren't there. They were the quiet colors living inside me, looking for a way out, echoed onto my phone's screen in pleasing shapes. Perfectly round spheres. Little flowers. The occasional tree or snowman.

Moves made a soft crunch, like footsteps on gravel. When the move created a match, a clear bell sang out a soft, "ting." The background music oscillated between jazz and a meditative drone, and I didn't feel cheap or ashamed when I answered its siren-call.

But on the phone, lives ran out. Half an hour ticked by too slowly before another red apple appeared on my tree of life.

A week later, I received my implant at the New Sofia Clinic.

"Valya, I don't think you understand how critical the device is to your progress." Orlov taps his full lips with a stubby finger. "It's easy to forget what life was like before you started this treatment."

"I remember what my head was like before. A mess." But those years of living on slippery edges have become a distant echo, as if they happened in another lifetime. "I just don't see another option. I can't afford a nanny. I don't have a partner. I'm a parent doing what I have to do." I take a deep breath and it's echoed by the hint of a hiccup in my belly. "I will give up what I need to if it means being the best mother for my baby."

"What if being the best mother for your baby means taking care of your mental health?"

His words sink into my ears like barbed hooks, readying the landing strip for his next approach.

"There is another option. Emerson Enterprises has a new clinical trial. It involves placing a tandem implant in your baby's brain." Orlov's words hit like a silent knife.

"An implant? In a baby? That's absurd."

Two years ago Orlov explained the risks of getting a Casual implant. A .05 percent chance it would not take, and a .006 percent chance it would damage my brain. A .003 percent chance the damage would be permanent and severe. All that for a 70% chance the treatment would ease my dexiety. Not a great tradeoff. But the risk was necessary. He was sure of himself and the tech. Now, leaning back, his fingers steepled in front of his dry lips, he hesitates.

"You know there are always risks with implants, Valya. But great advancements have been made in the past two years. It's safer."

"For babies?" Babies have tiny brains. Growing brains. They have years of connections to grow. Wouldn't a needle to the gray matter and little sinews reaching out to take hold of their imagination be riskier for them?

His mouth opens, but nothing comes out. His silence says everything.

A snort of laughter escapes me. "Has it even been done before?"

"Yes, it's been done successfully."

I narrow my eyes. "On how many babies?"

He looks away. He's supposed to be a professional—unfazed by these questions. The corner of his mouth twitches. He licks the spasm away before answering. "Two. One in Paris and another in Tokyo."

"Two," I parrot back to him, mulling the number over in my mind. How old are those two babies now? Toddlers? Or still infants? Two is not enough. They can't even get statistics from two babies.

"With the advances in sharing technology, a tandom rig could have great benefits for both the mother and the baby."

"What do you mean?"

"An infant couldn't control a full Casual on their own, but they could tap into your gaming experience. Not only would the device entertain them, they would also learn critical manipulation and reasoning skills," Orlov explains. His dark eyes gleam with possibility. He thinks I'll let them put a Caz in my baby. The man I've worked so hard to trust fades, becoming just another man from Padalo. That's what he is, after all—a man from my old neighborhood who happened to get out and become a psycher. He thinks we'll be their experiment. Why wouldn't he? He has spent years grooming me for this moment. Every man from Padalo thinks, if they put in enough time, they can take what they want. "The trial will pay for the placement, of course. It will cost you nothing."

Nothing? Everything costs something. Sometimes it isn't money, and those times are usually the worst. "No."

The word comes out calm, quiet . . . final.

Orlov doesn't argue. He nods with an acceptance that makes me think he expected my answer, but words continue spilling out of me, defending my decision. "She won't get Caz until she's old enough to decide she wants one for herself. She won't be your experiment because of my weaknesses."

"Then you want your Casual turned off? You're sure about this?"

I hesitate, trying to remember my life without Caz. Was it so bad? My brain can't latch onto anything solid in the elusive fog of my memory.

"Yes."

"Okay, we'll need to wean you off of it before you give birth. For the next two weeks I'd like you to try limiting your use on your own. Try to notice when you use the device and why. Think about what coping mechanisms you will replace your Casual with."

"Coping mechanisms?" I roll the term over my tongue, remembering its clinical, antiseptic taste.

"It wasn't that long ago. Surely you remember how traditional coping mechanisms work."

All I remember is how they didn't work. Long walks in the sunshine. Yoga. Writing. They never organized my thoughts or brought me joy and clarity, just made me tired enough to sleep.

Cutting. That was a coping mechanism that worked. Slicing into my skin, the searing pain getting stronger and sharper until the fog in my soul lifted and I felt light and adventurous again. Like Skylar. People like Skylar don't need to cut though. They don't need Caz. They're born happy. I admired that about him and had hoped it would rub off on me. Maybe, if our skin traded enough sweat and hormones, I would get some of his bottomless joy.

"I remember," I assure Orlov. "And I would like you to turn it off now. I'm ready."

Orlov stiffens in his chair and drums his tobacco-stained fingers on his desk for a few syncopated beats. I can't tell if he's frustrated or surprised, but I'll take either as a victory. Point for Valya. I settle deeper into my chair. It's been a long time since I've kept score, but it might be time to start again.

"I have to insist on a weaning period. As your psycher I cannot, in good conscience, turn it off so abruptly."

"Fine," I grumble. "But I'm not going to use it."

"That's great. I sincerely hope you will succeed. I'll turn off the prompts. It'll still monitor your levels, but you won't get a message telling you when to play. You'll decide when, and if, you need a session. I'll also set the device to require a long-start each time you play, to help you break your habits. It will be best for you if you can do as much of this as possible under your own willpower, and not because you no longer have access to the device."

CHAPTER THREE

MY LOCK IS the old kind, with an actual key instead of a palm reader. It sticks, and I have to jiggle the key until it pops to the left. After my daily stroll, meant to keep me in shape and stave off pregnancy pains, I hang the keyring on a hook and enter my apartment. The place is small but mine. If I was a more optimistic person, I'd call it cozy. But even Caz can't make me imagine the dingy one-bedroom conversion as more than what it is. A heavy woven blanket lies on my mattress during the day so I can use it as a sofa. I sling my purse onto it and glance at my desk.

My tablet is always on, waiting for me to tap its screen and start vlogging. Since my appointment with Janice, I've been meaning to do a piece on the laws regarding parents and Caz. A few tabs with research are still open.

Next to the computer my air filter whirs. I take off my mask and toss it on top of my purse. I need to give it a good rinse, but I leave it crumpled on the couch and go to the kitchen for a glass of water. I suspect my kitchen was once a bathroom. It's all tile, with a small drain in the center and a large mirror behind the sink. The table and two folding chairs take up most of the floor, and a microwave and an electric kettle crowd the counter. The water runs from the tap with a slight tinge of orange rust. Not enough to worry about when washing, but enough to make me keep bottled water in the tiny refrigerator.

The cool water, sweating against the plastic bottle, eases the flush in my cheeks from the walk up three flights of narrow stairs. But no sooner is the water in me than baby-girl kicks my bladder to get it out.

I can still maneuver between the rooms well enough, but I suspect in another month I'll be stubbing my toes and squeezing myself into the tiny area.

The bathroom is little more than a closet. The shower head is sandwiched between the sink and toilet. When I rest my heavy body on the toilet seat—cheap plastic that bends and threatens to crack—I miss the jacuzzi tub of our apartment. No. Not ours anymore. Skylar's.

○

After we made love for the first time, we lay tangled in his soft gray sheets, clean only moments before but then drenched with our sweat and covered with our colliding scents. My leg crossed over his hairy thigh, boldly possessive, as my long purple nails drummed idly on his wooden headboard.

"Wood." A rich, satisfying thud reverberated through me each time a finger fell. "It feels alive."

"I can assure you it's hundreds of years dead."

I stopped caressing his headboard and moved to caress his very alive cheek, probing its elasticity beneath the pads of my fingers.

"Where'd you collect so much death?"

Our eyes locked. I paused my roaming fingers and let the question hang heavy between us. The moment broke with his heavy laugh and he grabbed my hand in his, pulling me onto his chest.

"I love you, Valya." It was the first time he said it, but he didn't sound hesitant like the boys in high school who hid behind a deep blush when they whispered it after sex. He wasn't being proper, but honest. "You could move in here. Bring all that funny life you pack away. Save me from this oppressive death."

A nervous little rush of air, somewhere between a hiccup and a laugh, fell from my mouth onto his chest. He still hadn't been to my dorm, everything pressed in on itself, the furniture made of crappy chipped particle board. He knew I lived on basic income, but he didn't understand how basic that amount actually was. Not if he could afford an airy two-bedroom on his own.

"I can't afford half the rent on this place." It wasn't hopeful or coy. It was the truth.

"That would be a problem if I asked you to be my roommate. But I didn't. I'm asking you to be my girlfriend. You know, men used to take care of the women they loved. They enjoyed doing it. Call me old-fashioned. I'd love to take care of you. Make your life easier so you can concentrate on adding your beautiful insights to the world."

"You're a relic." I tapped his headboard again. "A relic surrounded by relics."

"Then bring me into the present." He laughed—that deep, free way he had—and flipped me over, pinning me beneath his solid weight. Then we kissed and made love, very much in the present.

Two weeks later, I moved in. He rented a self-driving pallet to deliver my plastic bins of clothes and trinkets. My stuff fit neatly folded into the drawers of his oak dresser and hanging behind the heavy doors of his wardrobe. A few knickknacks took up space on the buffet in his living room and my toothbrush hung in the vanity. But the apartment was still his, filled with his carefully selected collection from the ghost-villages that surround the city. I didn't mind being another piece of his curated anthology. I convinced myself I could be archaic, too.

The tapestries I found around town softened his hard corners. I added miniature crystal structures that mimicked the architecture of New Sofia. He didn't complain as I took away his space and made it ours, although his disdain for the crystals was almost solid enough to touch.

As I brought the apartment into the twenty-second century, I drifted there with it. Every crystal sculpture reminded me to assert my independence. The apartment was ours, even if he paid for it. I couldn't be his, even if he paid for me.

I try not to let myself miss anything about him. The breakup was a good thing. After I moved out, I was able to use Caz more regularly, and my mood finally stabilized. Orlov says I'm healthier than ever. Sure, I gave up Skylar's great apartment, but I force myself to take pride in this small place. My place.

When I moved in, I scrubbed it clean, filled the cracks in the walls, and applied a fresh coat of light orange paint, a shade brighter than the sky outside. I'm more careful with this apartment than the dorm I was living in when I met Skylar. The dorm was temporary—a waiting tank until something bigger and better came along. This place isn't any bigger or better, but I'm smart enough to know it's permanent.

Sometimes it squeezes in on me, and I think I understand how baby-girl feels confined by my womb. I want to stretch and push the walls just an inch or two further out. I'm not sure how I'll fit a baby in here, but for the first few months she can't take up much room. It'll be cozy—baby-girl and me sandwiched tight on the bed, taking showers together in the bathroom, eating together in the kitchen. I'll have to get one of those baby carrier backpack things, since there won't be room for a stroller. Sometimes they show up at Becca's secondhand store, and they aren't too expensive. It'll be intimate with her always tied to me.

My feet pulse when I prop them up against the wall, laying back on the colorful cover of my bed. The serious swelling hasn't started yet, but my legs appreciate the rest. I concentrate on the squirming of baby-girl inside me. The exhaustion started before I knew I was pregnant, and it hasn't let up since.

For weeks after I left Skylar's apartment, I was tired and emotional. Olivia helped me find this apartment and gather my few belongings when Skylar was out. The breakup was the kind of emergency she was always there for.

"It's normal to be sad," Olivia assured me. "You loved the asshole. It'll take time."

"How long?" We were sitting on my couch-bed, our backs against my wall, her dark brown feet crossing over my light tan ones.

"They say one-third the time you were together. Or three times as long. I forget." She kicked playfully at my feet and sat up straight. "Whatever. It just takes time, okay?"

Time. I refused to accept her answer, and I had a weapon that could stop the tears immediately. I spent hours of every day escaping into Caz. Whenever the sobs welled in me, I pressed the grain behind my ear. If I stopped playing, the memory of my final argument with Skylar rushed in on a wave of guilt that left a metallic taste in my spit. He was right. I leaned too heavily on the game instead of him. He was my boyfriend. We were trying to make a life together, a child, even. To shut the guilt up, I dove back into the game—deeper and longer sessions.

I played instead of sleeping, and the device sent a warning to

Orlov. He didn't bother to call me, just added a check-in to my schedule and let the confirmation receipt warn me of the meeting.

I took special care getting dressed that morning. My under-wire bra bit into the soft underside of my breasts, not resting quite right, so I opted for a supportive cami layered underneath a tweed tunic. The material was rough on the skin of my arms, but at least it distracted me from the growing ache in my heart. My skinny jeans were too tight, so I chose bright blue tights—my only thermal-wear—covered by a brown maxi-skirt.

Snow had fallen the night before, and my leather boots made a satisfying crunch as I walked from my apartment to Orlov's office in the center. Orlov had issued a bus ticket to my account, but the bracing chill of the day settled my nerves and distracted me from my memories.

"You've been using your casual quite a bit," Orlov said as soon as I hung my coat on his coat rack and sank into the buttery chair across from his desk.

"I broke up with Skylar."

We stared at each other for a long moment. His eyes combed my face carefully and I wondered if he was scanning me with his ocular implant, getting a new diagnosis on my mental health.

"That must be difficult," he said.

I snorted, shifting my weight to lean on the arm of the chair. "I expected you to congratulate me or something. You hate Skylar."

"I don't hate Skylar. I believe he's a troubled young man and most likely unable to have a healthy relationship at this point in his life. But that doesn't mean I can't understand how ending your relationship would be difficult for you. You were entangled deeply with him, and I respect your emotional process."

That's when the tears started. First in silent lines down my cheeks, brushed away by my fingertips. But as Orlov cocked his head to the side, his gray hair falling across his forehead and covering his thick, furrowed brows—the picture of concern—a sob grew in me. The sobbing was a weak, wretched sound, and I hated every revealing hiccup. But I couldn't stop. My fears turned themselves inside out and marched across his heavy oak desk, on display for him.

He pushed a box of tissues toward me and waited for me to gain control again. With a few quacking honks of snot into the soft tissues I stopped the sobs.

"Have you been crying often?" he asked.

I shook my head. "When I get worked up, I Caz out, and it goes away."

"How many times this past week have you used your Casual to keep these kinds of emotions at bay?"

The truth would have made me sound even more desperate and pathetic than I felt. My mouth did this weird fish thing, opening and closing several times without enough tension in my lips to form words.

Orlov held up his hand to stop my efforts, saving me from melting into another unnecessary display of weakness.

"Even with your history and inconsistent use of Casual until now, these reactions are more intense than I would expect in this situation. I'd like you to run down to the lab and have a hormone panel taken."

"Now?" The thought of showing my red, puffy face to the callous nurses in the lab made a weight settle over my lungs. I forced myself to take deep, even breaths to keep from crying again.

"I want to see if we need to add a course of medication to your therapy to help re-balance your hormones. Your neurotransmitter panels are within the expected range, but I think there might be something the device isn't picking up."

I leaned against the cool metal wall of the elevator. The crying episode had sucked the last of my energy out of me, and I struggled to keep my eyes open.

My head drooped, and I almost dozed off as the technician bound my left arm with an elastic band to draw my blood. As she slipped the needle beneath my skin, I yawned instead of wincing.

She snapped off the elastic, placed a cotton ball over the needle and withdrew it from my vein. The single vial of blood was dark, more brown than red.

"Orlov wants the results immediately." I wished the technicians wore name tags. Maybe using the sour woman's name would make me sound less demanding.

"Of course," she muttered. She turned to a large machine on the table behind her, keyed a sequence into the keyboard, opened the small door, and popped my vial of blood into a stand.

It only took a few moments of whirring and churning for my results to appear on the monitor. White numbers on a black screen.

My entire existence, summed up so medical professionals could understand without having to look at me. The tech scanned the screen, making sure all the tests had valid results. As one result came in, a self-satisfied smirk appeared on her small mouth.

"You know what's wrong with me, don't you?" The exhaustion lifted, giving just enough room for indignation to slip in.

"Well, I suspect. But only a psycher can officially interpret the results. I'll send these to your profile, and Orlov can discuss them with you."

It was the standard answer. Still, if she couldn't share the results, she should practice keeping a straight face when they came out. A deep desire to reach out and smack the smug smirk off her lips made my hand twitch. It was a strange impulse, but the image of my hand contacting the corner of her mouth was imprinted in my mind. I bit down on my lower lip to keep from acting on it and left with a nod, afraid to release my lip to say anything.

Orlov had the same reaction as the technician when he read my results. A surprised lift of the eyebrows and the twitch of his full mouth into that same half-smile.

"What is it?" I asked, irritation clipping my words. "It can't be something bad, since everyone thinks it's hilarious."

The muscles around his mouth quivered as if he was fighting with them to drop the smile. But the smile won.

"You're fine. Your hormone levels are in the normal range, for a pregnant woman."

A prickling grew over my flesh, and everywhere it ran, my skin fell numb. I exhaled, my eyes closed halfway, and I sank back into my chair. I didn't know how to respond to such a cruel lie.

"But I can't get pregnant," I said. "I'm . . . "

"Infertile?" He filled in the word I couldn't bring myself to use. "You know your mood disorder likely contributed to your infertility. With Casual regulating your mood, your body must have decided it is safe to have a baby. You were hoping for this, weren't you? Trying?"

My head nodded on its own, my thoughts far away from the mechanical action. Pregnant? The baby Skylar and I had longed for was now in me. Maybe it was a sign that our breakup was stupid, that we were meant to be together.

I went home, sat at the kitchen table, and thought of how I

would tell Skylar. I settled in the hard folding chair by the window and dreamed of showing up on his doorstep, a positive pregnancy test in hand. He'd wrap me up in those strong arms. The spicy scent of cloves would flood my nostrils. We'd forget our fight, and he would see how Caz helped me. Helped us.

But what if it didn't turn out the way I hoped? It was best to be civil. Delicate. I pulled out my phone and tapped my way into my contacts, down to Skylar's profile.

Skylar only allows those with an established relationship to contact him. Submit an explanation of your relationship to Skylar in the box below for confirmation if you would like to send a message. Or use his public email at this link.

I didn't know what to make of the message. It must have been a mistake. He couldn't have deleted me from his personal contact list. Not so soon.

But I couldn't bring myself to test my theory. Because what if he didn't want to see me? What if he was really done with me? I couldn't handle that. I'd wait and show him the bump, once I got one. It would feel more real.

Seven months later, I've fallen into a rhythm. I'm okay being home alone. Not exactly alone. Baby-girl is still with me, always kicking, doing her flips. The crying hormones settled down after the first trimester, and there's no sense triggering them again by thinking about what could have been with Skylar.

My hand worms its way beneath my head, massaging the base of my skull, releasing the tension from my neck. After a few rhythmic squeezes it sneaks around to the side, the base of my palm on my jaw, my fingers millimeters from my Caz.

"No, no," I tell my twitching fingers, pulling them down to my swelling bump. "We've stopped that." Instead, I rub my belly and wait for baby-girl to kick against my hand.

CHAPTER FOUR

LATE IN THE MORNING, with a mug of instant coffee and a bowl of granola swimming in re-hydrated calcium and protein supplements, I plop into the chair in front of my desk and turn on my tablet. A line of vlogs queue up along the side of my screen. Most of them I swipe away without bothering to open, but one woman catches my eye. Smiling a large, carefree smile, she looks directly into the camera, a picture of the Eiffel tower superimposed behind her. I've been watching Lindsay for three years now. I might have started watching because she's in Paris or because Edges recommended her, but over time I've grown fond of her. It's almost like she's a friend of mine, even though she never responds to my vlog. Of course, why would she when she has over a hundred thousand subscribers? I double tap on her image.

"Good morning boys and girls, and welcome to the latest edition of Masks Off, your critical examination of today's world. I'm your host, Lindsay, and this vlog is sponsored by Edges, the realest reality you'll get."

Edges. Even her saying their name makes my heart jump. My application for their syndication has been out with them for nearly five months, and today I finally have my interview with one of their reps. Without Skylar's support, I need someone to guide my vloging, and Edges is the best fit. I'm not as sultry as Lindsay with her matte red lips and smoky eyes, but I've got a real perspective. No fake news on my vlog. Edges curates authenticity. They'll find a place for me. They have to.

"Today we're going to talk a bit about flogging. You heard me right—feeling logging. Wait wait. Before you close your screens, I get it. Most of you are anti-tech. You know I hate it as well. But it remains our responsibility to understand the tech seeping into our lives."

I shift in my chair and roll my eyes. Talk about walking edges. Lindsay is leaning more pop every day. But I follow her bidding and half-listen as I crunch on my granola.

"As you may know, flogging involves a series of three implants: casual with the connect software, an ocular implant to record what a feeler sees, and a pulse implant to record blood pressure and rhythm throughout the experience. Yeesh! Invasive much? These experiences are recorded and uploaded for other Casual users to purchase. Today I've got Simone in the studio—he's a best-selling flogger with more than one million sales."

The camera pans out to show a wiry young man with large sunglasses.

"Thank you for having me Lindsay." His posture is twitchy, but his voice is smooth and low. "It's always a pleasure to share the concept of flogging with inexperienced users."

"Inexperienced would be an understatement. I don't even have a basic casual, so you'll have to start with a very simple explanation. Why do people buy feels?"

"That's the question a lot of people have before they make their first purchase. After . . . well, the question of why never comes up again." They both laugh and my lips turn up in response. "The attraction is quite simple, really. In the modern world experiences are restricted. Travel, for example, is nearly impossible. But with flogging it doesn't have to be. What is your favorite thing to do, specific to Paris?"

"Mmmm. Well, I enjoy going up to Sacre-Coeur around sunset."

"Tell me about it."

A small smile takes up residence on the corner of Lindsay's mouth. "You've been there, I'm sure. But I'll tell our viewers. The colors are amazing. Reds and purples over the entire city as yellow lights come on in the windows below. And it's lively. Musicians. Dancers. Children laughing."

I imagine my mother, what little I remember of her, enjoying a sunset over Paris. But try as I might, her face remains that of a generic woman.

"It's a lovely scene. Now, do you think your description captured it?"

"Parts of it. There's more, of course."

"What about a picture. Does it bring up the same emotions?"

The screen shows a photograph of the white church, its domes towering over small groups of people lounging on the steps leading up to it.

"No, not at all."

"Well, flogging can. It allows people to experience being places and doing things they might not have access to in their own lives. It gives them not only sight, sound, and your opinion, but smells, ambiance, and so much more."

I snort into my bowl. The experiences are still filtered, even if they're immersive. They aren't reality. Lindsay takes a different approach, discussing privacy and the intimacy of sharing what was once considered personal.

I shut off the vlog before it finishes. "You're slipping, Lindsay," I mumble to my empty room. "And I know just who can replace you."

I sit at my desk in a flowered tunic and tug at the stray strands of my hair as I check the clock on my tablet for the twentieth time. 14:26. Four minutes until my call with Brian from Edges network. A glass of water rests next to my arm. My heart flutters, but I'm ready. I have to be ready. This is my chance at a breakthrough.

If my Caz still gave warnings, it would tell me I need a session to help calm down. I let my fingers play on the lump beneath my skin. Four minutes. That's plenty of time for a quick race with the fox. I'll be more settled, ready for my interview.

I pull my hand down and take a small sip of water. It's not worth it. I can get a job without Cazing out. Otherwise, I really am junk for it. I tap on recent articles to distract myself. The top recommendation: *What's your baby doing in week 29?* I tap on it and scan to learn about size and positioning.

Apparently baby-girl's working on grasping motions. I picture her in my dark fluids, opening and closing her tiny fists. I do the same with mine.

"What are you grasping at, baby?" I murmur to my stomach. "I'm grasping at our future."

As if on cue, my tablet emits a low beep to signal an incoming call. I take a deep breath, straighten my spine, and press accept.

"Valya!" Brian booms as soon as his image appears on my screen. His smile is wide, his sandy hair tousled. "So good to pin you down in person."

"Hello, Mr. Brian." I stammer over his name and bite my lip. Did I just say mister? He probably has me pegged as a geek. "Nice to meet you, too."

"Right." His smile freezes, as if the internet has gone out. Then he's in motion again. "Well, let's get down to business, shall we?"

I nod, not trusting my stupid mouth to speak again.

"As you know, vlogging is all numbers. Any network or free agent will tell you that. Number of views. Number of clicks. That special, magical formula that gives us ad revenue."

I nod again and reach for my water. My throat is like a desert, but I try to sip instead of guzzling the drink.

"You've been on Edges' radar for a while now. I'm sure you know why. Dating Skylar? Living with him? That guy is just clicks on a stick, isn't he? People want to know more about the man who plans to lead the revolution. You were their in. We picked up on you as soon as your views started spiking. Three years ago, right?"

"Right." I wait for the giant but to drop.

"Now, I see you've started posting more regularly. Sometimes there's a vlog a day. That's great. A little strenuous for a one-person get up. We recommend five days a week, even three for some creators." He's leaning back, not looking at the screen, talking to the echoes in his office thousands of miles away.

"You've got consistency. We like that. But I'm afraid your numbers have been dropping. You were gaining viewers when you were with Skylar. Didn't matter that you weren't consistent. But I've heard you two broke up."

I doubt my microphone is sensitive enough to pick up my, "Yes."

"Damn shame that is. I should have caught you a year ago. No in with him at all anymore?"

I put my hand on my belly, out of the viewscreen. "No. But if you'd let me . . . "

He doesn't let me. "You're at what? Ten thousand subscribers?"

"Yeah." It isn't enough. He knows it, and so do I.

"I'll give you a month. No, two months. I'll give you two months to hit fifty thousand. If you can do that, then you've got the sparkle

Edges needs. Otherwise, I'm afraid we can't offer you a spot. Keep in mind, if you make it on Edges, we expect you to keep growing. Our smallest creators have hundreds of thousands of subscribers."

"I understand."

He flashes me a yellow-toothed smile. "Be cool, baby. Things are all good."

The screen turns black before I can answer. Things are definitely not all good.

My heart zips like a hummingbird, too fast for me to catch. I need it to slow down. I can't figure out how to more than double my subscribers with it buzzing around in there and baby-girl grasping and punching. My breath explodes in short puffs as if I'm a dragon starting up.

"Stop it!" I slam my open palms on my desk, sending the contents rattling. The water almost spills on the tablet. I breathe deep in my nose and out slowly but forcefully through pursed lips. Then two dragon's breaths, mouth open, exhales hot. "Okay."

The buzzing continues. I could silence it with my Caz. A satisfying long hold and then ten minutes with the fox. That's all I need to see straight. To think straight. To come up with a plan.

A plan. That's all I need.

I stretch out my fingers and put them to the keyboard to search for other channels with open content positions. Plenty of pubs need writers. Bloggers. Vloggers. Floggers. With the travel bans we've been under for the past generation, the net is all that keeps the world connected. Voices are in demand. It's almost considered a public service to share our experiences. But they all want someone with enough followers and daily, if not hourly, engagement. I stare at the screen until the classifieds turn into gibberish.

My eyes refuse to focus. A little game wouldn't hurt. Orlov said I am supposed to note when I need it, not stop completely. But if I can't find another way to focus, does that mean I'm junk for it? My fingers tremble in answer.

I take out my stylus and flip my tablet down to make a list.

To do:
—gain 40,000 subscribers

That's it. One simple task. Three words. Not so much once it's written down.

It's not even ten in the morning—I have an entire day to be productive. I pull my clothes from the drying rack and try to think about smoothing out the wrinkles instead of followers. No use obsessing.

Obsessing is a sign of my depression creeping in. Orlov taught me to watch for obsessive thought patterns back when I first started seeing him, but Caz has made me rusty. For two years it has warned me when my serotonin activity dropped, offering invigorating levels to keep them up before I even felt the depression.

I used to manage the pile of broken neurons and inadequate chemicals without the implant. Not well, but enough to get through the days. How did I do it back then? The release of cutting. A knife along my flesh brought me out of my head and into the moment. But cutting will land me in a group home, without baby-girl.

There was sex. The cocks and fingers shoved clumsily in me weren't as sharp as a knife, but they created enough distraction to keep the depression from pinning me down. Then there was the glorious, mind-blowing sex with Skylar, his forceful thrusting pushing the depression down into its cave in my heart.

I fold my last shirt and give a deep sigh. "No feeling sorry for yourself, Valya. Not now."

A walk should clear my head and give me some ideas for a few vlogs. I need something more engaging. More emotional than the surface-level news pieces I've been coasting on.

I pull on the beat-up secondhand running shoes I've been wearing for the past few months. They're ugly—gray and purple with scuff marks along the sides—but they're comfortable. I adjust my long, cotton skirt beneath my bump, and throw on a flowing, sleeveless top. I should wear a long-sleeve linen if I'll be under the sun for any amount of time, but it's too hot for even my thinnest long-sleeve. I'll deal with a light burning of the skin. I don't even run a brush through my greasy hair before pulling it into a ponytail, clipping a bright green face mask to it, and heading downstairs.

Most of the houses on my quiet street were abandoned when New Sofia was built. Sofia was one of the first cities to attempt underground architecture on a large scale. The caverns were carved out before the first bombs fell and sent the rest of the world scurrying to the safety of mountains. Anyone who had enough money became a mole-person, living in the depths of Vitosha Mountain where the air was scrubbed clean and acid rain never fell. No one left outside could afford the luxury of an entire house. They stood empty until the city acquired them and divided them into public apartments. Cheaper real estate with fifteen people crammed in a building meant for five. This was all back when my parents were kids. Since then Old Sofia has crumbled further, creaking in on itself and threatening to collapse.

The market on the corner has fresh vegetables out in baskets. As I pass, I let my hand run over a plump tomato. My fingertips can feel its wet juices move inside, and it's as big as the head of the cat looking down at me from its perch on the windowsill. My mouth waters. The red fruit probably tastes of pure sunshine and the rich dirt the vines grow out of. I bet it's full of vitamins, too. Healthy for the baby. But seven credits a kilo?

"Maybe on the way back," I tell the cat, patting the edge of the wooden crate. The cat is a tabby, fur too thick for the summer heat. Its sides puff out like bellows and its eyes narrow with a familiar wisdom. Like my fox. I imagine the creature with a bushier tail and longer snout. I reach out to touch it, but it shrinks away from me. We both know I won't be back for the tomatoes. My extra money, what little there is, goes towards baby things. I'm not asking Skylar for help. I'll get him to sign off his rights and it'll be just me and baby-girl. We'll watch our expenses together until I get syndicated.

My palms go sweaty as I think about syndication. Or maybe it's just the oppressive humidity of the day. Wet bulb is only ninety. But it still feels like death.

Leaving the corner market and its produce behind, I walk briskly, letting my arms swing at my sides. Within a few blocks my blood is jumping, my breath coming short and fast. I force myself to slow down, to not over-exert myself. With those first long steps I know this walk will not give me the satisfaction I need.

Satisfaction. The word brings me back to sex. In all the pregnancy blogs they never bother to write about how hormones can make a woman hungrier for touch than for those juicy tomatoes.

Skylar loved and matched my appetite. In those early summer days we competed over who would tire of our romping first. Which one of us, after hours of entanglement, would cry mercy and beg for sleep? Or food? Or an hour of cuddling and watching vids?

"You're insatiable," Skylar whispered in my ear late one morning. The words were more of an incantation than an observation, as if he hoped to stir my passion again.

"I have to get to class," I murmured, slithering out of his arms.

He gripped tighter, holding me against him. "Skip it."

"I can't." I brought my lips to his salty neck and let my tongue dart out. "It's my thesis."

"What are they teaching you that I can't?" His eyes twinkled with dual meaning. He was helping me get ready for my official launch after graduation, certain I didn't need syndication. Between lectures on business and vlogging, he taught me about my body and the spirit living beneath my skin, held together by bone and sinew.

I tilted my head up and kissed him on the mouth as a punctuation for the morning. But like the sun, he melted my defenses. I closed my eyes and fell into his deep kisses, letting our spirits become one. I was almost certain if I opened my eyes, I would see my own trembling, beige body, littered with scars, glowing with lust.

It was a transition I craved—to see myself the way he saw me. When I caught him looking at me, his lips twitched between a smirk of amusement and the rolling of awe. I wondered what in me evoked such emotions.

I stood naked in front of the mirror and stared at my skin, tracing the curves of my muscle and fat. I squinted until my vision blurred and yet the mystery remained. The only way to understand his passion was to fall into the shared pool of oblivion we created when we made love.

Before him, sex had been about the rush of power tucked beneath the thrill of newness. One day with Gregor, the next with Ivan, sometimes with Sarah Beth. It didn't matter who. All that mattered was that it was my choice. I made the rules, said where and when and how far. It was about control.

And now? Neither oblivion nor control. I'd settle for a satisfying orgasm to set me straight.

The walk obviously isn't serving as a healthy distraction, and I'm not getting any inspiration, so I turn around and head back to my apartment.

On the way home I stop at the electronics store. Computers and cameras clutter the floor to ceiling shelving.

"Looking for something in particular, Valya?" The owner comes from behind his desk to greet me. I open and close my mouth. Shake my head.

I'd love a new camera, maybe some new editing equipment. But gear is expensive. No sense getting more until I have a stable income.

"I've got this cool vlogger," the owner says, picking up a six-inch tube. "Dual camera. Records you and what you're seeing at the same time. Cuts down on editing and gives more in-depth possibilities for solo vloggers. High quality, good reviews."

I reach toward it. It's perfect for a solo-woman, and that's what I am. Just me.

"No, thank you." I snap my hand back before it can stroke the slick metal. I want to use the owner's name, but I don't remember it. He smiles, as if waiting for that one word. John? Jared? My chest heaves with concentration. Maybe it was Jake. Yeah, "Jake."

He squints and tilts his head to the side. No. Jake isn't right either. I'm an idiot. I'm backing up, stumbling against one of his racks. Things are falling behind me. Are they expensive? The metallic taste comes. I can't stop to pick them up. I back out the door. My chest squeezes. Heaves. Squeezes again. I slip off the step, jolting my knee as I tumble onto the sidewalk.

Three steps away from the shop, back against a cool brick wall, I pant. Put my head down.

Slow it down.

Slower.

I breathe.

Once the panic attack passes, I push myself off the wall, wobbly and drained. I take lunch and dinner from the automat near the market, my fingers trembling as I press my thumb to the red scanner, key in my PIN, and order lockers number five and seven. The automat takes a few seconds to process my order and subtract the credits from my account, and I zone out. My body fades and I'm a gelatinous blob within a still universe, unable to follow a strand of thought back to reality. A gentle click and a buzz bring me back to the moment. The lights on the handles turn green, and I take the dry packets out of each locker.

Vegetable soup re-hydrates nicely. The good thing about soup is the vegetables are supposed to be mushy anyway, so it doesn't matter if they've been dehydrated.

After lunch I try to clear my mind by playing Nature on my tablet. Not even a full week and I'm already having panic attacks? I need to get this under control. But chasing the animals around two-dimensional dots doesn't give the same satisfaction after years of a three-dimensional, immersive experience, so I turn it off.

I check my email, not hoping for much of a distraction. But there is one:

An Introduction to Casual Tandem

I tap on the email.

Dear Valya,

I was happy to hear about you and your developing pregnancy from Doctor Orlov. He thinks you may be a good candidate for the Sofia chapter of our Infant Tandem Program and, based on what I've heard so far, I must agree with him. Enrolling in the Infant Tandem Program will not only allow you to contribute to science and society, but it will also give you and your baby several new opportunities. I would like to discuss the program further at your earliest convenience.

Sincerely,
Emersyn

I groan and delete the email. That's all I need—more pressure to join Orlov's stupid experiment.

CHAPTER FIVE

"YOU'RE SHOWING." Olivia nods at my bulging belly with an approving smile on her boysenberry-painted lips. "How are you feeling?"

I sip my Viennese Coffee, the synthetic honey coating my mouth with sticky sweetness.

"Besides my new nurse?" I tilt my head towards the waitress, who's still glaring at me as she wipes down the counter. I had to explain to the waitress that the caffeine helps manage my low blood pressure and that my doctor approves of the drink before she agreed to bring me the beverage. Even then, she looked to Olivia for confirmation, as if pregnant women cannot be trusted.

Olivia rolls her eyes, turning into the saucy teenager I grew up with. "But I'm sure she got the highest degree in caffeine, health, and pregnancy a barista can have."

We both giggle, like little girls hiding in the closet, playing house with plastic figurines. The laughter melts away the weeks that have passed since we've seen each other.

"But really, how are you?" she asks.

"The usual, I guess. A bit of heartburn. Some new veins I didn't know I had on my legs."

"Oh yeah, I remember that. The varicose veins. So attractive."

"Did yours go away?" My legs itch as we discuss them. I shift back and forth, scratching them against my linen pants.

"Yeah. We're still young. Our bodies heal." Her eyes level on me as if there's a deeper meaning I should catch, but I shrug. Whatever it is, she doesn't press it. "I still can't believe you're pregnant."

"I still can't believe you have two kids," I counter.

No sense bringing more people into this miserable hole was

Olivia's mantra growing up. She got gel control as soon as she got her period, not trusting the boys in our neighborhood to get it themselves, even though the injections were easier for boys. It ended up not mattering. She wasn't interested in boys and had to pay a fertility specialist to combine her eggs with her wife's.

"How are your little angels?" I remind myself to ask about them. It's not that I don't remember she has kids, but we've always been so close I've never had to ask about parts of her life I wasn't involved in before. They simply didn't exist.

"Tani and Becker are fine." Olivia shakes her short, wavy mane. "Testing my patience these days. What about you? Did you have your checkup this month?"

"Uh-huh. Baby-girl's fine, me too. But they told me I have to get my Caz blocked." I tell her about my appointments with Janice and Orlov.

"Oh yeah. I read about that. A woman and her husband were going tandem and their baby almost starved to death or something. Tragic. But you could manage it, right?" She arches her eyebrow, demanding honesty.

My hand goes for my ear more than I'd like to admit, even to my best friend. But I'm not junk. A junker gives the last of their income to pay for more play. They waste away, chasing the next high. They get Connect. Chase. They always need more. I'm not a junker, just a bit addicted. "I had a panic attack the other day. It hasn't even been a full week and they are already coming back."

"Then why not keep it? Vlog about it. Get syndicated, and you can afford a nanny."

It's my turn to arch my eyebrow, thinner and lighter than hers.

"I'm just saying. It could be your in. It'd be interesting to people. Caz is becoming so common, more parents have it. Parenting with Caz. I bet it'd take off."

I point at the gold hoops in her delicate ear. Her shaved hair reveals the bare spot where an implant would be if she had Caz.

"Well, not all parents. But I'd still watch ya, hon," she assures me.

I stare into my coffee, the thick cream already dissolved into its brown depths. "It's a possibility. I need to find a unique angle. The syndication I thought I had only wants me if I'm with Skylar."

"Then you're better off without them." Her eyes go soft. I

always feel coated with something sticky-sweet when she looks at me that way. Like real honey, not the fake stuff they put in my Viennese coffee. She says it's love, but the only love I've known has been hard and rough.

"What about flogging?"

I snort with disgust at the idea of setting up a feel-log. "You can't be serious. I'm trying to turn off the crap in my head, not get more installed. Plus, have you seen the prices on a flogging rig? Even if I could afford it, who would want to experience my emotional roller coaster?" I don't mention the Infant Tandem Program. They'd probably offer to install the ocular and chest implants necessary to create a decent flog. They'd love the extra data for their study.

"You'd be surprised. Becca buys some flogs now and then. People want to experience everything. Roller coasters can be exciting."

I kick myself for not asking about Becca earlier. I always leave someone out, but Olivia's used to it. I remember Lindsay's vlog from the other day. What was that guy's name? The one with over a million sales? He is probably set for life and still making money. What kinds of experiences does he sell? Later in the program, when I was only half listening, he'd hinted about some pretty risqué stuff. Kinky, sexy feels.

"Yeah, I suppose it'd be interesting if you could get off it whenever you want. Nah. I'm done with all this. No more implants." Not for me, not for baby-girl.

"Shame. I bet you'd give awesome feels."

CHAPTER SIX

I HATE TO admit it, but Caz has done a good job controlling my dexiety. Although, I wonder how much I use it out of boredom. Too much of pregnancy is waiting. Waiting for the next exam, the next milestone, the next chapter of life. It's difficult to start anything new, and old interests are stripped away by exhaustion or multiplying aches. In the second trimester, I had settled into Caz as a source of entertainment.

A quick game in the morning gave me time to wake up. A session after breakfast let me digest before I looked for a channel with open vlogger positions or played with my vlog site. After researching and recording an entry, I would escape into yet another game.

The hardest part of weaning is how slowly time passes without the extra jolts of energy from the system. A day is just twenty-four hours. 1,440 minutes. It should pass quickly. But in this thick waiting, even the seconds crawl by, and there's 86,400 of those.

I check my phone. It's not even ten in the morning, but at least a distraction pops up: another email from this Emersyn person.

It goes into more details, letting me know Casual Infant Tandem will pay for an apartment in New Sofia. Trying to buy us. They would definitely pay for a flogging rig, and I bet Olivia's right. With flogging would come syndication. Then I wouldn't need Emersyn Enterprises, but I would be indebted to them.

At night, the anxiety pushes out the boredom with a slow-burning torture-session. It sweeps in and sets my heart pounding. My mouth aches as if stuffed with cotton. I teeter on a panic attack that never comes. The uninvited guest makes itself at home in my brain, drinks my best energy, and leaves me cleaning up after it well into the morning.

These days the anxiety has a stranglehold on my unborn daughter. It starts with normal parental concerns. Will I be a good mother? What if she's too demanding? What if I can't handle being a single parent? Once it's edged its way in with these innocuous questions, it starts with a more strenuous attack.

You're not good enough. You're not good enough. The distant beat of a war drum syncs with my blood.

You're not good enough. You're not good enough. It comes faster.

Once my nerves are at a peak, raw with the waiting, the real attack starts—from a different angle every night. Tonight it tells me I won't be able to protect this helpless little girl.

No. I'll protect her.

Tears tease at my eyes. I can't even protect myself.

Then the images come, floating on a bed of shame, the tips of my ears burning. There's my baby, tender and perfect. A red fox darts past her. It circles back and licks her face, its sharp teeth scratching her chubby cheek. The fox disappears, and the baby is whisked away by strange hands, white with dark hair on them. But they aren't quite human. Dread, thick and heavy, smothers me with the inevitable. The hands connect to the outline of a bone-white face. Angular. The edges are so sharp they cut my heart as my mind traces them.

I grab my nearest pillow—a small rectangle I stitched by hand from my favorite shirt when I was a little girl. Its bright pink has faded to a light salmon, and the white kitten face, once puffy and charming, looks like the hint of a ghost kitten. I throw the pillow over my face, press it down, and let out a muffled scream, begging for the images to stop.

Before Caz, I trusted Skylar to silence the nighttime anxiety. The first time it showed itself in front of him, it took the form of a night terror. I told him I didn't remember it, that I blacked out and woke up weeping in his arms, because lying was easier than trying to explain being both awake and asleep at the same time.

The sleeping part of me floated in a void, aware of something sweeping toward me without space or time. The awake me felt Skylar roll over in his sleep, press his smooth chest against my bare back, and creep his hand between my thighs.

In the dream, the sensation of being strangled without a body.

Constriction. I thrashed, and my awake self thrashed with me, kicked against Skylar's shins, tangled us in the sheet.

Above me, blurry and distant and yet somehow on top of me, a man. Skinny. Bones? No, not bones, but as hard and white as bones, sunken cheeks, eye holes to nowhere. He glowed like a film negative. The sensation of him grinning, of being laughed at, although the painted black lips didn't part. If they did, the teeth they would show . . .

The real me screamed. Loud and strong. In the dream I was silent, drowning beneath the man. Paralyzed.

Skylar's fingers wrapped around my biceps, held me down. His low and even voice, with the slightest hint of panic, reached through my thrashing to the dream self.

The dream disappeared. I was awake, panting, crying.

He didn't ask me any questions. He held me, safe and secure, as the images faded to nothing and my whimpering fell silent.

"Was that a panic attack?" he asked me the next morning over eggs. Real eggs, not the re-hydrated kind.

"A night terror, I think," I told him.

"You think? Has this ever happened to you before?"

"No, but they run in my family. My father, my grandfather, all my uncles . . . "

"The men," he extrapolated.

"Yeah, I guess."

He scooted his chair closer to mine, closing the six-inch gap between us. His arm wrapped around my shoulders, and his forehead fell against my temple.

"We'll just have to remind those night terrors that you're a woman." His breath danced hot on my cheek, soft as feathers. A thrill ran through me.

We made love, slow and lingering, and my mind was consumed with affection and desire. The terror had opened me up, exposed a rawness he tenderly filled, leaving no room for the dexiety.

After, I lay with my chin digging into his chest and stared at the stubble growing on his cheeks.

He stroked my hair, his fingers lingering on my back. "Did that help?"

I told him it did, and he assured me he would keep me safe. "We'll chase away those nightmares together."

After his tender promise, the terrors got bolder, more difficult to chase away. We had to work harder to keep me in the moment.

At first kisses and a slow exploration of my body had been enough of a distraction. We'd make love until I fell asleep, too exhausted to dream. But that gaunt, white face with filed teeth invaded my post-coital slumber. Skylar had to try harder to chase him off. He had to be more forceful.

I remember the first time he wrapped his hands around my neck. Well, not quite my neck. He wasn't choking me. He was on top of me, thrusting slow but deep, the way that sent a sharp twinge low in my stomach but otherwise felt too good to switch positions.

Usually that was enough to keep my attention, but that night my mind kept wandering. The terror had been coming in. I had been moaning in my sleep. Softly crying, "No, no, no," when Skylar brought me out of it. As we hit a rhythm, the nightmare edged back in.

Thrust, hard and deep. My eyes settled on Skylar's perfect face, his light curls falling around his forehead. Thrust, soft and gentle. My eyes darted to the corners of the room, searching for something that was almost there. That had always been there. That shouldn't be there.

When my eyes wandered, his sharp thrust brought me back to the safety of the moment, but even the sickeningly sweet pain on my cervix couldn't hold my attention.

Skylar moved his hand away from my wrist, down onto my chest. His fingertips brushed along my collarbone and he pushed with the palm of his hand, letting his weight settle on my ribcage.

My eyes flew open at the sensation, and instinct wiggled me back into the pillow-top, away from his crushing hand.

"Shh, relax," he murmured. His blue eyes were filled with soft love. "Trust me."

I trusted him completely. I stopped wiggling and lifted my chin to expose the soft line of flesh where my throat met my chest. I locked my eyes to his and silently told him to do what he would.

He pressed harder. I had never realized how fragile my ribs were. The way they moved beneath his firm weight, threatening to crack and give, made me aware of my vulnerability. All that could remain in that moment was his pressure and my breath coming slow and shallow as he took away the room for my lungs to expand.

I pulled in harder, but the oxygen wouldn't come. I was

swimming. Darkness took over the edges of my vision, and within the darkness, pulsing pinpoints of light bloomed in pink and purple and sharp white.

Without warning, Skylar's hand lifted. A lightness filled my chest. A tingling ran through my entire body, my fingers and toes vibrating. An orgasm rolled after it, pushing out any trace of fear I still held.

He rolled next to me, both of us breathing hard, and snuggled against my neck, his hair tickling my cheek.

"Wow," I breathed.

"Was that okay for you?" he asked in a soft, almost uncertain whisper.

"That was intense."

"Did you like it?" His head shifted, his question fell directly into my ear.

"It was fantastic. But is it safe?"

"Trust me." He kissed my temple. "I know what I'm doing."

After that, the sex got rougher, and I flourished in it. I never told Olivia the details because she would say Skylar was abusive. She wouldn't understand how much I wanted him to have that control, how much I needed someone to be in control when I couldn't be. It was a release I sometimes literally begged for, and I couldn't explain that to her.

Tonight I long for Skylar's strength. But he's not here. There's only me and this laughing anxiety that won't shut up, amplified by the protective hormones of a mother, hiding under a childhood memory that would fall apart if I washed it.

I can't take it anymore. I reach under the pillow to my ear and find the bump.

My finger hesitates, the sweat from my neck slick beneath it. I can get through the night without this. Baby-girl needs me to.

I take two breaths, but neither of them offers the deep, cleansing air I need. My hand trembles.

Click.

One, two, three.

Four. Five. Six.

Seven.

Blissfully distracting spheres appear in my mind, and a chattering squirrel chases away my fears.

CHAPTER SEVEN

MY NERVES PROPEL me to show up to Orlov's office ten minutes early. The light above his closed door glows red, so I pace the hall in front of it and wait my turn.

His door opens and an older woman with her hair pulled back in a severe bun exits. She's wearing therms—expensive, thermal-controlled bodysuits more common in New Sofia than out here—and no mask hides her thin lips as they curl up in a half-smile. She looks me up and down, as if I'm a piece of cake in the desert box at a cafe. The familiarity of her blue-gray eyes—too much like Skylar's—makes me shudder and scuttle into the safety of Orlov's office. I hate running into his other patients. They're all crazy.

Orlov glances over my statistics on his tablet. "I see you've used your Casual a few times over the past couple of weeks, more in recent evenings."

"If you'd turned it off completely, like I asked, I wouldn't be able to," I grumble, kicking my sneakered feet out in front of me. He should at least offer me a stool or something. I'm seven and a half months pregnant, and he hasn't bothered with that little bit of kindness. "Maybe if you tell the people at Emersyn Enterprises I'm not interested, and they stop emailing, I won't be so stressed."

His eyes widen. "Is Emersyn Enterprises harassing you?"

"Well, not harassing." I sigh, sinking into the comfortable trust of the room. "But they've emailed me a couple of times. Can't they get other women to join their trial and leave me alone?"

He pinches the bridge of his nose and nods. "Yes, they could get other women to join the trial. They will look for other women and enroll them soon. But you have a set of skills most other participants don't."

"Really?" I scrunch my eyebrows in disbelief.

"Yes. You have used your Casual for therapeutic reasons for a few years now. That means you have experience with the notification system, which isn't part of non-medical devices. You also have a greater understanding of the emotional and psychological aspects of the implant that recreational users don't."

"So it's not just because they think I'm desperate? Because I'm not."

"I know you're not desperate, Valya. You're in control, now more than ever. I didn't recommend you because I thought you would be the only woman on the planet to say yes. I recommended you because I think you're a woman who can actually help Emersyn Enterprises understand the possibilities of this technology and, to be completely honest, because I believe in the importance of this technology."

I flush beneath his words. Orlov isn't the type to flatter me. "Yeah, well, I don't feel like I'm in control. You've seen how much I used Casual this week."

"I'm not going to chastise you for using Casual, if that's what you think. It will take time to wean off it. You've done better than I expected. You have amazing willpower." He turns the screen around so I can see the charts and graphs. The lines and bars in bold colors mean nothing to me. I stare as if I'm reading the screen, my head playing along by bobbing up and down.

"Your overall usage, frequency of use, and length of each session have all dropped significantly. But I want to make sure you're not pressing yourself to stop too fast. We have another month to wean your usage and forcing it now could have negative effects. So, tell me, how have you felt these past weeks?"

It's hard to believe all that data doesn't tell him how I feel. I'm fairly certain the spikes lay bare thoughts I don't even know I'm thinking. But I humor him, answering questions he's only asking to lead me to some glittering self-realization.

"There were some difficult times," I admit. I'm not ready to talk about the panic attack or the strange dreams. "I think I was more bored than depressed or anxious."

"Bored? As in you have been using Casual to fill up your time? How are your social ties?"

He knows they're non-existent.

CASUAL

When I first started therapy, Orlov told me I needed more quality to my friendships. Besides Olivia, my friends were the type I could throw back a two-liter of beer and jump into bed with.

After all these years, not much has changed. He's still begging me to make friends. Except now even superficial ones will suffice. When did I become such a loner? During college, I threw myself into my studies, but there was still the occasional party invitation and always someone to grab a beer with. Until Skylar.

Skylar came to talk to our junior seminar before classes finished for the summer. We were a group of fifteen twenty-year-olds, somewhere between youthful idealism and the impending crash of disillusionment that comes with trying to find a first job. He sat in a corner of the classroom, assessing our faces as Professor Adlin introduced him.

"I'm sure Skylar needs no introduction," she said with a little laugh. "But allow me that pleasure. Skylar is a blogger with over five million followers—all in the written medium, without a vlog. With the competition for viewers and more interest in local content creators than ever, Skylar has achieved something many of you will strive for, but few of us will ever reach." Adlin's harsh voice continued, but I stopped listening. I knew about Skylar. We all did. He was one of the most famous bloggers of our generation. Born in New Sofia, he lived in the old city and led expeditions into the wilderness around the city. He wrote that he would live out there if it was permitted, and people ate it up.

He looked different from his pictures. He had a shocking whiteness about him, almost glistening, as if the sun had never touched him. The tips of his black, curly hair were frosted platinum, like his profile picture. But he had a vibrance beyond the simple charm a photo can hold. His dark blue eyes settled on me, and my breath quickened. He held me in his gaze as he strode to the wooden podium and the class clapped. His white fingers, the nails at least buffed and possibly polished, curled around the edges of the old wood, and he inhaled. All at once he released everything: his breath, the podium, and my gaze.

"How many of you already run blogs or vlogs?" he asked, his voice easy, his face relaxed.

Three students, one of them me, raised our hands halfway, as if he had asked a trick question.

"Why don't the rest of you?"

A boy in the front cleared his throat and answered, "We're still studying. Our senior projects won't be up and running until fall."

Skylar waved the boy's words away as if they were summer gnats. "The biggest disservice you'll do yourself is following the path the school lays out for you, waiting until they say you're ready.

"Don't misunderstand me, you're in a solid program with many benefits. Adlin's got plenty to teach. But you also need to try things on your own. Take risks. Fail. If you only do what they tell you, when they tell you, that's all you'll learn—to wait and tell other people's stories. That's fine if you're a producer. But no one in here is studying production. You're the creatives. For you, it's about pouncing on your own ideas before they're watered down by popular opinion."

I wiggled to the edge of my wooden seat, hanging on his words. Passion oozed out of him, sending tiny vibrations of excitement buzzing around my starry-eyed cohort. His words anchored my heart, beating with the rhythm of, "Truth, truth, truth."

He looked right at me, flashed his brilliant, easy smile, and said, "Some of you are ready right now. Bursting with creativity. I can tell. Don't let it go stagnant while you wait for your professors to challenge you. Challenge yourself. Or find someone who will push you."

Desire, wet and sweet, filled my mouth. I wanted him to be talking about me. Before my anxiety could tell me it was a terrible idea, my hand shot up.

"Yes." His smirk was more amused than cruel.

"In the Village Log, you talk about using our power to wake people up to social issues. But what if . . . " I faltered, realizing what I'm about to admit. "What if we don't have a social issue yet?" My face burned under the gazes of my classmates.

"I firmly believe your social issue will find you if you live your life authentically. You won't have to chase one down. The battle between right and wrong is going on every day. We're constantly picking sides."

His gaze flicked away from me, toward another girl with her hand up. Before I lost his attention completely, I blurted out,

"When you say authentic life, do you mean a life in the villages? That's what you wrote in your book, right? That the only authentic life is one close to nature."

A smile melted across his lips. "I did write that. I'm surprised you've read my book. Most people only know my blog. While I stand by my words, I'm sure you know the laws. Permanent residence outside city limits is, unfortunately, not allowed. Until it is, we challenge ourselves to find authentic expression within cities."

His lecture continued, peppered by questions from my classmates. But I heard none of it. I had already gleaned the most important part: I was ready. It was as if my entire life up to that moment had been a lie. But I was prepared to start living authentically. My cause would find me, and life would take on meaning.

"Earth to Valya." A hand waved in front of my eyes. I startled and focused on the girl behind the hand. Her backpack was already slung over one of her slight shoulders. "We're going to Linden's. You coming?"

The room was almost empty. Skylar fiddled with a light-brown leather messenger bag at the front of the room, occasionally glancing up at us, almost as if he was waiting for me.

"No, not today. I have something to do."

My jelly legs carried me down the steps to him.

He straightened to meet me and his face beamed with a smile that was impossible to not fall into. It was at once comforting and exhilarating and, in that moment, I would have done anything to keep it aimed at me.

"Do you want to go somewhere and talk?" he asked.

No words came to me, so I followed him silently, letting him take the lead.

We didn't go to a cafe or bar—the polite first date locations. We took the tunnel bus—the one that goes to the new city—and got off on the stop before the tunnel.

He held my hand, confident in his touch even though we had just met, and led me through the quiet streets to an open field. The grass was lush, and he tugged me down onto it. The blades tickled the backs of my bare legs, my anticipation echoing their needle-like sharpness.

He reached up to my hair and unhooked my mask. I held my breath as he unhooked the other side, removing the protective cloth.

"Breathe," he commanded with a laugh. "The air is fine these days. The pollution has decreased to almost pre-war levels."

The sun warmed my bare cheeks, or maybe that was a blush.

"You're beautiful. You shouldn't hide that." He stroked my cheek, near my burning ears.

I considered my nose, bumped and slightly hooked to the left. It was my mother's nose, and my father had called it a witch's honker. My smile was thin and lopsided. Did he really want to see that? I offered it to him furtively, and he returned an honest grin.

"What do you see?" He swept his hand across the horizon.

Vitosha Mountain stretched up into the sky. At the base of the mountain the tunnel stretched open like a giant mouth, the fluorescent lights dangling down like a soft-glowing uvula.

"New Sofia," I said. I couldn't see the city under the mountain, but it sounded philosophical and might impress him.

He shook his head, the frosted tips of his hair bouncing.

"Did I fail the test?" I joked, forcing my voice to stay nonchalant. The thought of disappointing him made my heart flutter.

He put my failure on the shoulders of society so it wouldn't weigh me down. "That's what they want you to see. Everywhere: New Sofia as the future. But it's a distraction. Look closer, or further, rather. The villages had a future, too, until that hole of a city made them a thing of the past."

I strained my eyes against the dark green foliage, trying to find a trace of the crumbling villages.

"New Sofia didn't take away their future. It was our ancestors with their factories and personal vehicles. It was politicians with huge egos, short tempers, and too many bombs," I protested, echoing a study blog from sixth grade. "New Sofia gives us hope for a future."

He patted my head like I was a puppy, stupid but cute. "It's hard to unlearn the things you've been taught, but stick with me, and I'll show you the invisible things you've been missing."

Lying next to him, I believed he was the key I'd been searching for. Professionally, his credentials backed me up. Anyone in my cohort would have died to be his protege, and he had chosen me. Sacrificing occasional beers with friends was a small price to pay to pick at the knowledge he was offering.

But it went beyond that. Both of us still, my hand a few blades of grass away from his, I could feel our hearts beating, mine slowing to match his steady rhythm. When they synced, I let myself believe he was the most important factor to my success in love. He was my future.

"My social life is about the same," I tell Orlov. "Well, no Skylar, but Olivia's there. Sorta. Sometimes."

"I don't think you're getting enough social stimulation right now. Not if you're using Casual out of boredom." As he speaks, he taps on his tablet.

"I can't afford a club," I remind him.

It all comes down to money. With so many people playing games in their heads, it's hard to meet people. Everyone who can afford an implant spends their time in their own perfect world, inaccessible to those left in the physical world. The loneliness of the less affluent created a business opportunity, and club prices skyrocketed.

I'm not poor. With basic income kicking in as soon as we graduate high school, no one lives in poverty. I've got an apartment and money for food. I can keep myself warm in winter, even if I can't keep myself cool in the summer. But I still have to make choices. Prioritize. A social life is even less of a priority than fresh tomatoes right now.

"Have you considered joining a pregnancy cohort? It would let you meet people and help shift your focus to a positive future instead of your current anxiety."

"Janice suggested I join one when she confirmed the pregnancy. But I waited too long and couldn't find one with an open slot."

He glances up from his tablet, giving me a stern, almost fatherly look. "There are three open spots in your month's New Sofia cohort. At this point a weekly trip into the new city might benefit you, and I can credit your transportation account to help offset the cost."

I sink back in my chair, my hand resting on my bump.

"You look unsure," he notes.

"I've been your patient for almost ten years, and I'm grateful I found you," I say. "But you know the reason I started coming to you, right?"

He dips his head, and I almost detect the slightest roll of his light brown eyes. "I'd like to think I offer my patients quality care and familiarity, but as one of few practitioners in this neighborhood, I'm aware most patients come to me because my location is convenient."

"It's not just the convenience. There's something unsettling about New Sofia. It's unnatural. I don't like being there." I stumble over my words.

"What makes you uncomfortable with New Sofia?" he presses.

Old Sofia has almost everything a young woman could need. It still has functioning schools, and our tablets access the same educational materials as the new cities. Cafes, clubs, and plenty of second-hand stores keep us entertained. The two general health clinics might be crumbling, and the doctors might not have the latest tech, but they are sufficient for routine medical care. The only thing we don't have is a psychiatric hospital. A few psychers, sure, but nowhere to take care of a mental emergency.

The first time I entered New Sofia, I was passed out. I woke up with leather cuffs pinning my wrists and ankles to a metal bed frame and a wooziness rushing between my head and stomach, begging me to go back to the oblivion I'd been resting in.

I couldn't find any lamps in the room, but the white lighting stung my eyes. I learned later that the city filters light through the crystal framework, making each wall a potential light source. In the hospital wing, they utilized that potential to the fullest with bright white panels for walls. The lack of shadows made the room feel unreal, and at first I thought I must be dead.

Confusion made me thrash. The cuffs clanged against the bed frame, and my head pounded. I tried to call out, but only a moan escaped from my dry throat.

My rasping caught the attention of a nurse dressed in dark gray therms.

"It's okay, you're in a hospital." His brown eyes were kind, but I didn't believe him. The room looked nothing like the dingy hospital I had spent three days in when my appendix had burst.

"You're in New Sofia," he continued, anticipating the questions I couldn't form. "You had an accident, and we're taking care of you."

An accident? Memories trickled in. My neighbor Gregor. Drinking rakia. He dared me to . . . I couldn't remember, but there was a ledge, slippery in the rain.

"Gregor?" I croaked.

The nurse shook his head. "You were the only one brought in. We've contacted your father."

"My dad?" Even with my dry throat and confusion, the nurse must have heard the fear in my voice.

"You're a minor, we can only release you to a parent or guardian."

I held my wrists up, not straining against the cuffs, but asking why I was bound.

"Sorry about that. They can be uncomfortable. But you tried to hurt yourself. Until a psycher can evaluate you, we need to make sure you aren't able to hurt yourself again."

I tried to hurt myself? Didn't he say it had been an accident? If they thought I intentionally tried to hurt myself, my father would be held accountable for the cost of my treatment—and I had a feeling this hospital, strange and clean, was more than we could afford on my father's income. I'd always been so careful, sure I'd never draw attention to myself. How had I messed up this time? More memories poked through the painful slush in my mind. A fight with Gregor. Yelling. Was that rain or me crying?

The nurse left and came back with a psycher a while later.

"I need you to lay back and relax," the psycher told me. She wore purple therms that stretched from her ankles up to her neck. Her black hair was pulled into a tight bun and she had a way of staring at me until I looked away.

"I didn't try to hurt myself," I said with a throaty sigh. The nurse brought me water and helped me take a few sips.

"Then this will confirm that." She pressed behind her ear.

"You're going to play Caz while we talk?" I asked with disbelief. The implants were still new back then, and most of us mocked the rich people in New Sofia who could afford the tech we secretly desired.

Her lips spread in a condescending smile, and I wasn't sure if it was because I was a teen or from Old Sofia, but I could tell she thought I was stupid. "No, of course not. I have an ocular scanner."

"An ocular scanner?" I asked.

She tapped the bone below her left eye. "Yep, right here. It lets me read your movements as we talk to help me diagnose you."

"You're kidding, right?"

"It's still experimental, but so far the results have been accurate. In the near future, a trained psycher might get a diagnosis simply by scanning you. Thirty seconds instead of hours of assessment. For now, it's just a suggestive tool to supplement my interview. It doesn't bother you, does it?"

It bothered me. It felt like she was looking underneath the thin sheet and paper gown, through me. But I told her, "No, of course not," because I didn't want her to think I had anything to hide.

"Let's get started then. It says here the police found you on the roof of a building. Why were you up there?"

"I don't remember." My heart raced because she might think I was lying. "I sometimes go up to the roof to hang out with friends."

"Who were you hanging out with last night?"

"Gregor." I was confident in that answer, at least, and my breath slowed.

She nodded and continued. "What were you doing with Gregor?"

"Drinking. His uncle makes rakia. Sometimes we go up there to drink it."

"I see, and you were just drinking?"

"No, we were making out." I remembered Gregor's rough hand slipping beneath my blouse as it billowed in the wind. His hands had the same roughness of all the men in our building who worked in the greenhouses on the edge of town. The hard callouses on his palm and the tips of his fingers scraped against my soft skin.

"Now tell me how you went from making out with your boyfriend to trying to jump from the roof."

Gregor wasn't my boyfriend, just a boy I hung out with, but I didn't correct her. His hand had abandoned my breasts and unbuttoned my jeans. When his rough fingers plunged beneath my waistband they met a roughness of my own—one he hadn't expected.

"The hell—?" He backed away.

I knew what he had found. Scars. Scabs. Long, thin, raised lines I cut into the inside of my thighs.

"You do that to yourself?"

I buttoned my jeans. Stood up to leave. Said nothing.

"You're sick, Val. That's messed up."

I shrugged, not caring enough to explain why I did it.

"Then why don't you jump? Get it over with. Or are you a coward?"

A slippery ledge. Hands pulling me from behind. After that, nothing.

"I don't know. I don't remember trying to jump."

"How do you feel now?"

"Awful," I said. "Hung over."

"And do you want to kill yourself?"

I shook my head. The fast motion caused the sloshing to return. I closed my eyes against the pounding that accompanied it.

"I don't. I promise."

If I felt like killing anyone, it was Gregor. How dare he tell the police I was suicidal. It was absurd. Now my dad was on his way to this cold, bright hospital, and this harsh woman was prodding me with questions. She paused, staring through me.

"Okay, I believe you. You'll be released tomorrow morning, under the condition you follow up with a psycher for therapy. It seems you have some unresolved issues."

"Unresolved issues?" I asked.

She nodded at my wrists, sporting similar cuts as my thighs. "This isn't your first time trying to hurt yourself."

I nodded. I would have agreed to anything to get out of that hospital room.

They released me to an angry father who sat silently next to me on the bus home. His clenched jaw only relaxed long enough to tell me he'd be paying my bill for years. I didn't even try to explain it wasn't my fault.

I wanted nothing to do with New Sofia's hard, clinical walls or harsh populous. It was a place to be tied down and judged. Old Sofia might be crumbling and poor, but at least I was free there.

I give Orlov a sullen shrug, unable to put into words the way the hardness of the city makes me feel like I'm walking on glass, about to slip at any moment.

"I won't push you, but I believe connecting with your maternity cohort could benefit you now and for years to come. I also think, when you're ready, exploring your disdain for New Sofia more might be necessary for your healing."

He says he's not pushing. It's not a requirement. But the way his thick eyebrows furrow down over his warm eyes as he waits for a response is enough pressure. He wants me to do this. Orlov rarely pushes me, so I cave to his suggestion. I owe it to him. Not just him. I owe it to baby-girl. If going to a strange, unearthly city once a week gets me off of Caz, I'll do it. For her.

"I guess I can try it."

CHAPTER EIGHT

MY CHEST CONSTRICTS tight around my lungs as the bus enters the Vitosha Tunnel. A dark shaft of heavy rock and concrete replaces the familiar orange-gray clouds. Lines of blue LEDs lead the bus deeper into the tunnel, casting a hypnotizing light against the windows.

The bus stops at the New Sofia platform and the passengers shuffle off of it. The road continues through the mountain to the cities on the other side, but I don't know anyone who has been further than the New Sofia platform. Most buses turn around here, wait twenty minutes, then head back out.

Skylar and I used to talk about continuing through the tunnel, seeing firsthand how the people in the smaller cities on the other side of the mountain lived. He could get a pass with his family connections. Without his help, the end of the bus line might as well be the end of the tunnel. I don't even cast a glance down the curving road.

The platform is a rectangle of concrete running for two bus-lengths in the tunnel's center. Light gray steps, slick as glass, penetrate its center. Their smoothness creates a distinct line between Old Sofia and the crystal city. I step onto them, my worn sneakers slipping. My toes tense, sending a jolt of nervous energy up through my spine as I navigate the steps.

At the bottom, a fat gate attendant sits at a large podium, eyes glued to the screen of a tablet. As each bus passenger passes the podium, they press a thumb to the red scanner and pause for a green light before continuing down the entry hall.

When my turn comes, I press my sweaty thumb to the grimy scanner and wait a breath. I smile at the attendant, but he doesn't even look up. A green light flashes, and I step forward into New Sofia.

The gray tunnel turns white and then translucent, a deep darkness covered by thick crystal, as if I'm walking through outer space. It widens until it opens into the Main Atrium. The map on my phone tells me it's the largest park in New Sofia, almost as big as the sprawling Borisova Gardens on the surface. Large trees and bushes grow from giant planters filled with soil. Near them, the floor softens into spongy lounge areas, tinted emerald — the crystal equivalent of grass. People lay on the soft sections, some barefoot but most wearing colorful felted slippers. I wonder what it would be like to glide down the polished floors in such soft footwear. My sneakers squeak when I forget to lift my feet, so I march with awkward high steps.

There are too many faces. No masks to hide the murmuring mouths as people talk low with their friends. I keep my eyes down.

Baby-girl turns a flip and kicks at my bladder as I pass through the cavernous room. Everyone else walks with confidence, not as if the floor might shift and slip out from beneath them. I fight the urge to drop to my knees and crawl. I remind myself it's shiny, but not ice.

I check the navigation on my phone and take the second exit off of the atrium. The large tunnel continues the same lie of exterior lighting from the atrium. I descend two floors, each with a ceiling pretending to be a blue sky and mottled green walls serving as a flat forest. Despite their three-dimensional effect, the halls squeeze in on me, threatening to crush me with unbearable weight. The filtered air, cleaner than the wild air outside, does nothing to slow my shallow breath and racing heart.

Room C17.

I press my palm to the white sensor and the thin panel of crystal that serves as a door slides to the left, disappearing into the wall so I can enter the fitness club.

A young woman sits behind a semi-circular desk, her painted-blue lips turned up into a smile as fake and hard as her city.

"Welcome to Active Neighbor." She touches her finger behind her ear. I can't tell if she's scanning me or pausing her implant to pay closer attention.

"I'm here for the September maternity cohort," I tell her.

She nods, holding up a well-manicured finger as her eyes track left, right, left, obviously reading something. She must have the business upgrade. Connect, they call it? Yeah, she seems connected to something.

"Ah, yes. They've already started in room two, first door on your left." She gestures down a hall, her attention shifting off me.

Five women sporting small abdominal bumps, and one with no bump, sit in a circle on white crystal blocks. Their heads swivel towards me as I enter, their faces blank, expectant.

"September cohort?" I mumble, edging into the small room.

The women wear expensive thermal suits stretched tight over their bumps. The non-pregnant woman wears an emerald suit that makes her blond hair look almost white. My Lycra pants and cotton tank top feel ragged and cheap against my skin.

"Come in, come in." The emerald woman waves me in with a smile. "We were just getting started."

I step through the doorway, nodding at each of the women—two in black, one orange, one pink, and one lavender. I perch on an empty crystal block. As the leader of the group congratulates us for entering the third trimester and explains what we have to look forward to this month, I continue to assess the other women in the group.

They aren't as similar as I thought they were when I first laid eyes on them. Two are blond, three brunette. All of them have the familiar swelling around the face I recognize in my own mirror, but beneath the pudge and glow, they have differences. One has high cheekbones, another a crookedness to her nose. These women are not just crystal clones. They look like they have personality. Maybe they're okay after all.

"I just don't know how I'll get through the first few months," the blond with the crooked nose wearing tight black therms admits. "The only nursery open is three floors up from our apartment, with no good elevator access. How am I supposed to manage all those stairs every time I need to feed the baby?"

"You can always pump and send the milk up by messenger," the brunette in orange says. "That's what I plan to do."

I bite my tongue hard and concentrate on the slight pain to keep fromlaughing.

The conversation finishes, and the leader invites us to stand as she walks to a panel on the wall. The lights dim and the walls turn a soothing light purple. Once we're standing, the cubes that served as chairs melt into the floor, which becomes springy beneath my feet. I stumble and let out a squeak, my toes splaying within my shoes to regain my balance.

The two blonds glare at me, one rolls her eyes, and they all settle onto the floor, sitting tall with their legs crossed. I copy them, willing the meeting to end as quickly as possible.

"We'll start a guided relaxation now," the emerald leader informs us. "Follow along as best you can, but remember this is about you and your baby. If you need to take a different position or modify the meditation, that's fine."

She instructs us to settle our breath, to breathe deep and steady, and to supply rich oxygen to our babies. Her voice—light and monotone—drones instructions so rhythmically that I follow along without hearing her.

My eyelids grow heavy. Either the wall in front of is pulsing with dark colors or my lids are falling shut and lifting open with my breath. The effect is relaxing, so I try not to distract myself with questions of how it's happening.

"This week your baby is developing blood cells within their bone marrow. Their bones are still soft. Let's concentrate on touching through their bones, to their marrow, and giving them the energy to make these blood cells that will sustain them." The instructor drones low and consistent, her words blurring together like the purr of a cat.

I run my hand under the curve of my belly, pressing into my skin, the pumping of my blood, the tough pink wall of my uterus. I press into the thick amniotic fluid to find baby-girl squirming with delight at my touch. The colors on the wall turn a dull, burnt orange. I hum deeply, tickling my baby with the vibrations of my chest. She stretches out, presses against my hand, and her colors grow stronger. Bright orange, like a crackling fire, fills the room, making me draw a deep breath. Just when I've adjusted to it, the brightness jumps again to yellow and, finally, an intense flash of white. I try to close my eyes against it, but it fills me, singing a high note like a clear ringing bell.

As the chime fades the regular lighting comes up and I'm not the only one wiping tears from my cheeks. The anger and anxiety balling up my shoulders and making me hate these women fades, letting me offer weak smiles and nods all around as I brush a drip of watery snot from my nose.

"Fantastic, ladies," the instructor says. "I'd like to remind you it's okay to feel emotional about your baby. Fear, excitement and wonder are all normal. Connecting with your emotions will help you connect with your child, so it's important to take the time to let yourself feel. Now, if you'll stand up and pair off, we will start confession."

I'm about to ask what confession is when a petite brunette in lavender therms that accent her shining olive skin grabs my hand and leads me two steps over to a pulsing white dot on the floor. The other women pair up and a set of thin, opaque walls grow up around each pair, enclosing us in small cubes with our partners.

I try to back away from the movement and end up bouncing side to side in the center of my newly formed cell. My partner lets out a deep laugh, masculine in its easy honesty.

"You act like you've never seen moving architecture before," she says.

"I haven't," I mumble, still eying the walls even though they've stopped moving.

A line creases her smooth, high forehead. "You're serious?"

"I don't come to New Sofia often." I can't bring myself to admit it's only my second time here.

She nods, gesturing to my sloppy, second-hand clothes as if she's just now noticing I don't belong here. "You know it's all fake, right?"

My jaw drops, and I reach out to tap the wall of our new enclosure. My nail gives off a light plinking sound.

She laughs again, louder and deeper, her bump bouncing with the energy of her chuckle. "Not the architecture. That's real. I mean the connecting with your baby bullshit. It's all a light show to make you feel like you're connecting, but it's Riker messing with your emotions, not you bridging your placenta to reach your fetus."

"Riker?" I ask.

She rolls her eyes and sinks to the still-spongy floor. "The woman who's never had a baby and is leading this class."

I let myself plop across from this woman, my knees spread to accommodate my hint of a bump.

"It's like Caz. It feels real while you're in it, but it's just a program pushing the right triggers in your brain. Nothing solid. Nothing you can touch." She reaches out and pinches my knee.

I jump and my hand leaps up to my ear in defense of the device, but my lips refuse to come to its rescue. She's right. My woodland creatures, while satisfying, aren't real. But that doesn't mean they don't help me. It's the same distinction Skylar could never make.

"Why do you still come if you don't believe in it?" I ask.

Her hand mirrors mine, petting her short black hair around her ear. "It feels good. I can know it's not real and still enjoy it, you know?"

Yes, I know. "So, what are we supposed to be confessing?"

She leans in and looks around as if she's checking for spies. "How much we hate becoming mothers."

"You're not serious!"

"Completely. This is our time to say how much pregnancy sucks and that we're frightened of being a bad mother because how on earth will we get our figures back and all that shit."

"You don't seem to have lost yours."

Her body is lithe and trim beneath her therms. Her bump sticks out to the front, but otherwise there doesn't seem to be extra weight to her.

"Yes, but just imagine your vagina. Or mine. Or let's say an unnamed vagina, passing a kid. There's no recovering from that."

We break into giggles and I forget for a moment that I don't want to be here.

"I'm Brianne, by the way."

"Valya." I stick my hand out. Hers is cool and dry when she takes mine.

I'm still holding her hand as the walls lower around us and the floor hardens to a glossy finish.

One of the other pairs is in a long hug. The other two women rest their arms around each other's waists. Apparently physical contact was appropriate, but my muscles still jerk my hand back from Brianne.

"Great job, ladies," Riker says. I can't keep my eyes off her flat belly. "I'd like to remind you I have several meditations available on Caz to help you connect with your baby and relieve the pregnancy aches you may feel these days."

"And to pad her bank account," Brianne murmurs close to my ear.

A smile tugs at my mouth, but I roll it between my lips.

"We meet again next week, at the same time," Riker finishes.

The other women linger, their chatter a buzz against my eardrums as I beeline for the door. No, she won't see me next week. I'll tell Orlov I tried, and it isn't for me.

As I reach the open panel, another body tries to squeeze through with me. I recognize the lavender therms brushing against my arm.

"You in a rush to get out of here, too?" Brianne asks as I let her pass. We fall into step naturally.

"I've got a bus to catch." It's a lie. The next tunnel bus won't be by for another forty minutes. I doubt she knows that, but my mind begins the process of replaying my error, sucking me into a loop of hot shame over my lie.

"Well, there's a great little sweet shop in the atrium. We could get a snack and wait for your bus if you want. My treat." Her friendly offer breaks through my shame-spiral before it can take root.

I stop walking and take her in. At first glance she looks like anyone else from New Sofia—well-fitted therms, subtle makeup, gelled hair. But her gentle smile reaches her eyes, making them sparkle with warmth.

"Sure, thanks," I agree.

The sweet shop is literally a hole in one of the massive walls of the atrium, something between a cave and a patio. A long, glass case displays a variety of cakes and cookies. It's been so long since I've had real sweets, that my mouth doesn't bother to water.

Brianne orders a wet-looking walnut roll, and I follow her lead, taking one for myself. She scans her thumb and we take the paper trays out to a small table in the atrium. I poke a bamboo fork at the roll, exploring its heavy texture with the tines.

"It's good," Brianne assures me, lifting a delicate bite to her lips.

I do the same and, when the bite hits my tongue, it sets off an explosion of sweetness that sends saliva out from every dark fold of my mouth. My eyes widen and then close as I let out the smallest hint of a moan.

"See, told you it was good." Brianne laughs, a high and free sound that eases the tension in my shoulders. How does one woman have so many laughs?

Listening closely, I wonder if she would let me record her and do a vlog about her laughter. I flush at the idea.

I need something to drink, but I don't want to ask Brianne to buy me anything else, so I take smaller bites. My body slowly adjusts to the sweetness, allowing me to enjoy it.

"It's my favorite bakery," Brianne says. "Do you not have a lot of bakeries in Old Sofia?"

"Oh, no, they're there," I assure her. "We love our sweets, too. But I'm saving money for the baby, so I haven't splurged much lately." Or ever. Another half-truth she doesn't need to know.

"Yeah, I get that. Expensive little devils, aren't they?"

Something about the way Brianne ends almost every sentence with a question puts me at ease. It's as if I couldn't possibly argue with her because nothing she says has rigid definition. Her softness tricks me into offering more details about my life than I intend to.

"Especially as a single mother," I admit.

"A single mother? That doesn't happen to many women who aren't rolling in enough money to think of a baby as a minor expense, right?" It's an invitation, made sweeter by the way she averts her eyes and concentrates on her pastry.

"Well, it wasn't exactly planned or unplanned. I thought I was infertile, and I broke up with the father a couple of weeks before I found out I was pregnant."

She gasps in an overly dramatic way that teases at shock and gossip. Her dramatic overture hits its mark, and I snort a heavy breath of air, almost a laugh.

She smirks, having achieved her goal, then leans in. "But seriously, shitty timing."

"Yeah, it was," I say. "But it made me realize I want this baby with or without him."

◯

Having a baby started as Skylar's dream. He drew me into it after an entire summer wrapped up in each other.

"I think you will be the mother of my children," he murmured. His lips brushed the peach-fuzz hair on my bare belly.

We were lying in the shade of the trees in the wild center of the Borisova gardens. Coming down from the excitement of our furious romp, I was nervous someone might walk by, but not nervous enough to move or cover up. Sex with Skylar had a way of sedating my racing mind. With him next to me, it didn't matter if someone stumbled over us post-coitally naked.

My fingers stopped roaming his stiff curls but stayed on his head.

"What's your dad like?" he asked.

I withdrew my hand, scooted away from him and reached for my clothes.

He placed his stubbly chin on my shoulder, stilling my frantic motion. "Did I freak you out?"

"No. It's just a weird thing to talk about when we're, you know."

"Naked?" He stretched out, letting the sun bounce off his lean but muscular chest, and I smiled despite myself.

"Yeah."

He tossed me my shirt. "So, what's he like?"

"Why does it matter? I'm not close with him."

He took my hand in his, brought my fingers to his lips. "Because they say a girl looks to have children with someone like her father."

I steadied myself with a deep breath and raised my gaze to meet his. "You're nothing like my father."

He kissed my hand again, then shifted to align his body with mine, his breath warming my ear. "I know you have a complicated past. It's written all over your body. I'm not about to push for anything. But you'll see. Someday, you'll figure out you're safe with me, and you'll want a baby together. I know it."

I tried to brush his words away with a kiss and light laughter, but the intensity didn't leave his eyes.

"How are you so certain?" I asked.

"Valya, Valya, Valya," he murmured my name like a holy chant. "I've been certain about you since the moment I saw you."

Our conversation planted a little worm in my ear that wriggled down to my heart, activated my ovaries, and demanded I create a child with Skylar. By the first snowfall, I was imagining an entire football team of babies running around our feet, growing strong on our unbreakable love.

Our love wasn't unbreakable, and the idea of managing a football team on my own is absurd. But this single life growing in me? She's loved and wanted and, hell, I'm excited about her.

Admitting it out loud to Brianne releases a flood of desire within me. My diaphragm squeezes down and I ache to reach inside myself and hold baby-girl. "I mean, why shouldn't I be excited? Babies are awesome, right?"

"Hell yeah, they are!" She nods along with me.

"What about you?" I ask. "Do you have the ever-supportive-partner?"

"Yes and no." Her bright eyes dim to a conspiratorial glow.

I raise my eyebrows, urging her to continue.

"Tony is my best friend. So, supportive? Check. And we're raising this baby together. So, I guess you can say he's my partner." She lets her voice trail off, leaving something unsaid.

"What's the no, then?" I press.

"We're not together. He was a sperm donor. In fact, I think he's going to ask his girlfriend to marry him soon. He would have already asked if it weren't for the baby."

"And you're okay with that?"

"I wish him all the happiness in the world. Like I said, he's my best friend. Besides, I don't care for male-types, you know?"

"So, you're one of those rich single women you were talking about earlier?"

"Maybe. But not like the women in our cohort."

"You mean the ones having babies just to put them into full-time care?"

"What's the point? They got pregnant on purpose, but it sure seems like they don't want a baby. So why? But I've always wanted a baby—more than a partner. Why wait for the relationship I don't want to have the one I do?" She laughs again, this time sweetly nervous. "I'm rambling."

"It's okay," I say. "Even a normal pregnancy is hard to describe, which it seems like neither of ours is. And I completely agree with you—what's the point of having a child you're not going to spend time with? But, if I'm honest, I wish I could afford a part-time nanny."

A hot blush burns my cheeks. I hadn't meant to bring up money, but this woman's charm has caught me off-guard.

Brianne arches an eyebrow and sits back, as if she has misjudged me, and I find my entire ordeal with Casual tumbling out in my defense. I tell her about Janice and the new law, and even give her some details I withheld from Orlov about my sleepless nights and the panic attacks threatening to return. I can't tell if she truly understands, but her judgment melts to a sympathetic frown as the words tumble from my mouth.

"I don't want full-time care," I assure her, "but I'm nervous. Weaning off is harder than I thought it would be, and I'm not sure I can do it."

She studies me for a long moment, and chews her bottom lip as if tasting the secrets I have shared with her. They are fatty secrets, laced with grizzle, but she doesn't spit them back out at me. Instead, she leans in close again, and this time it doesn't seem like she's pretending as she lowers her voice and whispers, "But you realize you have to, right? If they take your baby away, even for a year, you're not getting it back."

I frown. "It would just be protective custody, the city wouldn't strip me of my rights as a parent."

She leans in even closer, "Let me guess why you joined our cohort. Yours in Old Sofia was full, right?"

The tines of my fork make scratches along the top of my pastry, revealing cream flakes beneath the golden syrup. I press deeper, pushing the pastry open.

"Don't you wonder why ours isn't? More women here can afford babies. Why aren't they having them?"

I set my fork down. "Because they don't want kids?"

"No." Her voice is so low I have to lean almost to her lips to make out her words. "Women in New Sofia have a difficult time getting and staying pregnant. Something about living underground for generations messes with the reproductive system. If you give up your baby for that first, important year, a mother here will take it as her own. And you will not get it back."

I bite my lip. "But you're pregnant. You live here."

"I'm one of the lucky ones. So are you. Trust me."

I do trust her. I grip my belly and promise myself to do better.

By the time I leave for my bus, coming back to the cohort, or at least to hang out with Brianne, doesn't seem like such a bad idea. Looks like Orlov was right, again.

CHAPTER NINE

THE TRIP INTO New Sofia helps me shake off the boredom that crept up while not Cazing, but it doesn't keep it away.

I spend an entire day scanning job postings on my tablet even though it's pointless. No one will hire a pregnant woman in her third term, and it's not like there are a lot of traditional jobs in Old Sofia. All the good jobs moved into the new city. The ones that stayed outside—hard manual labor in the greenhouses, some administrative city positions, and the service industry—aren't reasonable options for me. Vlogging is remote work. Perfect for a single mother.

Brian said I have two months. That was almost two weeks ago. How does time slip away unnoticed while I'm bored, doing nothing?

My stats are crap. A handful of views over the past month. I have more views on old content—stuff about Skylar—but nothing that would attract advertisements or give me an in at a pub. Definitely nothing that will impress Brian and the people at Edges. No wonder he didn't offer. I need to try harder.

When I was with Skylar, my stats were decent. Each post had at least two thousand views. People wanted to hear about us. About him. I may not be with him, but I still have secrets of his I can share.

I set my tablet on its stand, open my recording software and adjust the height of my camera so it's square on my pimply face. A shower would freshen me up, make my hair less oily. But it's just a test run.

I give what I hope is a simpering, flirtatious smile, but it's hard to tell these days.

"By now you've all figured out I've broken up with Skylar. Or he broke up with me. Because let's be real, who would ever break up with the famous man who gives us all hope for a return to a simple life of freedom, out of the cities and away from the strict rules of the Global Governing Board?" I smile, give a whisper of a laugh, and continue. "But that's not the only reason I've taken a break from my usual vlogging topics."

I stand, turn to the side, and press my shirt down close around my bump.

"I'm pregnant! I fully expect all the likes and congratulations to stream in now. And yes, you're right if you think the father is Skylar."

I sink back to my chair and stare at the screen. My smile fades. I have a million other things to say, but no words come. I stop recording and press delete. Skylar deserves to find out about baby-girl privately, not through a public vlog. The view rate would jump, but I'm not that desperate. Not yet.

Heavy tears fill my eyes, threatening to fall. My implant practically pulses, begging me to turn it on. Is this the kind of emotion Olivia was talking about me flogging? A sorrow deep enough to fight off a person's own sadness. Even if someone could get off on my pain, I'm not sure I'd want to sell it. It's too much a part of me to share. Like baby-girl. Like Skylar once was.

I press my hands over my face and take a cleansing breath. Think of something else.

Sitting with Brianne, ideas flowed to me. I could do a series about laughter. People need uplifting news these days. That would be best with a flogging rig. Who wants to hear about laughter when they could experience it? I drum my fingers on my desk and close my eyes, letting the layers of Brianne's laughter run over me.

Even the memory pushes away my tears and self-pity. I open my eyes and turn on my camera.

"I met a woman the other day who had at least six different types of laughter. None of them were faked or forced. Within two sentences of hello she didn't have to hide behind a high falsetto. Instead, she gave a deep, true laugh."

My face smiles out of the screen, a dimple of pleasure showing at the corner of my lips. I give my own huff of stilted laughter, as if my disused well is springing into action for the first time in years.

"Her laughter put me at ease. It drew me into her as a

confidante. It made me trust her in a way I wasn't expecting. This woman has an entire vocabulary of laughter. She has a deep, unabashed, masculine laugh and a high, tittering, feminine laugh. She has the boisterous laughter of pleasure and even a conspiratorial whisper of laughter. I hope to bring her in as a guest soon and let all of you hear the depths and nuances of her laugh. But until then, I want to talk about my laughter and yours."

I lick my lips and let my eyes wander around my small room, looking for an insight I can pin down and share.

"Laughter is good for us. Physically, emotionally—it's healthy. It's also good for those around us. It puts others in a better mood, lifts them up when they feel hopeless or exhausted. True joy, shared through laughter, can be a medicine for a bruised soul. But just as medicine can be abused, so can laughter. There are the barbs that sting. The hidden laughter that excludes. These are the things I want to explore with you in my next series."

I press pause. It's rough but good. Optimistic. Something different. There's potential. But I can't risk Brianne seeing me swoon over her on my vlog. It's too embarrassing. Not worth risking our budding friendship. I close my recorder, but don't delete the piece.

I click on the AdStream app in the corner of my desktop. It's an inconspicuous little circle for the rush of information it contains. My screen fills with a flash of color.

Delish! The dish that makes a statement!

The words float across my screen before fading to a woman and toddler surrounded by a mess in their apartment. At least it's a story-line advertisement and not one of the subliminal ads. I can almost ignore the story-lines, with my camera still picking up the required amount of attention from my eyes.

"Hey, mom, what's for dinner?" a little boy calls out.

The mother, worn out from playing with a toddler all day, looks around in panic. She runs out of the room and down her apartment stairs to an automat. On the menu, *Delish!* flashes, surrounded by its iconic white half-circle. The mother types in a code and pulls out several packages.

Back in her apartment, she opens the packages and empties the contents onto plates. As she takes the plates from the microwave and sets them on the table, the camera pans out to show her apartment, immaculate now. The toddler giggles as she scoops him up and puts him in a high chair.

Despite myself, I laugh. *Delish!* isn't too bad, and only a little more expensive than other options. But it isn't about to clean my apartment and turn my child into an angel. Does anyone believe this crap?

The screen goes blank. In the bottom right corner, a number appears: .25 credits. To buy one of their stupid meals I'd have to watch twenty-five advertisements.

The next advertisement loads.

The screen turns into a series of flashes. I can't even distinguish the colors, let alone the words and symbols being dumped into my head. Nausea rises in my stomach, my breath comes faster.

I want it to end, but I can't turn my head away. I can't even blink. A sweet, sharp pain stabs at my pounding heart.

It's over as quickly as it started. My screen is blank. The corner reads: .5 credits.

I throw my tablet on my bed in disgust, fighting the urge to claw at my head and extract whatever they pumped into me. The need to scrub my brain makes my fingers twitch. But there's no way to get in my head, at least no way that won't land me back in the hospital.

"There's nothing there," I tell myself. "It was just an ad. It's normal. Safe."

I need a distraction. Something to stabilize me. I reach behind my ear.

No. Not something. Someone. I need Olivia.

My tablet rings six times before she picks up.

"Hey, how are you?" Her voice is strained. My eyes flick to the corner of the screen. 19:37. A stupid time to call. The pounding in my chest increases from a patter to a thud.

"I'm sorry, were you eating dinner?"

"Dinner? Oh, no, we were putting the kids to bed." Of course. The kids. I'm so selfish.

"Oh, so sorry, go ahead, we can talk another time."

Her phone microphone is sensitive enough to relay her heavy sigh. "It's fine. Really. Becca is taking care of it now. What's up?"

With anyone else I would apologize a dozen more times. But Olivia hates apologies more than interruptions, so I force myself to swallow my prostration.

"I just needed someone to talk to," I say.

"Are you okay?"

"Yeah, I . . . I tried to watch some ads, and it didn't go well."

"You know that's a bad idea." Straight to the point. She cuts through my blubbering bullshit to the heart of the matter. If my mind has always been a cloud of confused possibilities, hers has been a knife of precision.

"I thought I would try tonight. You know, in case the vlogging doesn't work out."

That heavy, tired sigh again. She doesn't even try hiding them these days. Deep in the background a muffled voice calls out to her. Becca needs her. I'm taking her away from her family. From her kids. My throat closes on itself and a stinging starts in the corners of my eyes.

"Valya, darling, I would love to help, but I don't know what to tell you. We're not kids anymore, and we don't live next door. It's not like I can come over every time you do something you know will set you off. Isn't there anyone else you could talk to? There has to be someone."

My eyes close and I go through my mental checklist. No family, at least none I intend on talking to. No school friends. No Skylar. Orlov is still a few days away. A face takes form in my mind. Smooth, olive skin, wide-set, upturned eyes. Straight, black hair. Brianne.

"Maybe there is," I murmur.

"That's great, sweetie. I know you'll get through this, and I'm sorry I can't help. Let's meet up soon, okay?"

"Of course." My tone lifts with my mood.

I find Brianne's profile easily enough, and her contact is public, but what if it's too late to call? Maybe she's eating dinner or . . . I'm already kicking myself for calling Olivia. I don't need more guilt to set off a round of anxiety. Plus, the long silences on the phone are too much of an edge for me, especially after frothing my brain with subliminals. I'm to the point where I can make necessary calls or chat with Olivia, but I doubt any amount of Casual or traditional therapy will completely eradicate my dread of speaking with people whose bodies are elsewhere.

Her profile doesn't tell me much about her. Her photo seems recent, or she doesn't change her appearance often. She works in the crystal nursery. Some scientist nurse or something. She's smart.

I hesitate. Doesn't Emersyn Enterprises control the nursery? What if they planted Brianne to win me over? My heart quickens. Orlov sent me to that group. Was it on purpose? I can't trust anyone.

Deep breaths slow my panic. She's not a spy, just another pregnant woman looking for friends. And yes, I can trust Orlov.

I continue down her profile. I don't want to make small talk about her job, anyway, and I hate that I'm supposed to. I'd rather skip it all and talk about . . . what? That's the real problem. I want to go deeper, but there is nothing to catch me when I peel back the layers.

I turn away from my tablet with a groan. Contacting Brianne was supposed to make me feel better, not worse.

An ache fills my chest, and the area around my implant burns. With a single touch I won't have to figure out the best way to contact Brianne or wonder whether it's pointless. I could be in a wonderland of soft music and simple, gratifying tasks. I could gain control.

I curl my fingertips into claws and rub them across the smooth desk. I exhale and send all the air rushing from my lungs, bidding my desires and anxiety to go away with it. The technique lessens the intensity of my frustration, but doesn't erase it. Not completely. It rests deep in my brain, close to my implant. I leave my tablet and go to the automat to buy a broccoli and cheese *Delish!*

CHAPTER TEN

THE DIGITAL JITTER of a call pulls me out of my morning slumber. After a night of tossing and turning, the early morning sunrise rocked me to sleep, letting me fall into the safety of the bright light of day. I'm not sure what time it is, but the fuzziness in my head says it's too early for calls.

"Answer," I croak from my supine position beneath my summer comforter. My spine relaxes against the lumpy mattress, feeling each bump and divot, waiting for me to sit up and twist to settle it all back into place.

"Hey, Valya?" The voice is bright, like the sunshine coming through my window.

"Yes?" I wait. Waiting is the best thing Orlov has taught me so far.

My father couldn't be bothered to sign me up for counseling, so I looked through the database and found a psycher downtown, close to my high school. Orlov's office had the same cream-colored walls back then. I stared at them during my first two sessions. Never looked at him. Said nothing. It wasn't until our third session that I gave him more than a grunt or sarcastic phrase. By then my resentment had faded enough for me to notice the warmth in his eyes. Or maybe it was because he told me he grew up two blocks over from my apartment. If he already understood what life was like in our neighborhood, there was no point in hiding my secrets from him.

"Sometimes life feels like too much," I admitted towards the end of our fifty minutes. He nodded, giving me time to elaborate, but I couldn't think of anything else to add.

"How does it feel like too much?" he probed.

"I dunno."

It was my favorite answer to give adults. It was as sullen and uncommitted as a shrug while being actual words. When I uttered those two words, whoever was bothering me gave up.

But Orlov didn't. He must have sensed the crack that had split open, just wide enough for him to sink his cerebral tentacles into, and he wasn't about to abandon it. "When is a time life felt like too much?"

His question forced a sharp flutter of images through my mind's eye. My teacher Kaya calling on me in class, asking me to explain the role of global warming in the social isolation movement. The answer shone clear in my mind—an entire lecture on the near-death of our planet and personal transportation—but with the eyes of my peers on me, waiting for me to speak, nothing but a hot blush came.

That was too much.

So was standing in the leftmost line at the market, waiting to get our weekly portion of prepackaged meals. Once I got to the front, I only had to scan my thumbprint and confirm my family's order. But the woman behind the counter watched me with hollow eyes, waited for me to fill the too-long silence between us. Her eyes were like Orlov's, expecting me to say something.

"Ugh, this, right here." I groaned, looking away from him.

"What about this feels like too much?"

"It's like you want me to say something, but I don't know what. Like we're staring in a vid and I never got the script."

He cleared his throat, then let the silence hang heavy between us. Finally he said, "Most people don't know what to say, and they're usually too busy thinking about what they should say next to pay much attention to how long you take to respond."

"That's not what it feels like," I grumbled. I slid my stubby thumbnail between my front teeth, found its edge, and nibbled at it.

"Of course not," he conceded. "But if you can trust me, I can give you some tools to help you get control over those feelings."

"Tools?" My eyebrows scrunched up in classic teenage contempt, but a sliver of interest sparked in me. "What kind of tools?"

"The first tool we will work on is simply waiting."

"Waiting," I mimicked, the spark of hope fizzling out. Waiting wouldn't help. I needed a way to answer faster or to make people stop asking me questions altogether.

"Yes, waiting!" His firm tone let me know my scoffing didn't put him off. "I want to help you learn how to give yourself time when you feel pressure. The more comfortable you become with waiting to respond or act, the more you realize that at least some pressure you're feeling is from your own expectations, not those of others."

"So how do I get comfortable waiting, then?"

He smiled a slow half-smile. "You've already taken the first step, which is to recognize the problem. For the next week I want you to practice something called interruption. Make a mental note of situations where you feel pressured to respond. Consider how you feel, what thoughts you have, whether you have a physical response. Take a step back and note it as a moment of pressure. We'll discuss these situations in our next session."

A week later I returned to his office with a list that filled two screens on my phone. Sweaty palms. Tight throat. Short, fast breath. Aware of my skin. The tips of my ears burned. I wanted to grip something. It went on.

We started at the top and worked our way down. Ten years later, I still follow the instructions he gave me: Breathe, sink into the tension, and let it sit until you're ready. Take control through waiting.

"Uh, Valya, this is Brianne." Her syrupy-sweet voice rewards my wait. "I thought you might want to hang out."

Brianne. The chances that she randomly thought about calling me the morning after I almost called her are slim. She must have seen that I visited her profile and wondered what I wanted from her. Is this a pity call? Is that why her voice is so gentle?

I breathe deeply, inhaling into my stomach, making my bump rise and fall. A sharp pain pinches my side and I wince. With another breath the cramp passes. *Focus.* The rise of swirling thoughts slows, solidifies, and dissipates. If only it was always that easy.

"Yeah, I'd love to," I say.

"Do you want to come here sometime today?"

My heart quickens and I have to sit up to control the flutter. I've got to get used to New Sofia if I'm going to continue going to cohort meetings, but I'm not ready to make the trip a daily excursion. Besides, tickets into the tunnel aren't cheap, and Orlov only credited my account for the meetings.

"Do you think you can come to Old Sofia?" A timid quiver crawls into my question.

"Yeah, sure, that's fine."

I'm surprised at the ease with which she accepts. Or maybe it's that hint of enthusiasm I can barely decipher. I haven't heard enthusiasm directed toward me, about me, in ages. Not since Skylar . . .

It's better to not think about him, and it's getting easier not to.

CHAPTER ELEVEN

A CONCRETE BUILDING painted brick red serves as the Old Sofia train station. Two trains come through from the north each day, drop off their goods at the warehouses, and continue to New Sofia. One returns. The other keeps going through the tunnel to the small, decaying cities south of the mountain. As a child, I listened through the steady hum of city noise for the rhythmic chugging of the trains. Three times a day my ears strained for the sound as if I was listening for news from afar. If I was honest with myself, which I rarely was, I would admit I daydreamed of the train carrying my mother back from Paris. I couldn't remember the train that took her away, but vivid images of the train carrying her back floated on the bold whistle of the archaic beast.

It was absurd. The trains carried neither secrets nor my mother. With the advancements in connectivity, taking a tour of another city was as simple as tapping into the public cameras or posting my questions to my favorite vlogger. Yet the rushing force of steel, actually having been there, awakened my adolescent will to wander. I suppose every teen had their own triggers that evoked a similar desire, but few teens had a parent who had gotten accepted to another city and left them behind. Starting university helped quell my thirst. I became interested in the life accessible to me. But returning to the train station to meet Brianne prompts a twinge of nostalgia for a past that never was.

I sit on a wooden bench, its thin slats creaking as my legs swing back and forth. Minutes tick by. The train should be here by now. It's like getting stood up, but by a hundred-ton beast of steel.

"Don't take it personally." My mantra steadies me. The rhythmic tapping of my tongue, three times against my hard palette, followed by the puff of air parting my lips soothes my anxiety. "Don't take it personally."

A familiar rumble in the distance takes over my ticking and puffing. The train—much newer than the station, but still older than me—hisses to an abrupt halt, and a small crowd of people get off. One holds her hand on the side of her belly as she swings down, a cream, linen tunic billowing behind her and her short, stretchy skirt showing off her athletic legs. A matching mask covers her lips, but her eyes are shining. The corners of my mouth tug up into a smile as I stand to greet her.

She leans forward, wrapping me in a loose hug as if we've known each other for years. Our bellies bump against each other beneath layers of fabric. The touch sends a strong flutter through my stomach and chest. If she notices my awkwardness, she doesn't let on.

"I'm glad you could meet up." Her mask muffles the clear tinkle of her voice and I almost think meeting in New Sofia would be worthwhile after all.

"I hope it wasn't too much trouble for you to come all the way out here," I say.

She waves my concerns away, her long, delicate fingers fluttering over the light summer breeze. "It's no problem. I've already started maternity leave, so I've got all the time in the world. Sorry I'm late. The train took forever to leave New Sofia with the checks."

"Checks?"

"Yeah, apparently there was some threat on the train system. A bunch of Chasers wanting to take over one of the trains or some nonsense." Her eyebrows wrinkle but her eyes hold that same conspiratorial sparkle as before.

"Terrorism? Now?" The isolation of each city is supposed to reduce the threat of terrorism that once plagued the planet. A shiver hits the base of my spine, making me sway. Skylar always wanted to take over a train. He said it was the only way to reconnect the wild areas with the cities. But he would never actually do it.

Brianne shrugs. "They didn't find anything. Probably someone blowing off steam. Threats with no follow-through."

We turn at the same time and walk, our feet matching pace.

She talks easily, words spilling from behind her mask. My fingers itch to take it off, the same way Skylar once freed me from mine. But I don't. Better safe than sorry while pregnant.

She seems to have the same approach, only bringing up safe topics: her work, the sweltering weather in Old Sofia, the joys of being pregnant. She carries the conversation, asking for nothing more than a few murmurs of agreement from me.

We walk a few blocks from the station before I'm ready to jump in. I reach out and grasp the edge of her long, thin sleeve, rubbing it between the tip of my thumb and middle finger before releasing it.

"I almost didn't recognize you without your therms. Do you come here often?"

The slightest twinge of sea-shell pink flashes along her cheekbone, running away as quickly as it came.

"They're left over from my internship. It was years ago. Are they ridiculous? Out of fashion?"

I can't decide whether she's serious or mocking me, but her low tone and shifting eyes make me give her the benefit of the doubt.

"They're fantastic. Besides, nothing in Old Sofia goes out of fashion. New fashions just layer on top of the old ones." I gesture at my full-length skirt and mismatched tank top. "If you're going to believe fashion advice from someone dressed like me."

"Aw, you look great." Her enthusiasm makes me believe her. "Anyway, I've wanted to come back to Old Sofia, and now I have an excuse."

"You want to come here?" I stare at the crumbling block apartments and cracked asphalt giving off shimmering waves in the heat. It's nothing like the perfection of New Sofia, which heals itself before anyone can notice the cracks. Letting my feet lead us without thinking, we've made it to Padalo, almost all the way to my old apartment complex. We stop and I make a point of turning my feet to lead her away from my childhood when we start up again. "Are you one of those people who hate New Sofia?" What I'm asking is *Are you like Skylar? Are you going to break my heart?*

"Hate it? No." she leans against a metal railing with flecks of blue paint, looking up at the gray clouds dotting the orange sky. "There are tons of things I love there. My work. Mild climate year-round. Some people. But there's always more to know, new people to meet. The world's bigger than just one city."

My teenage self would have said the same thing. Hell, she did, once or twice.

From this corner the park where Olivia and I spent countless childhood hours is visible. If I squint, I can imagine our bodies stretching out in the grass as we gazed up at the sky.

"I want to get out of here," I told Olivia.

"Everyone wants to get out of here." She tossed up a blade of grass and let it fall on her red silk mask.

"Not just Padalo," I said. "I want to travel."

"Travel?" She snorted as if I had said I wanted to take a rocket to the moon or join the mission settling Mars. "Maybe, someday, you might make it to New Sofia. But travel? No one does that anymore. You can barely afford a ticket to New Sofia. You think you'll ever have the money to go all the way to Berlin? Or Paris? Never."

"My mother traveled."

Olivia rolled over and threw a few blades of grass on me. I sat up to shake them off.

"Your mom didn't travel. She left. You have to come back to have traveled."

"Whatever. She got out. Went to Paris."

"If getting out means I never hear from you again, I hope you never travel."

I shake the ghosts from my head and walk away, leaving them to discuss how hard life would be. Brianne trails along with me.

"Couldn't you get assigned to another city for your job?"

"Nursery skills are specialized to each cave network. It'd take me a long time to learn another city's system, and few local governments would want to pay for that. Besides, I know people here. I wouldn't want to go somewhere new by myself."

We walk for over an hour. A few times my breath comes short, but the effort of the motion enlivens me. My body sinks into the rhythm, happy to be used, and our words come freely.

We meander from the safe topics into deeper conversation. I even tell Brianne about my dexiety.

"Dexiety?" She raises her eyebrows, thinks for a beat. "Depression and anxiety?"

I laugh as if I've never felt dexiety in my life. "Hey, you guessed it."

"It's a good phrase. Well, not good. But those things go together, from what I understand." She stumbles through her explanation and I hook my arm in hers, letting her stammering fade behind us.

When we arrive at a bus stop on the main road, I don't want our conversation to stop. Her liberal laughter makes me open to telling her anything. Well, maybe not anything, but more.

"This has been great," she says.

It's dinnertime. I can't invite her back to my tiny apartment, and I can't afford to treat her to a restaurant. Besides, that'd be too much like a date. It's time to say goodbye, but I don't want to let her go. I've had this problem before.

"Tell me more about Skylar," Orlov said.

It was late in the summer, and I had finally made my way to his office to explain why I had missed every one of our summer appointments.

"He's fantastic!" I gushed, aware of my shining school-girl eyes. I could talk about Skylar for the whole hour.

"What about him is fantastic?" Orlov asked with a gentle chuckle.

"Everything," I insisted. "At first I was amazed because he's such a good writer, so we have that interest in common. But it's more than that. The way he talks, it's like he's in my head sometimes. And he's interested in me, too, in what I think about things."

"You like the attention he gives you," Orlov summarized, as if my infatuation with Skylar was something simple and petty.

"You say that like it's a bad thing." My defenses flew up, creating a shell around me. I settled back into the shell and glared at Orlov. His acceptance had limits. I crossed my legs.

"I want to urge you to be careful. Your anxiety has prevented you from connecting with people in the past, so you're hungry for deep, intimate relationships," he warned.

"You think I'm imagining it?" My mouth rounded into an "oh" of hurt shock.

"No, no," he tried to settle me. "I think it's real, and that's what's risky about it. You may jump into an intimate relationship without assessing it clearly."

I didn't heed his warning about Skylar. But years later, his words echo back to me, telling me not to invite Brianne to dinner. I can't trust that she's as good as she seems. Maybe my need for intimacy is blinding me once again. We'll take it slow. If there's anything to take.

"Let's do this again," Brianne suggests, wrapping me in another of her belly-mashing hugs.

She boards the bus and sinks into a seat by the window. I wait for her to touch her ear or pull out her phone, but she waves at me, not breaking eye contact until the bus moves out of sight.

CHAPTER TWELVE

TODAY'S THE DAY. Tepid water falls from the shower, striking like needles against my aching breasts. It's not even warm enough to fog up the plastic-framed mirror. If I turn my head to the right and pin my left ear forward, I can stare at the small lump of my implant. I've tamed my habit of reaching for it every time I'm bored or stressed. I haven't been on Caz for three whole days and, more importantly, nights. I'm ready.

On the bus I wonder why they can't block my access remotely. It's not as if they're removing the actual implant. A few keystrokes on a computer somewhere and it should be deactivated. But what do I know? I barely passed programming one, and I somehow talked my way out of programing two, replacing it with a handwriting self-study. Maybe shutting down the device completely requires proximity.

The insertion clinic is on New Sofia's main level, past the central atrium. My clothes make me stand out, as usual, but most people are too absorbed in their augmented realities to even glance at me.

Near the far side of the large space, two blurs of color fly at me. The second is on a collision course with me. My hand flies to my stomach as I sidestep the chaser, a puff of air cooling my face as he passes.

The woman meandering a few meters behind me isn't as lucky, and the first chaser barrels hard into her shoulder, sending the woman into a spin as the chaser hits the ground.

Stopped, the blur turns into a young woman wearing therms. Unlike the chasers above ground, the only thing that sets her apart from the rest of the people in the atrium are the flashing jewels at the base of each finger and near her left eye. She doesn't even have the gaunt, sinewy look the chasers of Old Sofia have.

"Fuck, I lost it," the chaser mutters to her companion.

"Take it outside!" the woman yells, massaging her shoulder.

The second chaser lifts a middle finger at the woman and turns to his partner. The two whisper intensely and ignore the harsh glares directed at them. The girl chaser locks her gray eyes with mine. I blush and look away from her, down at the path.

They might not have the same sense of devil-may-care style, but these chasers seem as rude and wrapped up in their augmentation as the ones in Old Sofia. Maybe our two cities aren't so different.

Yet another hand scanner awaits me at the entrance to the insertion clinic. No wonder so many 1984 vlogs come from here. Almost every doorway has a scanner. No movement is private.

The young man sitting on a high stool next to the scanner offers no sign of recognition, but he looks like the same young man who was here two years ago when I had the implant placed.

To say I was nervous would have been an understatement. Fear woke me up before the sun was out, and by the time we sat down for breakfast, I was downright petrified.

"This is your choice. I get that you think you need to do this, but I can't support you in it," Skylar said when I asked him yet again to come with me.

"Orlov says it's my best chance of stopping the night terrors and getting control back in my life." I pushed around the scrambled eggs on my plate, unable to stomach them.

"Do you feel out of control? Here with me, don't you feel safe?" His blue eyes clouded with uncertainty and his hand reached across the table, falling just short of my fingers. "We've got things under control—you and me. Don't we?"

We did have it under control. When Skylar was with me, my dexiety hid from his bright eyes and booming voice. When it showed its stubborn side, he took me to bed and distracted me, making love in a raw, bestial manner that didn't leave room for thought. He slammed me into the moment and kept me there. He was persistent and creative, and I would never tell him his methods didn't work. They did, as long as he was there.

But on the days he went hiking in the wilds, gathering data for his next novel, I was alone. The dexiety flooded back into me. A casual implant would get me through the days and sometimes weeks he wasn't there.

"Fine, I'll go alone." I didn't mean to sulk when I said it, but the words came out flat, like a child trying to manipulate her parents into buying her a sweet.

He stood from the table. "Don't do that. Please."

"Do what?" I toed the leg of the table, refusing to look at him.

A rush of air left his lungs and swept over me. "Valya . . . "

Whatever he was going to say, he must have decided against it. Maybe it was too painful to say. Probably it wasn't worth saying. I wasn't going to listen, anyway. He grabbed his backpack and left without telling me when he'd be back.

The door slammed, splashing waves of guilt over me, but its force wasn't strong enough to keep me rooted to my chair. I was desperate enough to go on my own.

The tunnels slithered around me like snakes. They were too narrow and too short, and they all looked the same. Some glowed with faint blue hues while others blasted bold green, but to me the colors meant nothing.

I circled the main atrium twice, sticking close to the amber wall, before I turned on directions on my cell phone. The GPS, which I expected to falter so far below ground, worked perfectly, and I kept my eyes glued to the screen as a faint blue dotted line told me which way to walk.

Besides precise directions, the screen provided a legitimate reason to avoid looking at anyone. Six years after my involuntary hospitalization, the face of the harsh psycher, her forehead pinched in judgment, was the last thing I wanted to see.

A gentle buzz on my handset let me know I reached my destination. I looked up at the slack-jawed, glazed-eyed face of a young man pointing to a hand scanner.

"I'm here for an implant," I told him.

He jabbed his finger toward the scanner more emphatically.

I placed my hand on the scanner and waited.

"Valya. I have you listed for a basic casual, medical purposes, correct?"

"Yes, I have . . . "

He cut me off with a wave, not interested in why I needed the device. He pressed a button, and the door slid open to reveal a large white room with about ten white cots. Each cot had a small metal table and a computer console next to it.

A woman breezed up to the door. She wore her smile the same way she wore the large hoop earrings dangling from each earlobe.

"Valya, you're right on time." She motioned for me to follow her into the clinic and led me to a cot near a wall. Patients sat on three of the other cots, but the clinic was mostly empty. My clinician stood at a console as I sat on the cot next to it. Her lips moved as she read a few screens of information.

She motioned for me to lie back, my head near the computer and my feet facing the door of the room. "Everything is in order. You're getting a basic casual, and I'll give both you and Orlov access to your account, right?"

"Uh-huh," I murmured. Orlov had explained the implantation process, but I had been too nervous to listen.

"Where did you have your scans done?"

"At North Clinic in Old Sofia." The scanner was in the basement of Orlov's building, next to the laboratory.

"You should have gotten it done here. It's blurred. But for a basic casual, I guess it's fine. I would have to send you for another scan if you were getting connect."

Sitting still for the five-minute scan had been hellish the first time around. But I almost wanted her to send me for another one. What if the picture was too blurry and the implant was a millimeter off when it wrapped its tendrils around my brain? My heart started a familiar racing. My jaw clenched.

"Relax. I do this every day." She pulled on a set of latex gloves and took a long, thin, metal tube from a drawer in her table. She held it up for me to see.

"This is the insertion tube." She held a finger to the tip. "Your device is right here at the end. I'll take this air-gun, fit your tube, and a single burst of air will send the device beneath your skin. You'll feel a pinch and perhaps some pressure."

As she talked, she screwed the long metal tube into a small air-gun connected to the computer.

"What if you miss?"

"Miss? Not possible. Feel there, behind your ear. You feel that large, flat bone? That's what I'm aiming for. It will stop the device from going further into your head. There's almost no risk."

Almost.

"Ready?"

I wasn't, but I would never be, so I nodded anyway.

"Okay, hold still." The cold metal bit into my skin. "Exhale nice and long."

The air left my lungs and a sharp pain shot through my head. My jaw clenched, harder this time, and I winced. Then the pain was gone.

The woman re-holstered the gun next to the bed and held a cotton ball behind my ear. "Hold this."

I pressed the puff of cotton to my head while she took off her gloves and turned to the computer. Nothing happened. Maybe my device was broken. Or maybe Casual didn't work on me. I had heard stories about people whose brains couldn't decode the electrical impulses of the device.

"Okay, all set. I'll turn it on now."

My brain filled with bubbles, like the soft rush of a soda being opened. In the darkness behind my closed eyelids, the tickling, bubbling sensation was almost too much to handle. My mouth opened, ready to cry out, but before any sound came, a firm hand landed on my shoulder, steadying me.

"Shhh," the woman said, grounding me with her voice. "It's okay. Just relax."

Half a minute later, the fizzing sensation subsided, and I could make out the glowing lines of a familiar visual interface. It was the soft creams and browns of Nature, but so much more. I could almost touch the three-dimensional setting. The flat dots in the games became floating spheres. The flowers had actual stems with sharp thorns that made me wince.

I had no idea how to select a level or start a game, let alone how to play.

"You see the interface now?"

I nodded but didn't open my eyes. "I can smell it."

The flowers, the grass. All the greenness flooded my nostrils with a fresh, tangy scent.

"Great, let's teach you how to use it."

I spent four hours in the clinic, learning how to control my Caz. My teacher was patient, her voice soft and smooth. I hope I'll get her for deactivation, too.

○

"I'm here for deactivation," I explain to the boy at the podium as I scan my thumbprint.

"Deactivation?" He lifts one eyebrow, glances at the screen in front of him, back at me, back at the screen.

"Is there a problem?" I ask.

"Not exactly, but your appointment is with R&D, not here."

"Research and development? Just to get the implant deactivated?"

"I dunno, I'm telling you what I see here. We do standard deactivations remotely. There's no need to come in unless you're having the implant removed. Even then, not sure why R&D would get involved. But that's what it says. Room B12, down in R&D."

Another ten minutes of wandering the New Sofia halls before I find room B12 and palm my way in. A woman in a white lab coat sits in a high-backed chair, gazing at a large computer screen. I clear my throat to get her attention.

"Just a minute," she says without turning around. She continues typing. The room doesn't offer much to look at. A large metal cylinder with several buttons lies on a table, taking up most of one wall. Another wall has two rows of computer screens. The woman manipulates four of them with fast keystrokes. The final two walls are bare crystal, humming a calming green hue.

I wait, not sure why I'm waiting or who this woman is. Her fine ginger hair in loose curls irritates me. Everything about her poise irritates me. I hate that she called me to her, that she has power over me while I know nothing about her. My anger boils in the blood of my wrists, and I scratch at my scars.

After a few huffs, uncrossing and re-crossing my arms and considering leaving, my anger chills. Why waste energy being angry? It's just bureaucracy. I'll wait it out, she'll shut off my Casual, and I'll be free from this woman manipulating me like a marionette.

As if she was waiting for my anger to subside, she turns around. The makeup on her face is precise, accentuating her strength without making her appear harsh. The kohl around her bright green eyes serves as a flag, waving me into her tractor-beam stare.

"Valya." Her voice holds a deep intimacy, as if we're old friends, which would usually make me bristle. But the way she pronounces the "y" in my name, shoving two vowels into the space of one to make a hard "ia" before softening for the final, "a" . . . Only my father pronounces my name like that, with sounds that have been lost since English became the global language.

"And you are?"

She smiles with her whole face, her eyelids dropping over her eyes to reveal a pink shadow.

"How rude you must find me." Her lids left again. "I'm so used to everyone knowing who I am. My name's Emersyn."

My jaw drops, but I don't let my mouth fall all the way open. "As in Emersyn Enterprises?"

"Yes. Although, we're considering re-branding. Our projects are so much more than just our family now, what with chasing and connect and . . . well, I can't tell you the rest, but exciting advancements in our offerings will be available soon." The blue in her eyes shifts a shade brighter. She reaches back and pulls her hair into a bun, smoothing it tight before wrapping it in an elastic. That's when I recognize her as the woman I saw coming out of Orlov's office. Not a patient at all.

My heart thumps against my ribcage, sending blood roaring through my ears, making it difficult to hear. The room, Emersyn with it, seems far away, dim, pulsing.

"Are you okay?" she asks. Maybe those aren't her real eyes. Maybe they're some ocular implant that, when turned on, create cognitive dissonance in people. That explains the thundering that refuses to leave my head.

Somehow I'm sitting. She must have offered me her chair, guided me to it, helped me sit.

Breathe in. Breathe out. Concentrate on the slow pulsing of the crystal wall. In. Out. The rushing fades. Emersyn comes back into focus.

"Well, it's been a while since I've received such a, shall we say, visceral, reaction. I'm flattered."

It's just my anxiety, she shouldn't be flattered. But if it keeps her from thinking about how weird I am, I'll let her assume my reaction has more to do with her than it does. It's another one of Orlov's tricks: shift the focus onto the other person. It helps me feel like they aren't judging me.

"You're probably wondering why you're here. After all, you don't need the person who created your implant for a straightforward deactivation procedure," she says.

Not responding is the best way to keep a person like her talking. They don't like silence, and they love the sound of their own voices.

"Simply put, I'm here to convince you to join our little trial."

Of course. What else could the most powerful woman in Sofia want with a woman like me? Nothing, except my body for her science. Not even mine, but my baby's. Both hands fly to my stomach as if she might rip my baby from my womb.

"I told Orlov I'm not interested."

"Yes, you did." She stands and closes the distance between us, her face just a foot from mine. "But I feel like he might not have presented our case strongly enough. I see you're a protective mother, so I won't waste our time outlining the benefits you would receive from the trial. We'd need to monitor your baby, so we'd move you and her to an apartment near the lab in New Sofia. But that means little to you, right?"

My head nods along as if her ruby lips have put me in a trance.

"Right. You care about your baby, and I admire your selfless dedication. That's why I want to show you this."

She takes two steps back to the long metal tube. It reaches her navel, but the compartment that opens after she presses a series of buttons is no bigger than a tablet, whatever she extracts from the compartment disappears in her palm.

She waves me towards the small table in the middle of the room and waits for me to join her. Only then does she set down a tiny, translucent device, smaller than the tip of my pinkie fingernail. Its shape and size is familiar, and my hand reaches up to massage my implant.

Emersyn notices my hand and a smile flits over her lips. "Yes. It's an implant, but not like yours. This is our latest design, made from the same crystals that compose our city."

"Crystals?" The glowing wall catches my eye again. The device on the table is only a chip from these vast caverns.

"The amazing, revolutionary thing about crystal architecture isn't that we can build enclosed systems underground. It's that the crystals remain malleable after construction. We can continue programming them to suit our needs as our city grows.

"The problem with current implants is that once they're inserted, they can receive data, but their structure can't change."

"Software updates but no hardware upgrades," I murmur.

"Exactly. This is why implants aren't recommended for children with growing brains. It's why you're smart to refuse a standard implant for your baby. Why I don't blame you for ignoring my emails."

I flush, guilt washing through me. I should have written back and said no. I should have at least acknowledged her. I was impolite.

She picks up the tiny crystal, balancing it on the tip of her index finger. She holds it beneath my nose, and my eyes cross with the strain of focusing on it.

"But these implants will grow with your baby. We can reprogram their shape and the paths they take within your child's brain. Actually, we made it so it will reprogram itself to meet your baby's needs."

My face must show my confusion because she stops speaking, smiles gently, and sets the rice-grain crystal back on the table.

"How much do you know about the implant?" she asks.

"Enough to consent to its placement." My retort is bitter, covering how much of a mystery the device is to me. But Emersyn doesn't seem fooled.

"Standard implants are made from metal—a titanium casing and platinum-iridium electrodes. Before the casing is placed, your specific electrodes are coiled inside, waiting for deployment. We activate the device, and the electrodes slide into place. Then that's that. They stay there. Moving them, even for extraction, can be dangerous."

A slithering starts in my brain, as if the wires she's talking about aren't microscopic hairs impossible to be felt. Talking about the physicality of Caz always brings up these phantom sensations. A sharp pain, the younger, more annoying cousin to a migraine, settles behind the bridge of my nose and won't shake loose.

Emersyn pats my shoulder as if she can sense my discomfort and presses on in her explanation. "With crystal technology, the implant creates the electrodes after it's placed. They are so thin and precise that they can retract for removal and be reconstructed for new placement. Like braces. They continue to adjust to fit the brain."

"Braces change the teeth—their shape and the way they grow. They change a person's smile. I don't want braces on my baby's brain."

"Braces make teeth the best they can be. But don't worry, it's not a perfect analogy. We have no plans to shape the brain development. That's too complex of a task, even for us."

She thinks she's comforting. Her smug smile and the brisk excitement lighting her eyes betray her confidence. She thinks she'll win me over today. She's done her research, even talked to Orlov to find my weaknesses. But she overestimated her persuasive prowess.

"No, Emersyn. Convincing me it's safe isn't enough. The only way I would consider this trial is it was something my daughter couldn't live without. As far as I can see, you need us, but we don't need you. Now, can you please turn off my implant?"

If she's surprised, she doesn't show it. She scoops up the crystal implant and returns it to the tube. With her back to me she says, "It's already turned off. That's what I was doing when you came in."

"So you wasted my time, calling me here?"

She shrugs, turning to face me, the pleasantry gone from her lips, which have settled into a cruel line. "I thought we should meet. Because you'll change your mind, and we will work together closely. The baby is Skylar's isn't it?"

"Excuse me?" I haven't registered the father yet. Would Orlov have told her such intimate details about me?

"I feel protective of you and your baby. After all, we're family."

"Family?"

She tut-tuts. "Skylar doesn't talk about us. With all his anti-tech rubbish he can't let the world know he's the nephew of the CEO of Emersyn Enterprises. But I would think he'd at least tell the mother of his child. Oh well. Now you know. Have a good day, Valya."

This time, the familiar way her tongue wraps around my name holds no comfort. She closes her mouth, her lips constricting around the last syllable as if she's holding me prisoner.

Outside the laboratory, my strength fails and my back finds a hard wall to rest against. My breath comes fast, and hot tears spill over the rims of my eyelids, turning cold as they hit my burning cheeks.

I lift my hand to my ear, but pressing the nub does nothing. I press harder and harder, a bruise turning the skin beneath my ear tender. The walls close in on me, the panic rises. It's off.

94

CHAPTER THIRTEEN

MAKING IT OUT of New Sofia seems like an impossible task. But stumbling down the corridor, up two escalators, and down a short hallway to the atrium . . . I might be able to do that. At least the atrium will have more space. The squeezing and pulsing of the walls will stop. Hopefully.

Through the cloud of confusion settled around me, my thumb turns on my phone and finds Brianne's contact. Working on autopilot, it presses send. A distant ringing soothes me. Her calm voice comes through the tiny speaker, cheerfully unaware of the darkness overtaking me.

"Valya, you called!" she squeals. I concentrate on her voice, clinging to it like a lifeboat. It's buoyant enough for both of us.

My numb lips tell her something. Her cheerfulness falls to concern.

Move. Get to the atrium. Head down, avoid eye contact. I imagine my fox just around the corner, leading me to the safety of my new friend. Looking up, I imagine a flash of his red tail, sleek and low to the ground. I speed up to catch him and am almost running as I tumble into the atrium.

Brianne's waiting for me, her teeth grinding on her bottom lip. When she sees me, her eyes widen and she shifts her weight towards me as if she might tackle me with a hug. But before her arms wrap around my trembling body, her muscles tense and she freezes on her tiptoes. She lowers herself to flat feet and waits, saying nothing.

Relief floods me like seawater licking the sunburned beach. She knows what to do. What not to do. Either she's intuitive as hell or she's had a friend like me before.

"I didn't know who else to call."

"Yeah, hey, no worries. Do you want to talk about it?"

Not, "what happened?" Nothing demanding, just a possibility. Her patience warms me. My tongue releases, telling her about my meeting with Emersyn.

"Wow. The Emersyn? Creator of Casual? They must really want you for their study," she notes after I finish.

"Not really. I mean, there's nothing special about me except that I'm poor and fucked up in the head. Actually, I'm surprised they haven't hit you up. I would think New Sofia women might be more enthusiastic about that kind of technology."

"They wouldn't want me." She casts a glance around the atrium. People lounge on soft pads or move about the room with quick strides. Low voices hum like the beating of wings in a beehive. Everyone is involved in their own conversations. Despite Brianne's dramatic suspicions, no one looks over at us tucked away in a rounded alcove. She pushes her earlobe forward, revealing a spider web of raised scar tissue standing out as cold white against the golden warmth of her skin.

"What happened?"

"My brain rejected the implant. Every time they activated the device, I had a seizure. So they left it off. But even then, I kept getting dizzy and sick. They had to remove the implant completely. It was too dangerous to leave in." She shrugs as if the major brain surgery to remove an implanted device is no big deal.

I reach out and tuck her coarse hair behind her ear, running the side of my finger along the scar.

She grabs my hand away from her scar, pulling it to her chest. "Don't pity me. It just doesn't work for some people."

"See! I don't want something like this to happen to my daughter. They can't tell in advance if her brain will reject their tech, and it's so new it's even more likely than with the current Caz."

She shakes her head. I missed the point.

"Look around. Almost everyone here has an implant. They're immersed in their augmented reality, and I have no access to it. It's lonely without the implant."

No wonder she's willing to come to Old Sofia. There, the expensive devices distract less than half of us. She can feel normal. I squeeze her hand.

"You think I should do it?"

"It's different for everyone. Life without it is hard in New Sofia, sure. But there are risks as well. I'm not telling you what to do, not for your baby." She nods at my bump. "I wanted you to know about me."

It's then that I realize this happy, positive woman is as awkward as I am. I grin at her and pull her into a hug. Our bellies rest against each other and my chin snuggles down into the hollow of her neck.

"Thank you for coming," I say, not letting go.

On the bus home, I can't stop fidgeting. I haven't used the device in days, but now that it's gone, I ache for it. It's as if part of my brain has been hollowed out and I'm missing a critical aspect of my identity.

I glance around the nearly empty bus, unable to keep my gaze on a single point. I can't focus on the faces, and the gray buildings zooming by make me dizzy.

To keep from vomiting, I pull up Brianne's contact on my phone. I don't press call. Knowing she's there is enough.

VALYA:
MONTH EIGHT

CHAPTER FOURTEEN

T HE COOL GEL coats my abdomen, and seconds later, baby-girl appears on the screen. It's impossible not to see her as a human now. Her round head, her tiny fingers, the strong legs kicking out at me. Even in bits and pieces, it's obvious she's a baby. My baby.

As Janice focuses on baby-girl's face my heart skips up into my throat and I jolt to a sitting position. The grainy black-and-white picture on the screen, baby-girl's chin and nose in bright white, fading to gray and the eye sockets black . . . it's the white man from my dreams. The terror that usually stays tucked away in my sleep washes over me.

A squeak of surprise escapes my lips, and then I calm myself, sitting back on my elbows. Baby-girl's face disappears from the screen, and Janice holds the wand up, her eyebrows knitted down hard over her eyes.

"Are you okay, Valya?"

"Yeah, I just . . . " But there's no explaining the images that flashed through my mind. I could tell her about the night terrors, my history with the white man. It's logical. She would agree the ultrasound creates a similar eerie picture. But that's what Orlov is for.

"I got the measurements. You can wipe yourself off now."

But I'm not ready to wipe myself off. I don't want my last glimpse of baby-girl for the next month to be that one. Baby-girl is not an object of terror. She's a spirit of joy. That's all I will let her be.

"Can I see her once more?"

Janice nods me back down on the table and puts the wand to my stomach again. Baby-girl shifts and the screen picks up her profile. The tiny mountain of her nose dipping into the rippling valleys of her lips is less startling than the blackness of her eyes. *Not black. They have color. Either blue like Skylar's or brown like mine.*

As I wipe off the sticky goo, Janice reads the statistics. "17.5 inches, almost five pounds. You're on track for a healthy baby girl."

The statistics mean little to me, but her matter-of-fact tone comforts me.

"I see you had your Casual shut off." She moves behind her desk and pulls out her tablet.

"You told me I had to."

A laugh almost makes its way through her mouth, but she clamps her lips tight over it, glancing back down at her tablet.

"You're right, I did. But I've talked with Orlov since then. I know you had another option. As a doctor, I shouldn't influence your parenting choices. Ethically, I'm only supposed to give you medical advice and let you know the standards and laws that apply to your situation. The choices are yours. But I want to tell you . . . I think you're doing the right thing."

Despite the kindness of her words, I bristle at her judgment. Janice is practically a stranger. Sure, she's seen inside me a few times, but she doesn't know me. Not well enough to tell me what's right for me and baby-girl.

Before the words drill out from my lips, understanding washes over me. Besides me, Janice is the one who knows baby-girl best. She isn't talking about what's right for me, only for baby-girl. She's baby girl's champion, baby-girl's voice while she's growing in me.

"Thanks." The word cannot convey the gratitude overwhelming me. Tears well in my eyes—courtesy of the high hormone levels—and one spills hot down my cheek. That has to say what words cannot.

My walk hasn't become a waddle, not the way I imagined it would. Instead, it's a gentle rocking, left to right, like I'm dancing with baby-girl. She rarely kicks when I'm walking, so I assume she likes the sloshing of fluid around her.

"Can you feel your heaviness?" I ask her as I walk home after my appointment. "The doctor says you're five pounds now. Just about."

A buzzing in my purse interrupts our one-sided conversation.

I pull my phone out and check the message. It tells me a package is waiting for me at the automat near my apartment.

I can't remember the last time I got a package. There's no one to send me stuff. As I approach the low line of lockers, I realize that's a lie. I remember who sent me my last package.

Sending mail the "old fashioned way" was one of Skylar's romantic notions. He liked the way he could touch a necklace or book, hold it in his delicate hands, stroke it while thinking of me, and then send it to me. He told me it felt like sending a part of himself, as if his molecules seeped into the item and made their way to me. He wasn't amused when I pointed out it was his dead skin cells that sloughed off onto his precious treasures.

He sent me some trinket whenever he was gone for more than a week. He thought he was being sweet, but his tokens of affection frustrated me. He had to come back into town to find an automat and drop off the packages. Why couldn't he ride his bicycle the extra twenty minutes to come see me? Romance be damned, I would have rather been holding him than pretending his energy seeping through an old book satisfied me.

The closest I came to admitting how ambivalent his gifts made me was when he left for five weeks one summer. He sent two packages to make up for his prolonged absence. The first contained a long leather cord with a crystal wrapped in silver wire hanging from it.

His note read:

Valya,

This crystal grew wild in the mountain range south of here. This was before people decided they were better than nature at making crystals.

Love,
Skylar

I wanted to hate the necklace, but I couldn't help loving it. Crystals were a matter of contention in our apartment. They caused an argument almost every time I brought a sculpture home from the crystal singers.

The girls—every crystal singer I've ever seen was a girl—had a booth set up at the Southern open-air market.

People hauled everything to that market. Jewelry and art, made by wannabes and the best artists in town, were squeezed in close to found, saved, and stolen items. Pots and pans from when cooking was popular, nestled between clothes. Racks and tables and bins filled with colorful fabrics waiting for their next owner. As a teen, I walked along the narrow paths winding through the stalls, daydreaming about being able to afford to buy anything I wanted. Or anything at all.

I stumbled on the crystal singers my second year of university while walking arm in arm with Olivia. She dragged me from one booth to the next, ohs and ahs escaping from her mouth. A low hum vibrated beneath the bargaining and chatter of the market and we stopped walking. We shared one of those looks—wide-eyes beneath furrowed brows. We had to find the source of the humming. We both stuck our necks out and cocked our heads to the side, letting it pull us along as if our ears were tied to the noise.

The thick hum crackled with a sort of static. But at the same time it was rich with nuance. As we neared its source, a higher-pitched drone layered on top of it, oscillating up and down like a leaf blowing across the surface of a lake.

We turned a corner and gasped. A beautiful girl about our age, dressed in a plain cotton gown, black hair loose around her shoulders, had her eyes closed in deep concentration. Her lips, thin and dry, changed shape to direct the tone of the high drone. In her palm lay a tiny crystal, no bigger than a sugar cube. The milky white block had four copper wires connecting it to a small black device, a bit bigger and blockier than a cell phone.

An older woman, dressed in jeans and a t-shirt, touch the girl's belly, adjusted her posture, and pinched her jaw. The low note dropped even lower, the crackling strain of her vocal chords cut out, and a deep vibration rushed through the crowd.

The droning stopped and the girl's eyes flew open as she reached up to turn off her casual.

"I think I did it!" she gushed to her tutor.

"There's only one way to find out," the older woman answered.

She reached out and pressed a series of buttons on the blocky machine.

We waited. The old woman, the girl, Olivia, me, and the small crowd that had gathered all held our collective breath.

At first, nothing happened. The girl's face crumpled, losing the rigidity of her excitement. But then, slowly, the crystal transitioned. It grew rough, almost scaly. One side expanded out, the other down into a point. Wherever the crystal changed, the scaliness rushed over the surface, almost like a fizzing soda. Then it was over. On the table lay a delicate crystal heart as large as my fist.

"Amazing," I breathed.

"Beautiful," Olivia agreed, keeping her eyes on the girl's face.

"Crude, but a successful singing," the older woman commented.

We returned to that stall almost every weekend that fall. The singing, and the shapes it produced, drew me. The girl drew Olivia. By the time I moved in with Skylar, I could afford my first sculpture, and Olivia was talking kids with the girl, who had dropped out of her apprenticeship and was managing a secondhand store.

With my modest student budget freed by Skylar's support, I could buy two or three sculptures a year. The sculptures reminded him of New Sofia, and he hatedthem cluttering his home, so when he sent me a crystal, I took it as a truce. I hung the necklace around my neck as a sign that my boyfriend knew and loved me even if he sometimes left for weeks.

The thoughtful gift made my anticipation for his return grow into an ache to express my gratitude with caresses and kisses. But instead of him showing up at the door rugged and unshaven, I got a second package.

Walking down the road to the automat, my chin hovered a few degrees above horizontal. I had a boyfriend who loved me and a package waiting for me. No one else got packages, and if they did, the contents were never as thoughtful and creative as the ones my boyfriend sent.

But after keying in my code and giving my palm print, my smug superiority dropped. The box contained an antique brandy set made from clay. The small cups, dark brown with blue and white waves around the rims, had hooks for handles that allowed them to hang from a ridge on the wide mouth of the matching decanter.

After the initial disappointment, anger flared in me. These didn't show that my boyfriend knew and loved me. They were careless. Stupid. I had stopped drinking when I went on SSRIs a few years earlier. Because Skylar found alcohol to be a crutch for weak, unenlightened people who needed to numb their pain, I never started up again. We had no use for a brandy set. Sure, it was gorgeous and hand painted, the blue the same color as Skylar's eyes, but it screamed that he didn't understand the life we lived. Or at least not the one I lived.

I tucked it back in its box and, head hung down, walked it home.

That evening, Olivia examined the clay cups carefully. "They're gorgeous. Over the phone you made it sound like they were hideous. They're probably worth a lot, too."

"Yeah, they're nice, but I don't drink. He knows that."

"Maybe it's time to give it a try again." She pulled a plastic bottle from her purse. I recognized the light ginger-colored liquid sloshing inside it as her uncle's homemade brandy. "You're not on meds anymore. You're an adult. No reason you can't enjoy a night of unwinding." As she spoke, she poured the apricot brandy into two of the cups.

I glanced around the room, looking for a place to display the set. It was beautiful, but even among the antique furniture, it would look pretentious.

That was what had been bothering me about the set. "It's so pretentious. Everything has to be from a different time, from the villages. He can't appreciate anything from the city. He can't accept that we live here and now."

I didn't add that he couldn't appreciate me, since I was part of the society he hated.

She nudged my cup over to me and lifted hers. "I hate to break it to you, darling, but you're dating a pretentious guy."

After that statement, I couldn't remind her I no longer drank because Skylar looked down on it. So I clinked my cup to hers and shot down the burning brandy in one gulp.

I fought back a sputter and let the burn spread through my throat—too much at first and then comfortably warm.

"Smooth." Olivia gasped, and we both let out ragged laughter.

With the first shot down, it was easier to keep drinking than to stop. She refilled the cups, and we sipped them, losing track of time along with how many times we topped up the tiny cups.

Olivia and I melted across the couch cushions. I kicked my feet up on Skylar's prized oak coffee table. Olivia inverted herself, her toes kneading the back of the couch, her head hanging upside down by my hip.

When the door swung open, we struggled to right ourselves, but the alcohol made us slow and sloppy. An empty cup fell off the table, landing on the thick carpet with a bounce.

"Are you drunk?" The first words Skylar said to me in a month: a cold accusation tinted with disappointment.

"You're the one who sent the brandy set. What was I supposed to do?" My speech was thick and slow.

"Apparently forget who you are and go back to being a stupid teenager." He gestured to Olivia as if she had caused my reversion just by existing.

Olivia stood, unsteady on her feet but her eyes cold and focused. "At least as a teenager she could be herself."

"What's that supposed to mean?" Skylar laughed, but the sound was short and cruel, more like a snarling dog than his usual melodic laughter.

Olivia gestured erratically, her waving hands encompassing the whole apartment before settling on me. "This. All of this. You keep her like a fucking pet in your perfect apartment. You make her take on your hate, your superiority. It's not her. This . . . is not her. Valya is . . . better than . . . this."

She ran out of steam, her words slurring beneath the brandy. Skylar's face became rigid, as if a smile would shatter his skin.

He stepped away from the door, leaving it open. "I think you should go."

Her eyes flicked towards me. I met her fierceness with a subtle shake of my head, and the last of her fire died out.

"Yeah, whatever. I'll see ya around, Val."

As soon as the door clicked shut behind her, our fight started. At first it stretched out tight between us, our words skipping across the tension we created like the pebbles on the surface of a trampoline. As we threw our statements with more force, they bounced wildly, flying beyond our control. Then the tension dissolved into a thick, almost wet, ring of animosity. It coated us, and our voices lowered to primal growls.

"I don't know what makes you think I want this stupid crap." I took the crystal from my neck and threw it at his feet. It bounced off his muddy boot and skidded beneath a cabinet, hiding from our anger.

"This stupid crap is our heritage! It's what our life should have in it. What it was before the government turned our cities into islands!"

"It's trinkets you steal from dead people's abandoned houses."

"They never should have left!" he roared.

It was an old argument that had nothing to do with me. Skylar's rage had gone beyond my drinking to his disdain for the way the world abandoned its villages.

"They couldn't have stayed," I reminded him. My anger dissipated beneath my need to comfort this deep ache in him. "Not after they took away the cars and the busses stopped. Not when the rain was acid and poisoned their food. Not when they could barely breathe the air."

"You really hate the brandy set?"

I took the cup off the carpet and held it as I sunk to the couch. "Yes. I understand the villages are important to you, but for me they're places that take you away from me. That's what this reminds me of. That next month, you'll be gone again."

He took the cup from me, ran his fingers over the pattern. Then he set it on the table and took me into his arms instead. His lips covered my face and neck in the hungry kisses I had been missing.

"She's wrong, you know," he murmured between kisses. "You're not my pet. If anything, you're the one keeping me, changing me, making me a better man."

A swirling sensation of intoxication surged in me, more intense and pure than the brandy had offered. Power had the ability to fill me completely, to make me soar. I held him close, returned his kisses, and silently promised to protect him.

Guilt rides the summer breeze, tugging at my hair and caressing my cheeks. I didn't do enough to keep us together. He always played at being strong, but deep down he was counting on me, and I forgot my promise. I let him break up with me.

With the guilt comes the tiniest glimmer of hope. Only Skylar sends me packages.

At the automat I key in the package number from my phone. The numbers on the keypad depress with satisfying clicks. A seven pops up on screen.

My thumbprint opens the locker. Inside is a brown package about the size of my fist and as light as spun sugar. A glance at the label—typed, not handwritten—crushes my hope. It's not from Skylar. It has nothing of his careful style. But curiosity crawls up in hope's place before I allow defeat to sink into me.

No return address. Not even a name. I fight the urge to rip off the brown paper right in the street. My apartment's two blocks away. I can show decorum. Wait.

I'm out of breath by the time I open my door. I tear off the brown paper, revealing a plain white box.

I hesitate. If not Skylar . . . ? Before my mind can fill in the blank with more silly hopes, I thumb open the box.

A folded piece of paper fills the opening. Beneath it rests something I can't quite comprehend. A black disc, half an inch thick and maybe two inches in diameter with a small toggle switch. One surface has a shiny chrome finish, and on it rests a coil of delicate, clear rope.

I unfold the note. Typed as well. My eyes skip down to the signature. Emersyn.

Dear Valya,

It was delightful to meet you. I hope this note finds you well, and that your pregnancy is progressing without problems. I had one of my lab technicians create this to help you understand the new implant. I believe as soon as you turn this device on, the artistry of the piece will thrill you. However, I want to be clear this is not an attempt at bribing you. A bribe would be unethical, and I in no way think I can buy you with a sculpture. I simply want to showcase the responsiveness of our advanced programming that would be used in a child Casual. I am sending you a device that I hope will give you a better appreciation for our latest crystal technology.

If you have any questions, I am always happy to answer them.

Emersyn

The device has no instructions, only the single toggle. I slide it over until it clicks into position.

The crystal rope responds immediately, uncoiling and lifting away from the platform. It stretches its full length, then keeps stretching, getting thinner to gain height, until its top end hovers at my eye level. Then it splits from the top down, separating into five strands that spiral around each other, joined at the bottom. Each strand is as thick as a few pieces of hair, almost invisible.

The movement stops, and the crystal strands hover, catching the late-afternoon sunshine, casting delicate rainbows on my table. I reach out to touch the sculpture, but it bends away, making room for my hand. Once my hand is drawn into its cage, the strands close, grazing my palm and wrapping around each of my fingers.

I gasp, not wanting to move and break the device. The crystals grow rigid around my fingers, but as soon as I get the courage to flex my fingers, the strands bend as if they are not even there.

I pull my hand away from the sculpture. It releases me and spirals back into its gorgeous cylinder, waiting for someone else to interact with it.

Emersyn has a point: the crystals are responsive and beautiful. But they're not beautiful enough for me to trust them worming their way into baby-girl's brain. I switch off the device and place it on my single shelf in the hall, next to a crystal necklace and a series of hearts, boats, flowers, and tiny clear animals. It probably cost three times as much as my most expensive one. More. Enough to set me and baby-girl up for a few months if I can find a buyer for it.

CHAPTER FIFTEEN

"YOU KEEP SAYING you can't afford anything. Are you going to feed this baby gold?"

Olivia returns the three-quarter sleeve tunic to the rack and continues flipping through the sea of green. We're in Becca's second-hand store, so Olivia can swing a discount, but the perks don't extend to me. I run my hand idly over a rack of blue clothing. Cotton, silk, and chiffon ripple beneath my fingertips. It's like touching the sky from old pictures. I inhale and imagine clouds puffing by.

"No. Money's just tight, living on my own now."

She side-eyes me, and I can't tell if she's trying to figure out if the avocado top in her hands would clash with the olive undertones of my skin or letting me know she thinks my excuses are bullshit.

"You're too cautious. I've been there, and I can tell you with the way you live, the child credit will cover your expenses. And if you breastfeed, you'll have a bit left over." She punctuates her sentence by tossing me a dark green, long-sleeve top. "Keep the sculpture. And buy the shirt. It'll be a great nursing top."

I toss it back to her. "It's hotter than hell out there, and I still hate green."

Olivia has been trying to get me to wear green since we were teens. She can wear almost any shade of green and look great. I put on a neutral shade and look like something crawling out of a swamp.

We continue searching the racks. Olivia tosses potential items in a basket at her feet. The three items at a time rule doesn't apply to her. I drop a pair of buttery-soft, wide-banded yoga pants into my empty basket, just to try something on.

"What about the syndication? Any news? Progress?"

"Not much. I lost followers last month. Brian will not be impressed with that. Although I have a great idea for this series on laughter."

She stops flipping through clothes and looks me up and down. "Laughter?"

"Yeah, laughter." I shrug. "What's so strange about that?"

"You're such a serious person. I didn't have you pegged as an expert on laughter."

As if to prove a point, I let out a snort of laughter. "You don't have to be an expert to vlog about something. I'm vlogging about my exploration of laughter. Viewers can learn to appreciate laughter alongside me."

"Mmm hmmm." She turns back to the clothes. "What sparked this interest in laughter?"

I tell her about Brianne and her many forms of laughter. A flush rises over my skin, especially in the tips of my ears. She doesn't accuse me of harboring the crush unfurling within me. The slight smile tugging at the corner of her mouth says enough.

"It seems like you're in more desperate need of an outfit than I realized." She drops the short navy blue dress she's inspecting into my basket.

I insist it's not like that, even though it's exactly that.

"Tell me, is this girl better than Skylar at least?"

"That's not fair," I protest.

She drops the pretense of shopping, her face losing the hard edge created by years of adult responsibility and softening into the one I spent semi-drunk nights sharing my teenage dreams with.

"Valya, it's fair. It's fair because I'm the one you turned to every time that jerk flipped the emotional roller-coaster he had you strapped to. I love you, but I'm not sure I could handle seeing you that way again. Honestly, I don't think you could survive another relationship like that."

Olivia always disliked Skylar. Of course, she only got the bad stories about him. I went to her when we fought, when he left town for almost a month without telling me, when I felt insecure. How could she see him as anything other than a monster?

"He's not that bad."

"He left you when you got pregnant! I bet you're still going to have to fight him for child support."

"I'm not fighting him for anything. I'm going to ask him to sign over his rights. When I tell him."

"When you tell him what?"

"That I'm pregnant."

"That you're . . ."

"He didn't know. He still doesn't."

Her mouth falls open, but no words come out. Apparently, I'd left this detail out. It isn't my fault. We've been spending less time together. She's busy with Becca and the kids, and the breakup was such a messy time that the pregnancy announcement, if it can be called that, got rolled up in the rest of my depression. This whole time she must have thought he broke up with me because I got pregnant.

The day we broke up should have been gray and snowy. It would have been more appropriate. But a hazy orange light that passed for good weather bathed the peaks of the Old Sofia buildings, and the week was warm for winter. Skylar was leaving on one of his village expeditions, taking a team of his closest friends out of the city, deep into the snow-crusted wilderness. I wanted to go with them, to see the sky as blue as it's supposed to be. Or maybe I wanted to be closer to Skylar. Each day he slipped further into his obsession with the villages.

"What are you doing out there that's such a secret?" I asked.

His nervous anger lifted and his eyes shone in a familiar way that made jealousy rise up in my throat. "You'll see soon enough. If we get funding for this project, it can change everything. The way you and I . . . and everyone lives."

"Then let me be a part of it." I tried not to whine, to only show my enthusiasm, but he insisted it was men's work.

"There's no such thing," I teased, a sliver of wickedness growing in me.

He squashed the growth with a set jaw. "There is. This is it."

He pressed his lips to my forehead as if putting a period on the conversation.

"You're a relic." Pleading with him to change his mind wouldn't dent his decision, but I could wrinkle his perfect facade with a streak of guilt.

"You used to love that about me."

He left me alone in our apartment. I collapsed into a chair and laid my head on the table, the smooth grain pressing into my cheek.

When I found the energy to lift my head again, I rang up Olivia. She would understand, even if she had the perfect girlfriend and two kids. Growing up in the same building in the heart of Padalo, her family two concrete floors above mine, gave us an intimate understanding of hot-headed men and their drama.

My phone cooed at me, assuring me it was searching for her. My heart calmed, waiting for her to tell me I was being petty. Skylar was better than any of the boys from Padalo—more of a man than both our fathers combined. The things she would tell me soothed my anger before she even picked up.

But Olivia didn't accept the call. I tried not to take it personally. She was probably elbow deep in diapers or the chicken pox mutation hitting the daycare centers. I tried to convince myself she wasn't rejecting me, but my anxiety rose.

Because what if she was rejecting me? What if I had done something wrong? Called her too often? Forgotten to ask about Becca and the children too many times?

Waiting for her to answer was like that moment on the bus when the doors hiss, just before they shut, and there's no turning back. Fear rises in my body, and I want to jump off before it's too late, but the doors close, the moment passes. Or it doesn't, and I've become an animal trapped on a moving bus.

I depended on her too much. I never called to check on her or stopped by to ask how she was doing. She thought I was selfish. She had been through so much more than me. The worst of Padalo.

A soft fizzing sensation behind my forehead stopped the train of thoughts from barreling further into my brain. My vision went fuzzy around the edges, softening the hard lines of the wooden furniture. I closed my eyes.

The game interface faded into view.

If Skylar was around, I would have pushed the notification away. But without Skylar at home, I let myself sink into the game.

Casual fed me a neutral screen, all creams and beige with the smallest traces of pure white. If I could have thought while playing, I would have realized my impending anxiety must have been significant to require such gentleness. But the whole point was that I couldn't think.

The first level was easy. I matched small dots into groups of four, building cubes that floated away in a pale yellow sky. Every time I cleared some dots, new ones faded in, taking their place. I didn't have to hunt out moves or calculate a strategy. I flowed with the game for several minutes, letting it lull me into safety.

Eventually the washed-out background solidified into snow with trees, and my little red fox friend jumped around the grid of dots. Outside of the game, I had no idea what my face was doing, but inside, a smile grew—the warm, expectant kind.

I waited until the friendly little fellow curled up in a cluster of dark blue dots and made a cube around him. His image disappeared, sending a jolt of warm, wet pleasure through my head and neck. The fox in the snow, wet and dirty on my tongue.

We played together, the fox and I, the only friend I needed. He pushed Skylar's burning glance and Olivia's rejection from my mind. The happier I felt, the more the fox jumped and teased until, after a satisfying level I didn't quite win, the interface went dim.

Balance achieved. The game had served its purpose. My cortisol levels decreased. I no longer teetered on a dangerous edge of anxiety. I could turn off my game and go about my day. If Skylar was there, I would have.

But Skylar wouldn't return from his men's work for hours. I didn't want to do nothing and wait for him. My finger crept behind my ear, found the hard nub below my hairline, and long-held the device.

One-two-three. The game came alive again, this time with a colorful, swirling, pulsing background. An army of bees I had to dodge replaced my fox friend. The bees melted like sugar in water when I captured them, and the corresponding buzz of pleasure reverberated halfway down my spine. If I collected them faster, the sensation pushed lower, almost into my pelvis. It was like walking the edge of an orgasm, tightly controlled by my mind.

The slamming of a door pulled me out of the game. I flicked the interface off, my eyes adjusting to the dim light of dusk.

Skylar had already dropped his bag next to the door. He stared at me as I lounged on the sofa. I pulled my feet up under me. I hadn't even gotten dressed.

"You've been playing that stupid thing all day, haven't you?" Skylar's lip curled up, revealing a flash of his perfect teeth.

I was too shocked by the late hour to lie to him. Besides, he was Skylar. My Skylar. I never lied to him.

His temper often ran hot when he caught me using Caz. He yelled or growled, his booming voice taking a deep tone that both frightened and excited me. My heart raced as I waited for the screaming and what would come after. His hands, rough on my arms, pinning me down. Sometimes it hurt, making my chest pound and breath come short until the moment he entered me. Then his passion for me would overwhelm his anger against me.

But this time his voice remained icy. Not even a tepid swirl of emotion in it.

"You've turned into a vapid tech head." He took a step toward me and the room closed in tight around us.

"I need it for my anxiety," I reminded him.

"All day? No. You like it. Besides, we had your anxiety under control before you complained to your psycher and let him put that crap in your head."

My hand flew to the nub behind my ear as I waited for his voice to reach a peak. Why was he so quiet? What was different? What had I done? Mentioning the anxiety invited it to our fight, and it was fighting on his side. In me, but against me.

"I can't do this anymore." He let his shoulders drop and turned away from me to gaze out the window.

I stood, my legs weak under me. The three steps to touch his back and draw his gaze were impossible. "I don't want to fight either. It's stupid. Let's forget about it."

"No."

The word sunk me back to the couch.

"I mean us. You made your choice, Valya, and you didn't choose me. You chose your stupid implant and your crackpot psycher."

"That's not fair," I started, but he raised one of his deceptively delicate hands to silence me.

"Don't you get it? I don't love you anymore. I can't love you. With that thing in, you're barely human. I fell in love with a woman, not a machine. Now I look at you and you disgust me. I don't want to see you anymore. Get out of my apartment."

He turned back to the window. It was our last conversation.

"He doesn't know?" Olivia echoes back. The shock on her face looks like I've slapped her.

I want to explain why I haven't been able to call him, but I can't. I shrug, and there's a moment even our ancient friendship can't bridge.

She reaches across me and grabs the handle of my basket.

"Come on, let's try these on."

In the dressing room I fiddle with the zipper on the short dress. It's snug, but the way the fabric wraps around my bump and swollen breasts gives the sensation of support rather than confinement. When I catch a glimpse in the mirror, I feel sexy for the first time in months. I pull my hair loose from its high bun and let it cascade in waves over my bare, acne-scarred shoulders. Olivia lets out a low whistle when I step out from behind the curtain.

"I won't be able to manage heels with it."

"You won't have to," she assures me. "You look fantastic just like that. Now you only have to decide whether you want to wear that when you tell Skylar or the next time you see this Brianne girl."

Her impish grin lets me know she thinks I should wear it for Brianne.

CHAPTER SIXTEEN

CONCENTRATING IS BECOMING more difficult. Sitting across from Orlov, I can't focus on his face for a full thirty seconds before glancing away. My mind touches on the blue dress hanging on the drying rack outside my kitchen window. Before the image forms fully, a visual stutter takes me through a barrage of faces and places.

"A lack of focus is a normal withdrawal symptom," Orlov assures me. He's surprised I'm not experiencing worse symptoms. Headaches, nausea. Between my pregnancy and anxiety, I should be a complete mess. Barely able to function. Why didn't he warn me? Maybe he did, and I didn't listen.

"This is why you wanted to wean me slowly."

His eyes are gentle, concerned. His voice is far away. Did I say something wrong? The answer floats in a deep sea, unable to find the room I'm sitting in.

My finger scratches behind my ear, finding the nub of the implant and pushing it back and forth. My nail wraps around it.

"Valya! stop!"

I yank my hand down. A thin film of blood is slick on my fingertip. "Sorry."

He asks me how often I have trouble concentrating. Answering is difficult, and he shakes his head. He wants to prescribe me some upper for a few days, but he has to talk to Janice first. When is my next exam? I'm not sure, but soon. I can't remember when I'm supposed to switch to bi-weekly exams.

Even Orlov, with all his patience and training, can't hold back his sigh or hide the slight clench of his teeth. He looks up the answer himself, reminds me of the date and time. It slips out of my head even as he says it.

"I'm not always this bad," I say. "It's so stuffy in here." I need to tell him something else. Something about a face or a dream or . . . I can't remember.

He stands. His long, spider-like legs carry him to the window. It slides open easily, letting in a gentle breeze that hits my face. Allowing the air to caress my bare skin is a bit of a rebellion, but it's too hot to be refreshing.

"How did your meeting with Emersyn go?"

I sit up straight. Everything sharpens. I'm here, in Orlov's office, and I'm in control.

"You set me up," I accuse.

"You wouldn't have gone otherwise."

He holds my gaze with a steady warmth, and I find my head nodding. It's a nod of recognition. This is the moment our relationship grows beyond ethics. Ten years of therapy and I'm ready to go beyond personal to a place that's real.

"She's emailing me almost every day now, just to check in. Sending me crap I don't need, trying to win me over. Can't you tell her it's pointless?" I won't admit her crystal sculpture is my favorite, or that I actually read her emails before deleting them now. "You know I saw her in your office, right? You two are in this together."

He shrugs. "I'm not in this with her any more than I am in it with you. I'm here to help you see your options."

"You think I should do it." My voice catches as if I'm whispering to a lover across my bed. I cough, trying to cover the thickness of my words.

"I do."

"Why?"

He brings his fingers to his forehead and runs his thumb and middle finger across his eyebrows as if I've given him a headache.

"Casual therapy is an effective method for managing your anxiety. Some psychers believe it's too effective. Instead of forcing you to confront the root of your mood disorder, the implant allows you to function on a normal level without facing what caused your problems to begin with. They say it doesn't heal you, just distracts you. I would argue the new habits Casual helps you develop is a type of healing, but that's neither here nor there. The point is now you're off of it and in a better place. Your mind may decide it's time to deal with those root causes."

I rub my belly, letting silence flow between us.

"Without Casual, some deep memories you've repressed may surface, and I'm not sure you will make it through them without external support, whether it's chemical or mechanical."

"Repressed memories?" I pretend to not understand what he's talking about, but I do. I remember too little about my childhood. My memory is Swiss cheese, with events and people slipping through the holes. Even now it's difficult to form memories and hold them for more than a few months. But my childhood? It's a blur, and this isn't the first time the blur threatened to come into focus.

○

Coming up on sertraline was like nothing I had experienced before. The other things I'd gotten my hands on, which weren't many, were fast. From half a minute to half an hour, I was where I wanted to be. But the sertraline took half a month to kick in.

I weaned off the benzos while the sertraline adjusted my serotonin patterns. Orlov warned me not to freak out if I didn't notice any change.

"Sertraline is subtle at first, and it can take a month or even more before the positive results register. Just stick to our schedule. Give it the benefit of the doubt."

The day I met Skylar I was still on half a pill, slicing the tiny ovals with a kitchen knife. A month later, I was up to a pill a day, and I had fallen in love with Skylar.

"Okay, this month we will bump you up to seventy-five milligrams," Orlov explained as he typed the new dosage schedule into his tablet.

"But I feel great where I am," I whined. "Better than great. I feel alive. Vibrant. I think it's enough."

He brushed away my concerns with a wave of his hand. It was the only time he had been dismissive towards me. Or maybe I was finally healthy enough to recognize his dismissiveness. I wasn't sure, and that uncertainty made me nod weakly when he insisted on upping the dosage.

"You're still under the recommended therapeutic dose. I want to make sure we're supporting you as well as possible. Even seventy-five milligrams is at the low end."

I echoed the words back to Skylar when I met up with him that evening.

"But I thought you were coming off it."

"Not so soon, no." I reached out to stroke his arm, but he turned away. "It's a long-term thing. Not a forever thing. But I need a few months of stability before I can come off it."

Every week I bumped up my dose. A pill and a quarter every morning, taken with a small pull of coffee with real honey stirred in. How Skylar got his hands on real honey, I never bothered asking. It was too good to question. Then a pill and a half.

That was when the night terrors started. Those dreadful dreams that gripped me and refused to let go.

"It's the pills," Skylar insisted. "Tell your psycher and get off of them." The way he spat psycher made it clear he didn't think of Orlov as a medical professional. Or maybe he had no respect for the medical profession.

"But you don't understand! This is the first time the world has ever been . . . beautiful. Sharp. Clear. I feel in control! I can't give that up because of some bad dreams."

I was twisted in Skylar's sheets, wet with sweat, glancing around his dim room for the face I had seen in the depths of the darkness. Every time, the dream was only the sensation of being pinned and that one face. White as china and yet pure darkness. Thin. Sharp. Terrifying.

I told Orlov about the face, and he agreed with Skylar.

"The night terrors are most likely a side-effect of the pills. How do you feel during the day?"

"Great!" I assured him with too much enthusiasm. "Everything is crisp and vibrant. I feel fantastic. And I can meet people's eyes. I want to talk to people. It's amazing."

"Vibrant or vibrating?" he asked, latching on to a single word that gave away my euphoria.

"What do you mean?"

"Do you feel like you're buzzing? Any eye tremors? Feelings of . . . dissolving?"

Downcast eyes and introspection even though I knew the answer. A nod.

We lowered the dose. My days remained productive and beautiful, but they lost the extra buzz. Not every good thing sent my heart racing, but I still noticed them. It was a good place to be, and I stayed there for two more months. But the night terrors still rushed in on unexpected nights.

Skylar alternated between begging and demanding for me to stop taking the pills. His plump lips sweetly pouting one day and set hard the next.

"Why's it so important to you?" I moaned the question, thick with irritation. I was nearing the edge of my patience, even with the extension the pills had given it.

We were in his shower together. Steam filled the large bathroom, protecting us from the fall chill outside. I sank onto the teak bench, level with the firm muscles of his thighs, while he slathered shampoo in his curly hair.

"I've never known you off of them."

"And what, you're afraid you wouldn't like me?"

I flicked the water drops nearest me with my fingernail.

"No, it's not that at all. I know who you are. But, I wonder if the things you're feeling right now are because of the pills." He put his head under the water and the white lather cascaded down his tanned skin, racing in and out of the ripples of muscles along his shoulders, disappearing around his back and showing up in a puddle near the drain.

"They're not."

I was certain. After all, the pills didn't change who I was. They let me manage my symptoms. Except, who I had always been was a scared girl who could barely make eye contact with a stranger without her breath coming short. Here I was looking into the most stunning blue eyes I had ever seen without flinching. Was it so bad if the pills let me do that?

"I need to come off the pills," I told Orlov the next week.

"I thought you were doing well on them. What changed?"

I couldn't meet his eyes. The whole reason I wanted off was Skylar. I promised him I would prove our love was real. But telling Orlov the night terrors were still happening wasn't quite a lie. They had slowed down in frequency and intensity, but they hadn't stopped.

"I'd like to do a scan of you." He motioned over the length of my seated body. "An ocular scan. It's a new technology, integrated into connect, that helps doctors make a diagnosis based on physical cues we might otherwise miss."

"I know what an ocular scanner is. The psycher in New Sofia had one."

"And you didn't like it?"

I shook my head. "It didn't hurt or anything, but it's invasive. Unsettling."

"I respect that. If you don't want to do a scan, we don't have to." He settled back in his chair. It wasn't a game of wills with him. He honestly meant I didn't have to do it.

"I think maybe it would be okay with you. I trust you."

"It might be a little uncomfortable, emotionally. I'll be staring at you for quite a while. But if you tell me to stop, I will."

Over the years, Orlov got faster at doing his ocular scans, to where he could conduct one without me noticing. But that first time, it was awkward as hell.

I stood in front of his desk, one hand resting on the hard wood, and faced him. He touched the back of his ear, closed his eyes, and waited. His eyes opened and darted over me, licking me like a hundred little tongues. His curiosity became tangible fibers growing between us. It felt pervy, like he was a lech, memorizing every curve of my body—especially when his gaze slowed down and stroked me, inch by inch, from head to toe and back again.

When he finished, he nodded and sat back down, motioning to my chair and saying nothing.

"What did it tell you?"

"I'm not perfect in the usage. So, there's a possibility I made interpretation errors."

It was my turn to wave his concerns away with the flick of a wrist. "Bullshit. What'd you see?"

"According to the scan, you hold intense trauma in your body. Early trauma. Something in your childhood. The medication is creating a buffer, making you feel safe for the first time in your life. And that distance is allowing you to access those memories."

"My childhood? I mean, yeah, life in Padalo is crappy for kids. You know that. But it's nothing like those dreams. I would remember if it was."

"Well, the man in your dreams is likely a symbol. But it's the first step to accessing those memories. Your trauma is surfacing, so to speak."

"Did your fancy machine tell you what the trauma is?"

"There are a few possibilities. It could be as simple as you not having your needs met as an infant and being allowed to cry for extended periods of time. But in your case, it is likely more intense: witnessing violence, physical neglect, emotional abuse, physical abuse, sexual abuse, maybe even your mother leaving."

He swallowed and his voice lilted up when he said, "sexual abuse." It was obvious he thought that was the one messing me up. Who did he think did it? My dad? A neighbor? The questions flooded in, but the anger that carried them was too strong to allow them to create words.

"So I stop the pills and the dreams stop?" is all I squeaked out.

"Yes, but this could be the ideal time for you to process . . . "

"No," I said. "It's not."

○

"So you're saying this time I will have to process those repressed memories you've been itching to get at?" I mumble.

"I have not been itching to get at them." Orlov closes the window. "But I believe you have to face them to move forward with your life. So this might not be a bad thing. I just wish you were in a position for me to offer you more support."

"You mean drugs again?"

"Yes. But I don't think Janice will approve of starting any medication this late in your pregnancy."

"The dreams? Will they come back?" My voice sounds far away. Like a little girl's. Is this the memories coming up already? Am I remembering how it feels to be small? I shake the feeling away with a shudder.

"Perhaps. In the third-trimester dreams tend to be vibrant anyway, due to the hormone balance. But you know I'll be here for you, anytime you need me you can reach me."

We're back to, "Call anytime." It's like being seventeen and on suicide watch. Great.

CHAPTER SEVENTEEN

THE NEW DRESS hugs me in all the right places. I'm safely covered, yet sexy. The mirror in my bathroom only shows my top half, and even for that I have to press my back against pipes on the opposite wall and stand on tiptoe. But what I can see makes me pucker my lips and do a little jiggle with my shoulders. The neckline plunges down in a sharp v, revealing my improved cleavage. At least I get some benefit from the nausea-inducing sensitivity of my breasts. If I had eye-liner or a red lipstick, the effect would border on stunning. But Skylar thought make-up covered our true selves, so I got rid of mine. I wasn't eager about throwing away my hard-earned liners and shadows, powders and creams. But he kept insisting I was beautiful without makeup. In the morning, he would wipe at the carefully applied liquid liner, making dark smudges all around my eyes. I rarely had time to do more than wash the makeup off, leaving my eyes red and raw. Eventually I gave up and let him toss it with our weekly plastic trash. Until now, I haven't had a reason to buy more.

Stepping into the Mountain Cafe, I feel overdressed. Maybe I should have arranged an evening date. Not date. It's just a meeting between friends. The dress is ridiculous. Desperate. That wet shame grows warm in my sinus cavities. She will take one look at me and know what I want from her.

"Would that be such a bad thing?" Orlov's steady voice comes to me.

I was nineteen, still struggling with cutting, and leaning too hard on the benzos. We should have been discussing that, but I came to the session in the middle of a meltdown.

"It's embarrassing. Wanting sex, sure, everyone wants sex. Hell, guys love when girls want sex, right? But to want more? That's so weak. Pathetic."

"Tell me, what's the absolute worst situation you can imagine if Gregor learns you love him?"

"I didn't say I love him. I just, maybe want to date him, okay?" I narrowed my eyes to slits, not because he had over-estimated the situation, but because I knew "the worst situation" wouldn't sound so bad. Gregor would reject me. I was sure of that. Maybe he'd have a laugh over it with some of our friends, but probably not. He wasn't always an asshole. Admitting it out loud made it seem petty and shallow. My words wouldn't carry the terror that wrapped its thin tentacles around my throat and chest, squeezing the air from my lungs as I played out the scenario in my mind. Even safe in Orlov's office, the certainty that part of me would shrivel up into nothing if scrutinized too closely was building.

I gripped the arms of the chair. My chair, even though dozens of other patients used it. When I was there, the chair was mine. Orlov's time was mine. The room was mine. I was in control.

Orlov waited while my breathing slowed and my fingers loosened their grip.

"Rejection can be frightening," he explained. "Especially if you haven't experienced it much. But the weight you give your imagination can be worse than the reality of the situation."

If anyone else had told me that, I would have thought my panic was justified. They were belittling my concerns as some teenage drama. But I fought the urge to bristle at Orlov—to get uppity, as my dad called it from his lounger in the living room, a beer pressed to his stomach. But Orlov and I had a rule. I always had to give him the benefit of the doubt. My certainty told me everyone was against me, but the doubt . . . it created enough space to believe Orlov might work with me.

He was right. Rolling calm on half a benzo, I told Gregor I wanted more than our drunken hookups once a month.

"Yeah, sure, college-girl. I knew you couldn't get enough of me."

The way he called me college-girl made me feel cheap and fake. He had gotten a job at the solar plant right out of high school. Most of our classmates got jobs, too. Even Olivia. How could he make me feel stupid for something I had to be smart to do? But the benzos weren't letting me feel stupid right then, or anything else for that matter. I raised my probably-glassy eyes to meet his. His were also dull, but for no reason. He wasn't drunk or high. Definitely not on tranquilizers. He just didn't have enough emotion towards me to make his eyes shine.

Stupidly, I pressed the question, clarified myself, forced a full rejection. It didn't hurt at all, even once the benzos wore off.

This time I'm going in clean. No tranquilizers, no Caz, just seven more years of therapy and enough rejections to know Orlov was right. It's better to know when someone doesn't like me. At least then I can move on.

Brianne slumps in a metal chair at a table near the bubbling splash pad where a few toddlers run naked. That'll be baby-girl in a year or two, maybe running around with Brianne's kid if we're still friends. The picture brings a smile to my lips, and I remove my filter so Brianne can see it.

Her eyes shine back at me and she takes down her own mask. She launches out of her chair, the way we have to these days, and her flowing pink sundress cascades over her bump. A fine dusting of sparkling makeup coats her smooth skin, making her look like she's heading to a maternity shoot. Glowing. Perfect.

She pulls me into a hug and kisses each of my cheeks with her warm, dry lips. Her makeup smells of peaches with a trace of that familiar acidic scent of pressed face powder. Inhaling deeply, I catch a whiff of her perfume, light and floral. Her close, easy contact brushes my anxiety away, and I lower myself into the chair next to hers. I mirror her sunken position, letting my knees drift apart to accommodate my bump.

"Oh we must be a pair!" she raises her sweating glass and, since I don't have a drink yet, I nod my agreement.

I order a club soda with lemon, extra ice.

"Being pregnant in this heat!" she teases. "Did you do something wrong in a past life to deserve this?"

Today is mild. A gentle breeze lifts the heat off my neck and forehead and wherever else beads of sweat form. But to someone from New Sofia, where the temperature's perfect every day, even a little heat must be oppressive.

"You couldn't imagine the evil I've done," I say with a wicked smirk.

My drink comes and I take a long sip, relishing the cold bubbles as they dance in my throat.

"I can't stand soda. It reminds me of the cleaning solution we use in the nursery."

As we sip our drinks, she tells me about her work. I have a hard time imagining the crystal nursery. A dark, dank room, like a cave? Or is it well lit, each crystal isolated from the next? She says it isn't a nursery at all because the crystals are rocks, not alive, but they're cared for like babies. They feed them every few hours, bathe them twice a day, and Brianne even admits to singing to them.

"I know they're not alive like us, and maybe it's group hysteria from working there for so long, but after a while they feel like babies. They develop personalities. And when they get cut and taken away, I miss them." As she speaks, her face softens into a dreamy, wistful look. A low excitement radiates from her lips. Her love? Her passion, at least.

"Have you ever been in a room made from a crystal you grew?" I ask, trying to keep her passion on display.

"I dunno. I have no idea what they do with them when they take them away. Rooms? furniture? No clue."

"And you don't think you'd recognize the feeling? Know one of your babies?"

Her hand goes to her belly, and she bites her lip.

"Kicking?"

She nods. "But not that. You hit a tender topic for me. It's one of the things I'm scared of. What if I can't recognize my baby? What if they're like every other baby to me? What if that magical connection they talk about isn't there?"

It takes all of my concentration to keep from laughing at her absurd fears. But I do, because that same uncertainty—the one that creeps in on something no one else seems afraid of—has pinned me down before. People laughed at me, called me silly, and that was the final pin, holding me paralyzed. Nothing is worse than being dismissed as silly.

"But you'll be with her the whole time. She'll come out and you'll see her, and there won't be any question."

"Unless there are complications. You know, I've read stories of infants being switched at birth, going home with the wrong mother. The families didn't find out for decades . . . "

"Stop." I reach over and cover her hand with my own. My fingers fall between hers, and the tips of them feel a gentle *thump-thump*. It's strange for the kicking to come from only the outside.

The fear melts from her face, and she exhales a deep breath. I can feel how completely gone the anxiety is, and a twinge of jealousy rises in me. If only mine faded with a single word.

She squeezes my hand before removing it from her bump. But our fingers remain threaded, dangling together between our chairs.

The touch sparks my bravery. "I wanted to ask you for a favor."

Brianne arches one eyebrow in her usual conspiratorial gesture. I'm already laughing, the tension of the previous moment gone.

"For my vlog. I want to do a series about laughter, and I was wondering if I could interview you."

"Me?" She gives a full smile and half a deep laugh. "Why me?"

A thin blush flushes my face then recedes. "You're the one who inspired it. You have such wonderful laughter. So many types. It sounds very true and authentic. I want to explore that."

"I guess. My place or yours?" She winks and my heart flutters.

I hadn't planned what I would do if she said yes. But I can't imagine pinning her laughter in my tiny apartment. Nor do I want it echoing off the crystal walls. "Neither. There's a park I go to sometimes. Almost like pure wilderness, right in the center of the city. We'll film there."

"Shall we pay and go, then?"

I sip my soda. "No rush. I need a day or two to get my thoughts in order."

CHAPTER EIGHTEEN

BRIANNE MEETS ME early in the morning. Thick fog rolls down from the mountain, covering the city in a blanket of wet air that permeates my clothes and makes my skin slick.

"It's more like swimming than walking," Brianne comments as we make our way towards the Borisova Garden.

"Do you have a pool in New Sofia?"

She side-eyes me. "Of course we do. Three pools, actually. One on the main level. One on C-level, and a private one down on E-level."

"Private?"

"Yeah, E-level is where all the rich people live. They don't enjoy mingling with us commoners."

My laughter stops my steps and doubles me over. "The rich people? You realize all of you in New Sofia are rich, right?"

Brianne takes my hand and guides us along the cracked sidewalk, even though I'm supposed to be leading. "It's all a matter of perspective."

It's not all a matter of perspective. That's something well-off people say when they want poor people to think they understand being poor. But I let it slide. Her smooth hand in mine and the privacy the white sheets of fog provide put me in too good of a mood to ruin it with semantics.

By the time we make it to the park, the sun is burning off the fog and revealing dark green leaves and damp grass.

"It's beautiful," Brianne says.

It smells of piss and stale beer, but she's right, it's beautiful anyway. I lead her deeper, past where the kids party, into the depths of the park where there are coves of privacy created by twisted vines and overgrown shrubbery.

"Downright wild." Brianne almost floats off the path as she gazes at the greenery. I have to tether her down, and while I like the image of me grounding her, I laugh at her naivety.

A flash of rust red burrowing beneath a nearby bush breaks my concentration.

"Did you see that?" I ask.

"What?" Brianne looks around the clearing, unable to find anything out of place to focus on.

"It almost looked like . . . " I let my voice fade out. Impossible. There aren't foxes in the Borisova Garden. It must have been my imagination. Again. "Nothing. Never mind."

Brianne squeezes my hand, but lets the topic drop. "Is this where you want to record?"

"Yeah." I plop down on the grass. "I don't think anyone will interrupt us."

I distract myself by pulling out my camera and hooking it up to my phone. Its small plastic stand pops out from the back and I adjust its angle until it's recording both of us without us sitting too closely.

"I feel weird," Brianne admits. "What am I supposed to say?"

"Just ignore the camera. Talk to me. It will feel weird at first. But eventually you'll forget that we're recording and you'll start being your normal, charming self."

"Charming, eh?" She flashes me a wicked smile that I catch and swallow down as I press record.

I introduce Brianne to the camera as a friend, as if we've known each other longer than a month, and then we continue chatting about the park and Brianne's excursions into the old city.

"You said before that you wanted an excuse to come out to Old Sofia. Why is that?"

She gives a laugh low in her throat, without opening her mouth. "I don't know. I guess curiosity. You can only learn so much through the experiences of other people. At some point, to truly know a place, you have to go there. I might not be able to fly to another country. But I can at least come visit you and learn about your life, right?"

"Right. Now I want to get to the heart of this conversation and talk about how you laughed before you answered."

"Did I?" She furrows her eyebrows. "I didn't even notice."

"You did. It was a low, subtle laugh, like this." I mimic her laughter, my shoulders rolling up and back with the contained force of the sound. "Can you tell me what about my question made you laugh?"

She leans back and cocks her head to the side. "Hm. Nope. I can't. Maybe a bit of embarrassment because I didn't know the answer?"

"And what about this laugh?" I reach out and brush her side with my fingertip, digging in to tickle her ribs.

Her laugh is high and full and free, and she falls onto her back, squirming to get away from me. "That tickles!"

When I stop to let her catch her breath, she goes on the offensive. Beneath my squirming and screeching laughter, there's a deeper sensation of connection. It's been so many months since I've had this kind of touch. Not quite sexual, but more intimate than friendly. Beyond professional. While my body arches away from Brianne's probing fingers, my heart leans towards her, begging for the moment to last.

But all moments come to an end. Our tussle leaves us both breathing hard, flushed, and smiling.

"Now, where were we?" Brianne asks.

I smile. The questions come easier. Her answers flow. The back-and-forth feels natural. Just what the camera wants. Just what I need.

We talk until the sun is high in the sky, pounding down on us through every crack in the canopy of green.

My camera flashes a red light, indicating a low battery, and I turn it off.

"That was great," I say.

"More fun than I expected," Brianne says. "I didn't know vlogging could be so liberating."

"Well, that's the first step. There's still editing, commentary, more research. It's not all tickle wars and good conversation." I pack up my camera and phone in my bag.

"But some of it is. So I think you're lucky. Want to go grab lunch?"

We both scramble to our feet, a task all its own these days. I dust the damp dirt from my butt. "Sure."

Before we start walking, Brianne turns to me, the laughter gone from her eyes and her small mouth serious. "But I want to ask you. What did you see when we first sat down?"

"Oh, that." I hold my hands out and bite my lip, unsure how to explain without sounding crazy. "You know I use Caz. In my game there's a bright red fox, and now that I've turned it off, I sometimes catch him in the corner of my eye. Just my mind compensating for the change I suppose."

Her eyes narrow, not in judgment, but in slow consideration of me. "I've played Nature on my phone before. There wasn't a fox."

"It's not on the phone. The Caz version has a lot more detail."

After lunch I walk Brianne to the bus station and return to my apartment to edit the footage. It's good. The lighting is sweet and soft, giving both of us that classic pregnancy glow. Brianne is a natural in front of the camera.

I stop the footage more often than necessary, just taking in her face and the easy shapes it morphs into. Between my jittery brain and my obsession with Brianne, the sun falls before I've created the clips I need for my vlog. But before crawling into bed, I render a ten-minute introduction to my exploration of laughter and press post.

The full moon shines through my window, keeping me awake. Instead of counting sheep, I count potential viewers. I toss and turn, trying to get comfortable, and keep myself from flicking on my phone to check the stats.

"Give it time," I mumble, closing my eyes against the yellow light.

A run with the fox would distract me, stop the racing of my imagination and calm the thrill of possibility enough to let me sleep. But it's off. There's no relief there.

I prop myself on my elbows and layer my pillows beneath me to play the game on my phone. Brianne was right. There's no fox there. How have I never noticed?

My eyes close halfway, my thumbs slide over the glass screen on their own. Sleep is at the edge of my brain. But there, in the hallway, my fox comes. I startle, almost wake up, but sigh and let myself fall asleep, dreaming of my lost friend.

CHAPTER NINETEEN

WALKING TO MY appointment with Orlov, the crisp powder blue therms catch my eye from across the street. Sure enough, the set is topped with ginger hair, pulled back in a severe bun.

"Valya!" Emersyn waves at me.

I put my head down and walk faster. I may have the time, but I don't have the energy to deal with her.

She crosses the street and cuts me off.

"Didn't you hear me calling?" she asks, out of breath from her short jog.

"Must not have." It's a lie, but when someone's stalking me, I no longer consider lying such an offense.

"Well, then I guess it's lucky I caught up with you."

I roll my eyes like a sullen teenager and wait for her to continue, since it's obvious she's not about to let me get away.

"I wanted to talk to you about Skylar."

"Skylar?" The new twist in her pitch tightens my chest.

"Yeah, do you think he'll be a good father?" She cocks her head to one side, waiting.

"Uhm." I stutter, unable to say anything coherent.

"Because, you know, he's looking for funding for some village renewal project. Been having a hard time crowdsourcing it . . . "

Dread creeps up from my ankles like a small, furry animal, racing to burrow into my stomach. "Skylar would never agree to your experiment. He hates Casual."

She shrugs. "Which is why we think you would make the better parent. You would be right there in it with your baby. Skylar would never take part. But, for the right price, he'd let us set the child—your child—with a surrogate in tandem."

"He wouldn't." Spit gathers in the back of my throat and I'm overwhelmed with the urge to hurl it at Emersyn. Instead, I swallow. Breathe.

"You think you know him? Skylar has a habit of giving up everything for these fancies of his. Did you know that?"

Like he gave me up. The creature in my stomach leaps up to my throat, clawing and fighting. "Why are you so obsessed with me and my child? Just leave us alone."

"I would if I could. But this trial is too important. And you and your child happen to be desperate enough at the right time. As much as we need you, you need us. You'll see that, eventually. I'm not going to drop this." She smiles widely, looking almost like a skeleton with her pale skin. "Have a good day, Valya."

"Have a nice chat with Emersyn?" I ask Orlov before I even sit down.

He presses his lips together in a thin line. "Yes, she was here discussing the trial."

"Discussing me." I slide down into my chair, the heat and scent of cigarettes oppressive.

"Trying to think of other potential participants, since you don't seem interested. We'd love you in the trial, but with or without you, it needs to happen."

Breath rushes out of me in a snort, such a close sound to laughter but without the humor to carry it further. "We?"

Orlov folds his hands together and sighs. "Emersyn. Emersyn's trial, okay? Now, shall we get started?"

The way he changes topics so quickly makes my head spin, and I feel as if I'm flying off a merry-go-round. I cling to a wisp of a thought before it fades. "Sure. Let's start."

"Tell me, how are you adjusting to life without Casual? Any issues?"

"There's one, but it's kind of weird."

He settles back, comfortable with me again. "Weird is what I'm here for."

"It's just that in my game there was a fox. A bright red one. And a friend pointed out the fox isn't part of the phone game. And now, when my mind is racing, I imagine I'm seeing the fox. Just flickers you know, not a hallucination or anything. Like, he catches the corner of my mind. Is that insane?”

He smiles broadly, and the tension melts from my chest. My breath comes easier, as if baby-girl is finally making room for my lungs.

“No, it’s not insane at all. The implant, as opposed to the screen game, keeps track of your interests and, in your case, your needs. It can accommodate your preferences.”

“Like AI learning?” I wrinkle my nose, imagining some intelligent creature crawling through the slimy folds of my brain.

“Yes. Your game has always been a conversation between your brain and your implant. You interpret that conversation through images. What’s interesting to me is the images you’ve seen. A red fox, you say?”

“Yes, bright red, sleek coat, a white tip at the tail. It looks so soft.” Just thinking about the fox settles my mind.

“Looks soft. So you’ve never caught it? Never touched it?”

I think back to the games I’ve played. “Huh. I guess not.”

“Foxes have a lot of symbolism. A fox usually means some sort of deception or perhaps cleverness. But a red fox, in particular, symbolizes passion, energy, and confidence. I wonder if these classic representations have any meaning to you.”

My heart flutters. Baby-girl kicks hard at my belly button. My thumb rubs the spot to make sure she didn’t pop it out. “I’ve read the children’s stories with the clever foxes. And, yeah, red means passion to me.”

“And what do you think it means that this fox is there, so important to you, and you’ve never caught it?”

I shrug.

“Do you feel frustrated that you never caught it?”

“No.” My answer is immediate and sure. “I feel happy that it’s there. Excited. I don’t need to catch it.”

I walk home thinking about my fox friend—the one I made up—and for the first time since getting my implant turned off, I don’t feel like he’s gone. How could he be gone if I made him up?

I walk up the stairs with new energy. My breath isn’t as short as usual. I wonder if baby-girl has dropped, whatever that’s supposed to be. I definitely feel lighter.

After re-hydrating a bowl of soup in the microwave, I park myself in front of my tablet, ready to slurp my dinner and check out how my latest vlog is doing.

Two-hundred views. Not bad for two days. But I need more. Especially because only two of the viewers subscribed. Boosting it to the mid-level networks for a day will only cost twenty credits. I can afford that. Sometimes, spending a little money is necessary to get a vlog lubricated. It pains me to press accept on the transaction, but I remind myself that with syndication I won't have to watch my money so closely and twenty credits will be nothing.

A single noodle rests on the bottom of my bowl. I should at least put it in the sink. Preferably wash it. But instead I look up Skylar's blog for the first time in months. There's his smiling face, as handsome as ever. Next to it is a thumbnail for a crowdfunding campaign. My heart stops and I remind it to beat. I click the video.

Skylar is in front of a run-down house in some village, talking to the camera. He's handsome when he's still, but his face in motion and the easy way he arches his back or spreads his arms makes me swoon.

"There's a truth the city is hiding from you. That truth is simple. The danger from the wars is over. Deep down you already know this to be true. Every month, more and more people discard their masks. Why? Because the air is breathable again. But shedding that protective strip of cloth takes a leap of faith. What else is possible with a little faith?"

The camera pans out, showing a large garden, red and orange vegetables hanging heavy on vines.

"This. It's possible to grow food in the wild again, to cultivate life beyond the strict confines of the city. The government doesn't tell us this. The government wants to keep us in a confined space, dependent on government-controlled greenhouses. I'm here to give you another option, though."

The camera swings back to Skylar, so close in on his face that I stroke the screen, expecting to feel the softness of his smooth skin.

"With your help, I'm starting a program called, 'Back to the Village.' Next year, I want to have a crew of at least fifty people living and working in a self-sustainable village. But to achieve this, I need basic funding. We will need supplies, initial stores of food, and emergency funds to make this dream a reality. You can help liberate us from city life."

I stop the video. I've seen enough. Emersyn wasn't lying. He's going through with his dream of moving out of the city, and he's looking for funding. But would he trade our baby—my baby—for his dream?

A few weeks ago, I thought he had held a train hostage. My whole body turns cold, like a cloud passing over, then through, me. Yes. He would sell baby-girl. My head swims, and I can't see the room. Everything is too far away.

CHAPTER TWENTY

THE PREGNANCY BLOGS say I should sleep as much as possible: surrender and let my tiny energy-vampire suck up enough of my life force to keep growing. They say to sleep now because I won't get any sleep once the baby makes her way into the world, as if her crying will be more distracting than the stretching of my uterus, sinew, and skin or kicking of my vital organs. I'm thinking these mommy blogs are all run by bots. Live women who have lain awake at night during the final two months, begging for sleep, couldn't have written them.

Each night I stumble to my bed early, hoping to get comfortable enough to enter that deep, rejuvenating sleep that evades me.

Lying in bed, I look up sleep tips on my phone. *Sleep hygiene 101: Don't go to bed until you're tired.* No problem. I'm exhausted all the time. But when my head hits my lumpy pillow, sleep skitters away like a shy, frightened animal. Like my fox. I close my eyes and try to imagine his sleek fur and laughing, lolling tongue.

My body longs for Skylar's king-sized bed, the temperature-control, pillow-top mattress that felt like nothing beneath me. It wouldn't make a difference. My body is bent out of shape, not my hard mattress. Even so, that rectangle of heaven haunts my near-sleeping mind. His bed had so much room, and Skylar's body would make the perfect prop to throw my leg over. His hip or back would support my heavy belly. His always steady heartbeat would lull baby-girl to sleep. He'd stroke my hair, right at the roots, turn me into a cat. He could put me to sleep.

My thoughts tangle like our bodies used to, and I'm no longer sure whether the ache I feel is for Skylar or sleep.

The sun goes down, but between the waxing moon and the

streetlamps, my room is still bright. I need to buy proper blackout curtains before baby-girl comes or neither of us will get any rest. Yet another expense.

I wipe the tears from my cheek and turn onto my left side with my right leg thrown over a pillow—the way Janice says I should sleep. She said it's good for baby-girl and me. Something about proper blood flow, and optimum comfort. It puts me facing my wall, my back to the room and the open doorway. I force my eyes closed, but the skin on the back of my neck tightens.

A familiar sensation of being watched washes through me. It grows into dread. Fear, even. My heart picks up its pace. Did I lock the door? Who would come into my apartment? If not who, then what?

A shadow races across my ceiling. Was it a tree branch waving in the wind outside my window or something in my room, by my bed, close enough to touch me? It's not my fox. Nothing friendly about it.

It's my imagination. If I turn around, I'll see there's nothing there. But I can't turn over. What if, this time, there is something? Seeing it will make it real.

I stay rigid. Listening. It's too quiet. A shout from the street startles me, but the danger I feel is closer. Reaching into the depths of my courage, beneath my runaway heart, I throw my sheet off. In one awkward motion I slide out of bed and hit the light switch.

Nothing. My desk. My bed. Me. A moon out in a dark night. I try not to think about the darkness. I grab my phone from my desk and flick it on, trying to lose my fear in two-dimensional trees and dots.

The external game can't compare to the implant, but it provides enough of a distraction for my heartbeat to slow to a steady rhythm. Every time I pull my eyes away from the screen, I see the flicker of a shadow or hear an impossible rustling in the kitchen. It's safer to immerse myself in the game than to investigate my imaginings.

I play until sunrise.

"I'm an adult. I can't be afraid of the dark. It's pathetic."

"It's more common than you might think." The window in

Orlov's office is open again, but I take off my mask, anyway. The small strip of fabric is suffocating me these days. The smell of stale cigarettes makes me gag. He never smokes in front of me, but he must burn through cigarette after cigarette when he doesn't have patients. At the tips of his first and second fingers, there are two golden patches of skin, a shade darker than the rest of his worn hands. My father has the same marks on his calloused fingers.

"But why now?" I moan, even though we both know it's because I stopped using my implant. It gives me too much time to think during the day, and the anxiety builds, released at night in the form of irrational fear. "Can't you give me something to help me sleep?"

"Janice would have to approve it."

In other words, no, he can't. Or he won't. He almost seems like he can't wait for the memories to rip me apart so he can examine my darkest corners. No, that's the anxiety talking. I have to give him the benefit of the doubt.

"We can discuss the infant trial again, if you think you might be second guessing your decision."

Maybe the way he edges forward in his chair, listening intently, isn't excitement. It could be his own anxiety for me, because he wants me to get better.

"No." I tap the arm of the chair. It's solid beneath my finger. Smooth, but solid. I flick my fingers harder against it to keep the tears from rising. "I've told you no. Again and again. No. Can't you see I'm trying to be a good mother for this baby? I'm trying!"

A few hot tears run down my cheeks. I grind my teeth and don't bother wiping them away.

"I see that, Valya. I do." Orlov taps his cheek, his finger slower and more even than mine. "But you're exhausted. You don't seem to be coping right now, and I'm worried for you."

I stop tapping and cross my arms over my belly. "Worried for me? But it's not about me. Not anymore."

"It will always be about you. Yes, you need to be a good mother for your baby, but what does that mean? It means being there for her. Will you be able to be there for her if you're falling apart?"

I glare at him, and he glares back as the minutes of our hour tick away.

On the way home, the heat melts the frustration out of me. I drag the toes of my sneakers over the weeds fighting to grow out of the cracks in the sidewalk, and hang my shoulders. Part of me feels like an ape. A huge, disgusting ape with knuckles grazing the ground. I tug at my sweaty tank top, trying to cool myself, but nothing helps.

Inside, I peel my wet clothes from my clammy skin and sink onto my couch. It's been years since I've gotten in a fight with Orlov. Being at odds with him is worse than fighting with Skylar. Orlov is the one person who's always there for me.

I pad to the kitchen and pull a water from the refrigerator.

Always.

He won't hold a grudge. I'll go in next week and he'll be calm and collected. We'll talk about what happened, if I'm ready to, and everything will be fine.

Baby-girl kicks at the chill coming down over her. I tap back at her. "It has to be fine."

I press the cold water bottle to my forehead and make my way back to my bedroom. A notification is up on my tablet, so I head for the desk instead of the bed. The name makes me sit up straight.

Brian.

I click to open the message.

Valya,

Edges has been following your vlog with interest. It's obvious you took our last conversation to heart and are ready to make some changes to your style and earn some followers. Unfortunately, the new direction you've taken, with the exploration of laughter series, does not fit our aesthetic. Also, your follower numbers have not increased significantly in the past seven weeks.

We wish you the best of luck with your vlog, and hope you find a following that is passionate about your perspective. Unfortunately, that is not likely to be the Edges following, so we can not offer you syndication at this time.

Best of luck,
Brian

My jaw goes slack. He didn't even bother to call. I don't even get the chance to defend myself or explain my project. Just like that, he wipes out all hope with a damned email.

I throw the water bottle and it bounces off the wall. Just a damned email.

VALYA:
MONTH NINE

CHAPTER TWENTY-ONE

JANICE SMILES WARMLY at me from behind her desk.

"Things are coming along nicely." It's the same thing she says every month, and I wonder if she says it to every woman who passes through her office. Is it a lie? Does she get bored with reassuring us over and over again? Surely I don't look like everything is coming along nicely with the purplish circles beneath my eyes and greasy, unwashed hair hanging in my face.

I close my eyes against the pounding in my head. The train of words, rushing over me, is getting harder to stop.

"You don't look so good. Have you been sleeping?"

I don't even open my eyes. "It's difficult. Uncomfortable."

"It's to be expected at this point. You're sleeping on your left side, right? If you sleep on your back or right side anymore, the lack of blood-flow can wake you up."

I open my eyes, but only to raise my eyebrows at her. "I'll keep that in mind if I ever get to sleep."

"It's difficult in the last month, Valya, but you need to keep a positive attitude. It's better for you and better for your baby." She taps on her tablet. "I'll see you again in two weeks, right?"

Wait. I'm not ready to go. There was something I was supposed to ask her, but I can't remember what it is through the fog floating in my brain. Ah, there it is.

"Has Orlov talked to you?"

She scowls at me. "Orlov? No. Why?"

"It's just, I'm not doing so well since we turned off the Casual. I think the anxiety could be what's keeping me awake. He says he needs your approval to put me on any sleep medication or anti-depressants."

The wrinkles on her forehead relax. "Of course he didn't come to me. He knows what I would say. It's too late in your pregnancy to start those kinds of drugs. You're going to have to tough it out until you give birth. Then you can figure out a new medication regime."

"But . . ."

She clicks her tongue against the roof of the mouth, cutting me off with a sharp, wet sound. "They would be bad for the baby at this point. Maybe if you had been on them during your whole pregnancy, but you can't start them now."

I blush, tears welling as I nod.

"You're a strong woman, Valya. You might not feel like it, but you are. And over the next month, you will see how strong you are. But for now, believe me, you can make it through this. You just have to keep making the choices that are best for your baby, all right?"

"The self-righteous bitch." Olivia stops walking and turns to me. "She said that?"

I shrug and continue down the path. "She has a point. I'm going to be a mother soon. I need to get in the habit of making the best choice for baby-girl."

"Yeah, but maybe the best choice is to have a mother who's able to sleep. To think clearly. To relax. The stress can't be good for her, either."

As if she agrees, baby-girl does a flip in my belly. I pat my stomach to calm her and she presses out against the tapping. "You sound like Orlov these days."

Olivia narrows her brown eyes at me. "Is Orlov still pressuring you about this trial?"

"No, it's not like that. He's just . . . you know, Orlov."

She keeps her eyes on me and I squirm under her scrutiny.

"I'm allowed to pressure and suggest, because I'm your best friend. But no one else is allowed to. Not Janice, and certainly not some creepy psycher from Padalo. He's supposed to be a professional, but I wonder what's in it for him."

"If I join the trial? He has a patient in a fascinating trial. That's got to be interesting for a psycher."

"That's all?"

"Sure, what else would it be?" I turn to walk again, but don't take a step. "I'm more worried about Emersyn."

"Emersyn?"

"She said she'd take baby-girl through Skylar."

Olivia steps in front of me, so close I can smell her breakfast. "She threatened you? You have to tell someone. At least Orlov. Maybe the police."

I step back. "It probably wasn't serious. It's not like she's going to come snatch baby-girl away in the middle of the night."

She takes my hand. Her slick palm reminds me I have to pee. Again. "You would tell me if you felt in over your head, wouldn't you?"

I throw my arms around her slim shoulders and she stumbles back beneath the weight of my sudden embrace.

When I pull away, my face is wet with tears.

"Sorry, the hormones. You know how it is."

"Yeah." But there's a cloud of doubt in her eyes.

CHAPTER TWENTY-TWO

"YOU KNOW YOU'VE got to tell him."

I lie close to Brianne on one of the lounge-pads near the wall of the atrium. We've tilted one edge up to serve as a backrest. Two iced drinks make dark rings on the crushed velvet cover.

The nuance of the synthetic sky distracts me. It has all the subtle variations in color as the real sky, but without the streaks of clouds and smog. The air is so clean, so pure, that I'm tempted to stop breathing, lest I taint it.

"It was raining when I came here before class. A little chilly, too. You would never guess. Down here it's always perfect, isn't it?"

Brianne untangles her fingers from mine and rolls on her side to face me. Her glare hits me hard, but I pretend not to notice it.

"You're avoiding the topic," she says.

I let my head roll to the side and take in her pinched eyebrows and pressed lips. She's cute when she's angry. My lips twitch with the desire to feel hers beneath them, but we're still not there yet. Or maybe we are, and she's waiting for me to close the foot of space between us and initiate contact. I can't tell, so I do nothing.

"Don't take it personally. I'd just rather not talk about it. About him. I shouldn't have said anything about it." I don't know how the conversation always comes back around to Skylar, even when I'm with Brianne.

She sighs and strokes my cheek, her moist eyes shining as they stare into my own. "I get it, but ignoring it won't make it go away. He's got rights, and as soon as the genetic tests come back, the hospital will notify him, if Emersyn hasn't already told him. With her in the mix, I don't know. Maybe you should get a lawyer. Things could get complicated, especially since you say he was the one who wanted the baby. It's better to deal with it now." Her mouth falls open, and she recoils from me, snatching her hand away. "Unless you don't want the baby."

"Of course I want to keep my baby." The words are right, but my tone is too exhausted. There's no fight in it to prove my point, and Brianne doesn't seem convinced. She turns away from me, her hand on her own bump where I can't grab it back.

I know the laws on custody, at least well enough to know Brianne's right. Skylar has more of a claim to the child growing in me than I do. He wanted her more. When I was ready to stop trying, he was the one who convinced me to keep going.

Three months before we broke up, I was ready to call it quits. I didn't even need a pregnancy test that month. My period rushed in early, soaking my favorite pair of underwear and letting me know my body had failed, yet again, to produce the child Skylar wanted. I cleaned myself off in the bathroom, flushed my tears down the toilet, and tried to put on a brave face. But by then it had been two years of brave faces, and a stony grimace was all I could muster.

"Why so mopey?" Skylar asked over lunch at his favorite cafe— the one with vegetables so fresh he claimed he could taste the green in them. Our table was close to a stream, and the waterfall running down the rocks kept capturing my attention, interrupting our halting conversation.

I lowered my voice in discretion, but the rushing water masked my words so even Skylar couldn't hear them.

"I got my period," I repeated a second time after his annoyed mocking of my mumbling.

"Ah, that's it? So what? It's no reason to get mopey. We'll try again next month." He shrugged off my bleeding as if it wasn't some kind of epic failure. I suppose I should have appreciated that he didn't blame me, but his certainty grated against the raw emotions exposed by my rushing hormones. Some bodies aren't built for carrying a child, and mine was giving all the signs it was one of them.

"I don't think I want to keep trying." I stared down at my tomatoes and sheep cheese laid over a bed of quinoa. The little balls of grain, their tails popped out from boiling, reminded me of sperm. Combined with the crushed red tomato, dripping its succulent juice . . . I pushed the plate away.

"Don't be absurd. Why wouldn't we keep trying?" Skylar took my plate and swapped it with his empty one, unaware of the carnage I imagined as he ground my salad between his perfect teeth.

"It's just too sad. Too much pressure. I need a break."

He laughed that full, warm chuckle that always made my stomach flutter. "What would stopping even look like? You can't be on hormones because of your *anxiety*, and I sure as hell am not getting that stupid injection in my cock. So what? Are we going to stop having sex?" He kicked my foot under the table to separate my legs and thrust his hand in the gap he created.

I pushed his hand down to my knee, glancing around to make sure no one had seen his bit of indecency. But even embarrassed and sad, the mere touch of his hand brought an almost burning warmth to my pelvis. I ached for him, and there was no way we would stop having sex. He was right. I was being stupid.

"Maybe we could, I dunno, not talk about it?"

He laughed again, squeezing my knee tight enough to make me jerk it away. "Sure, whatever you need. But how will you ever forget? That's why you got this stupid gadget, right?" He pressed two fingers into my implant, making it connect with my skull and sending a sharp pain down the left side of my body. But before I could register the pain his hot breath was on my ear, his tongue ticking at my lobe. "Let's go not make a baby."

Conversations like that kept me going month after disappointing month. If we both filed for rights to the child, a judge would only need to listen to one of those conversations to decide I had no real desire for this baby. Would I deny they took place? Try to lie? Probably. I'd fight for baby-girl. But it wouldn't matter. A court would look at his finances and my history of mental illness and decide she would be better off with him. But as long as I don't tell Skylar about her, I can pretend she is only mine.

I want to make Brianne understand all of this, to ease her wrinkles of judgment and let her know I'm just trying to hold on to my baby for as long as possible. But there's no simple way to say all that, so I say nothing. I rub my belly and watch the muscle in the back of Brianne's jaw clench and unclench.

"It must be hard," she says, slipping her hand back into mine. "I've had Tony's signature on our arrangements since the first trimester, so I can't imagine how you must feel."

I can't imagine it either. Yes, part of me is afraid to tell Skylar about baby-girl because he might take her away. But isn't another small part of me holding off on that conversation out of hope? As long as I haven't told him, I can imagine him seeing my swollen belly and taking me into his arms. Forgiving me for choosing Casual over him. We could still be a family.

But if I believe that, why am I here holding hands with this sweet, sexy woman, wondering if she wants to kiss me? Plenty of girlfriends hold hands—it could mean nothing more than she's comfortable with me. And that possibility frightens me more than telling Skylar.

As if she can read my mind, Brianne's gaze shifts to our hands. She pulls our loosely clasped fists in front of her face, studying the way our fingers entwine. She traces my index finger, stopping at her knuckle. Then she lifts her eyes to my face and, holding me in her stare, presses her warm, dry lips to the back of my hand.

My stomach flutters, but it's actually baby girl changing position. I let loose an explosion of nerves and joy and amusement. Brianne returns my laughter, and for a moment we're just two pregnant women enjoying the day with no worries beyond flutter-kicks and gentle kisses. I let myself sink into the moment.

A flash of red near one exit catches my eye and I jerk upright.

Brianne covers her mouth and wrinkles her eyebrows. "Are you okay?"

There's no fox. I know this, but I continue scanning the small crowd of people, searching for a sign of my friend. Instead I see an old woman with a severe bun watching us from the corridor. Emersyn? I rub my eyes and she's gone.

"Did you see . . . ?" I mumble.

Brianne sits up and brushes my bicep with her fingertips. "There's nothing there, Valya. It's okay."

My eyes narrow at her. "Why do you care so much?"

She sits up. With her towering over me I feel foolish. "What do you mean?"

"What's it to you? What do you get out of it if I tell Skylar?"

"Nothing." She runs her hands through her thick hair, the softness we had been building squished beneath her frustration and my accusations. "Why do I have to get something out of it?"

Confusion flares in me. Anger leads me in one direction and desire in another. I stay somewhere in the middle, my words flat. "It's convenient that we met right when Emersyn wanted me to enroll in this experiment, and you're always fighting for what she wants. Pushing me to do it. Why?"

"That's ridiculous. You can't think—" The fire in her dark eyes simmers, then extinguishes beneath a heavy sigh. "You have to trust someone at some point. Not everyone is out to get something from you."

She's right. The paranoia is exhausting. But like a puppy gnawing on a treat, I can't let it go. "Until now it's been true."

"You don't want to trust me, fine." She fires the words from a tight mouth. "But you're so worried about being a good mother. You're giving up everything for your baby—your health, your lifestyle—at some point you're going to have to at least trust yourself."

I open my mouth but have no answer. I want to make her anger settle down, to fall back into the easy moment we had built. How did things go so wrong so quickly?

Brianne heaves herself to her knees, then stands. She glowers at me. "If you trusted yourself, you'd know how you feel about me. And you'd know I'm not trying to hurt you. But until then, I don't know if we have anything to say to each other."

She stands, her struggle righting herself almost muting her fury. But when she's upright, it's still there, and she stamps away, the weight of her steps vibrating the cushion beneath me.

I fight the urge to call after her. She's right. Unless I trust myself, and her, there's no point.

CHAPTER TWENTY-THREE

IF I WANT to be with Brianne, I have to tell Skylar. If I want any sense of chance with Skylar again, I have to tell him. If I want my baby safe, I have to tell Skylar. It all comes down to what should be an easy task: tell the father of my child I'm pregnant.

But it's not easy. I spend days lying in bed, tossing and turning against the stifling heat but refusing to get up for more than a glass of water, infinite trips to the bathroom, and the occasional meal packet.

Right now, everything is possible. But as soon as I knock on Skylar's door and he sees me, choices will be made and the possibilities will shrink. I imagine what it would be like to catch my fox. I feel his rapid heartbeat beneath my hands. His fur isn't soft at all. It's ragged, matted. I crush harder, trying to find the thrill the fox always gives me, but dirty and smelling of small game, it provides nothing. Its small bones crack beneath the squeeze of my hands, and it lies limp in my arms. I never really wanted to catch it.

But some day, I'll have to.

And that day is today.

Skylar's apartment building still feels like home. Even after eight months, walking up the lit path to the steps makes a tightness in the back of my neck relax, like I'm coming home after a long journey. If only my new apartment possessed such magical powers.

Hesitating in the courtyard, the magic fades. The solar lamps by the main door used to glow blue, but now they're green. Two bushes close to the door seem new, too. It's enough of a change to remind me I don't belong here. It should make this easier, but my heart sinks and I have to steel myself against running away.

The heavy glass door scrapes on the concrete entryway, like it always has, but a pack of Chasers run by, breaking the familiarity. They're far away—just quick shadows in the night—but their low whistles and clipped shouts echo off the buildings as they close in on their digital prey.

The noise must drive Skylar mad. He chose this neighborhood because it had fewer Chasers and more people who seethed against implants. Five years ago, no one in his building even had a Casual. Of course, that was changing even back then. The backlash against Casual died down, and most people came to accept it as the modern normal. But not Skylar. Every time he learned someone else got an implant, he would curse and moan about it.

"A disease on society," he called them. He meant a disease within me.

The first time he used that phrase, we were sitting on the campus quad during my break between classes. He had brought turkey sandwiches with a tart sauce that stained his lips red. My own red lips were sore from biting them to curb my urge to lick the drip from the corner of his mouth. All summer it had been just us—in his apartment, in the fields, in quiet parks—and his modest decorum on campus let me know he wasn't the type to appreciate public displays of affection on a campus where he sometimes lectured.

Eventually my staring, along with a discrete scratching of my mouth, tipped him off to the spill and he wiped it away with a napkin. He was leaning towards me, about to reward me with our first public kiss, when a flurry of feet flew between us, breaking us apart and sending sandwich wrappers flying.

"What the—"

A barrage of sharp curses from Skylar cut off my startled question. He strung together innocuous phrases into hate-filled tirades the way only a writer could. People around us stopped what they were doing and watched his pale face turn red as he collected the wrappers.

Please don't yell after her.

It wasn't that she didn't deserve his anger. She was an inconsiderate brat, so wrapped up in her own world that ours didn't exist to her. But lashing out at strangers always made things worse, especially when the stranger was a Chaser. These kids—and they almost all were in their late teens or early twenties—wore the ripped jeans, chains, and spikes to show they didn't care. They shaved their heads, as a general way to say, "Fuck off." If their message wasn't clear, they had no problem yelling it at anyone who dared point out their inconsiderate behavior. Their entire purpose was to be inconsiderate.

I could forgive chasers because they were just doing what they do. Like animals following their nature. But the normal people who tried to change them? They made me boil with a mix of shame and anger. How could they be so stupid, trying to engage a Chaser? I wasn't ready to think of Skylar as stupid.

It took a few moments, but Skylar's muttering stopped, and his coloring faded back to its usual soft cream. As soon as it became clear he wasn't about to unleash on the Chaser, the eyes left us and we returned to our new-couple bubble.

He offered me a light smile and rolled his eyes. "Sorry about that. I hate them. They're so weak, complete slaves to their game, not realizing they're wasting their lives away. A waste of humanity, if you ask me."

"Chasers? Yeah, some are rude, but they're not all like that. Besides, I bet the experience is pretty intense. It's no wonder they get caught up in it." Back then I was still curious about implants. I still thought they might be fun or exciting.

"Trust me, they're all addicted to the tech. They're more machine than human."

In that moment, sitting on the grass, beneath the fall sun, my hate for New Sofia entwined with my concept of Chasers and Skylar's view of tech. It was all evil.

This was back when chasers only had a couple of additional implant options. Over the next few years, finger jewels grew in popularity and ocular implants jumped from the medical field into the more lucrative field of gaming. Chasers chased not only imaginary digital animals but a deeper, more realistic augmentation to their reality. Now they've moved into the hipster neighborhood where Skylar had been sure he'd be safe from their thirst for the game.

Part of me hopes their distant whooping and the patter of their combat boots on pavement keep Skylar awake at night. Satisfaction washes through me as I imagine him sharing the lack of sleep involved in carrying his baby. Even if he can't feel the other aches and pains tormenting my body, he can stay up at night and float through his days exhausted and cranky.

In front of his door my body stops functioning. My arm won't lift to grasp the brass knocker—yet another find stolen from a nearby village house. At least my throat's still functioning, producing a sweetly sick bile that fills the back of my mouth. My heart works, too. It's pounding out my presence in Morse, loud enough for Skylar to hear if he's home.

Turning around and leaving isn't an option. I have to do this, and who knows if my courage will ever rise enough for me to try again. My hand lifts. Like a balloon, it floats to the knocker. My fingers grasp the ring. It doesn't feel as heavy and solid as it should, as if it's made of plastic, not metal.

Tap. Tap-tap. Tap. Maybe he's not home.

There's a slight jingle of metal behind the door as the chain slides, then the solid click of a lock. The door swings in. My eyes rise to meet Skylar's, but his face is wrong.

It's dark and narrow, not creamy and round. Bushy eyebrows top dark brown eyes, and between the eyes glitters a green jewel. No, it's not glittering. It's glowing. An implant.

My eyes sweep up and down the girl's body. A black leather vest is laced up over a gray t-shirt, squeezing her young breasts up and out. A green jewel, matching the implant, shines from the piercing in her belly button. She plays idly with the piercing. Two green jewels, implants again, rest between her knuckles. Short black shorts hang over her matchstick thighs, a few glittering silver chains drag on her smooth, dark skin. She stands with her legs apart, her half-laced up combat boots like two massive islands on the shining wood floor.

Skylar doesn't allow shoes in his apartment.

"Yeah?" she prompts.

"Skylar?" It's a question, a squeak, and a call for help. Please let him come and make sense of this impossible girl. Could he have moved out? Did she break in while he was away in the villages?

She rolls her eyes and turns to call over her shoulder. "Babe! Some chick for you."

CASUAL

She doesn't leave her post at the door. Instead, she turns back around and assesses me, her eyes roaming over me the same way mine did on her. Her scan pauses at my belly, and she smirks. Even one of her teeth has a glittering green jewel in it.

Skylar appears behind her. He drapes one arm over her shoulders and kisses her cheek. If he's surprised to see me, he doesn't show it. His eyes don't even hesitate on my bump.

"Go on inside, Lala," he half-suggests, half-commands. The girl—she can't be over twenty—ducks under his arm and disappears into the living room. In the glimpse before Skylar shuts the door, the living room is the same as it was months ago. The same hand-woven rug and the same leather sofa. Even the sculptures I left behind are still there. The only thing different is the out-of-place Chaser.

The hallway smells of disinfectant, and beneath the astringent detergent, Skylar's spicy cologne drifts to my nose. It smells of years of sex and cuddling and trust. It burrows down in my nose, invades my lungs, makes me forget what I need to say.

"You're pregnant," he notes. "Congratulations."

"It's yours."

His gaze flits to the closed door, then back to my belly. He doesn't meet my eyes. "Nah, it's not mine."

I fall back a step. "There was no one else . . . "

He cuts me off, holding up a strong hand to silence me. My mouth is eager to comply and clamps down on itself. "Sure, biologically, it's mine. But I've got a new project going on and a new life." He jerks his head toward the living room. "You got the baby you wanted so badly, good for you. But don't rope me back into this. Me and Lala, we've moved on."

I search his face for some sign of softening. His gaze finally settles on mine and there is a moment, just a flicker, of something I've never seen in his face before. Pain? Fear? I didn't think it was possible, but my heart jumps even faster, making my world spin.

"You can't mean that. You wanted . . . "

He looks to the corner above me and laughs, a brief snort of derision. "You're confused, remembering things wrong. You were the one who was always so baby crazy. Guess I dodged a bullet with that, got out right on time." He leans back against the door jamb and looks me over, taking his time. His eyes, once full of love, are cool and calculating. "I've gotta say, Valya, pregnancy looks rough on you."

My cheeks fill with stinging heat, as if he'd slapped me. "My Casual got turned off last month, for the baby."

"Is that so? Shame. It kept all your crazy nailed down. Without it . . . sheesh. You're barely holding it together."

Tears burn my eyes, but I blink them away and go on. "Your aunt, Emersyn. She wants to put a Casual in the baby."

I don't know what to expect, but I certainly don't expect him to laugh so hard he has to put his hands on his sides to hold himself together. "Is that so?"

I wait for him to turn protective, to shout that he won't allow such a crime. But he doesn't.

"I thought you should know. She said you would let her, in exchange for funding."

"I wouldn't." His voice drops low, almost tender. The hard lines of his face have melted. He flicks a glance at the door, then takes a step towards me, close enough that I can feel his breath light on my cheek. "I wouldn't sell my baby."

His blue eyes hold me. I'm oozing beneath their power again. But before I melt into a puddle at his feet, he turns away and raises his voice. "Look, I'd love to catch up and all, but Lala's waiting on me. About the baby, is there some form I file now? Or after it's born?"

"She. After she's born."

"Great, you'll send it over then?"

My head nods without a thought. "No, I meant the baby is a she, not an it. The form, you can sign it now."

He groans. "Yeah, whatever. Just send it over, okay?"

My eyes water at his frustration. My throat closes and my breath can barely squeeze down into my lungs.

He leans over, and I lean into him, like a magnet I can't resist. "Don't trust Emersyn. The woman's batty. Keep the baby safe from her."

I'm about to explain that I have no intention of letting Emersyn put an implant in baby-girl, but he disappears behind his door, leaving the brass knocker to stare at me, a laughing semi-circle.

The hallway that seemed so familiar only ten minutes ago now feels foreign. Every crack in the floor seems new. The pattern of stripes—dark gray, light gray, dark gray, light gray—are alien, as if someone came in and laid new tiling while we were talking. Even the steps seem to be the wrong height, causing my knees to buckle beneath me as I descend.

I don't bother with my mask. I'm too numb for anything to matter.

The cool evening air should be refreshing after a hot day. But it hits my face and knocks my breath from me. A choking sob escapes my throat, followed closely by another. My body crumples to the wet grass, droplets soaking through my leggings. I crawl to the new bushes before I expel my lunch and dinner on Skylar's lawn.

Except it isn't Skylar's lawn. That wasn't Skylar. It wasn't the man who had loved me so tenderly and completely. It was not the father of baby-girl. My head settles into the lawn a foot away from my vomit, and the tears come between broken hiccups.

CHAPTER TWENTY-FOUR

T HE NEXT DAY is a fog. I get out of bed and pop a meal packet in the microwave, but I wander off, forgetting it before it even gets warm.

Maybe a quick rinse, lukewarm, border-line cold, will shake me out of the fog. But somehow I lose an hour beneath the water and come out shivering, my head no clearer. The day's no good, not worth being awake for, so I head back to bed.

Did I fall asleep, or have I been staring at the paint bubble on my wall for the whole morning?

Beneath the fog a deeper, more complete confusion threatens to break free and overwhelm me. Something happened. Something terrible. Tragic, even? But its memory sits beyond the mist. If I reach for it, I might be able to wrap my brain around it, but as long as I stay in the fog I'm safe. Whatever happened, however my world crashed, remains hidden from me.

I need help.

I should call someone. Olivia. Her steady voice always helps. She's confident, reasonable, stable . . . like a rock. But trying to anchor at a rock in this fog, I'm just as likely to crash into it. Besides, there's something I need to remember. She's mad at me? No. She didn't sound mad the other day. Just tired. Exhausted by my depression.

So am I.

I pull the sheet over my body even though it's too warm, but flashes of clarity creep under the cotton. They wrap their icy truth around whatever part of me they can find. I'm not sure if it's the sheet tangling my legs or my memories pulling me down.

Sleep was a bad idea. There's something waiting in my dreams that I don't want to meet.

Orlov. He said to call anytime. Benefit of the doubt says he won't judge. But it's too much effort to give him that benefit today. All I've got is the doubt, and that half doesn't do much good on its own.

Most of the day I'm not even coherent enough to feel trapped in the fog. I'm bored in it. Tired of it. Finishing a thought takes so much effort and . . .

The sun goes down, taking enough of my confusion with it to let me sleep. Despite my exhaustion, my mind doesn't fall into the cool, black oblivion I crave. Instead, it jolts around from color to shape to picture, making me even more restless.

I throw off my sheet and hit the light switch as if it were a fly buzzing around my head. The exposed bulb chases away the gray shadows in my room but not the mist in my head. Close my eyes and drift off to sleep. That's the stuff. A sweet, swinging sensation. Back, forth. Back, forth. Like swinging in a hammock. Inhale. Exhale. I'm just about there . . .

But no. My mind won't allow it. Out of bed again. Look out the window. Calculate the six hours until sunrise. But what good is sunrise? The fog will still be here. And beyond it, Skylar will still have . . .

He'll have done what? He did nothing wrong. He didn't yell or even raise his voice. He wasn't cruel. So how did he send me spinning into this? I haven't felt like this since . . .

I need something to focus on to prevent my brain from oozing out in all directions.

I settle into my chair and tap-tap against the glass screen of my tablet.

The face staring out at me is ragged. My hair is stringy from sweat, and my skin's shiny with oil. Each pore on my nose is huge, like pits I could fall into. It doesn't matter. It's just for me. I press record.

"Skylar wasn't himself last night. Or last night was the first time I've seen him as himself. If that's true, then the past five years have been a lie. A fabrication. Of mine or his? Or did we share guilt in building a reality that never existed?"

The words spill out fast then slow then fast again. My mouth goes dry. I pause long enough to swallow and remind myself to breathe.

I keep talking, telling myself my secrets and fears. The clock counts up. Twenty minutes. Thirty. My confessions are far from complete, but a familiar burn fills my heavy eyes.

Exhaustion.

I barely make it to my bed before sleep rushes in.

When I awake in the morning, my emotions are raw, and there's an aching deep in my chest.

I feel the hangover guilt that used to haunt me after a night of drinking. I tell myself it's just exhaustion, but there's a niggling in my brain. What did I do last night?

My phone buzzes with my tablet echoing. New follower. New subscriber. New. New. New.

I click through to the responsible post. There I am, looking like a ghoul, confessing my darkest secrets—and Skylar's—to all of humanity.

By the time I make it to Orlov's office, I think I might burst apart.

Before sitting down, I smack my phone down in front of him. His hands flutter around like two frightened pigeons, but he picks up the device before the screen goes dark.

He presses play and my weak voice, scratching like an excavator hitting pavement, fills his office. It's impossible not to stare at him. Pacing doesn't help. Why isn't he saying anything yet?

"You went to see Skylar?" He finally speaks, but they're the wrong words. He sets the phone down and motions to my chair, ready to start our session. "Please, sit, Valya."

"Yes, but don't you see?" I ignore his suggestion.

"It seems to have been a difficult interaction. I'm not surprised by that, given Skylar's own issues. If you sit, we can discuss it."

Skylar's own issues have been among Orlov's favorite assumptions for years. He assumes Skylar had a rough childhood. He assumes Skylar abused me. Every time he brought up these supposed issues, I reminded Orlov that he didn't know Skylar—had never even met him. Not officially. Seeing him across the parking lot or out the window shouldn't count.

Orlov insisted he could understand a lot about Skylar from my descriptions of our relationship. He listened to what he referred to as my "blind loyalty," and from that extrapolated Skylar's plethora of issues. At least that's how he claims to know about Skylar. But I know why he's so sure of himself. He scanned Skylar.

It was back when he had first gotten his ocular implant. After that first scan, it wasn't so bad. To help him calibrate it, I allowed him to scan me during our sessions.

"Is it that accurate?" I asked. "It can read my health on a weekly basis?"

"It's more general," he explained. "A suggested diagnosis, if there is a clear one, along with early warning signs if a patient is getting worse. I want to make sure I can use it properly despite a patient's mood. That's why it's helpful for me to redo your scans every week."

"So you're hoping it comes up with the same type of crazy every week. Consistently crazy."

"Valya, you're not crazy. You have a chemical imbalance that results in mood disorders. That's far from crazy."

Our session went over. We took fifteen minutes to start talking about things that mattered, so a fifty-minute-hour was never enough to cover anything. Orlov usually scheduled me for evening appointments—so we would never have to rush. That evening we left his office together. He walked me down to the lobby, held open the door for me, and wished me a lovely evening.

I called goodbye over my shoulder, forgetting about him and our session as soon as I saw Skylar waiting across the narrow parking lot. I bounded over to him and threw my arms around his broad shoulders, letting him spin me around as if we had not seen each other in weeks instead of hours.

Skylar's arms stayed wrapped around my waist, but he kept glancing over my shoulder. Turning, I saw Orlov still by the door, staring at us.

"Who's that?" Skylar asked, barely moving his lips.

"That's Orlov, my psycher."

"Why's he staring at us?"

From across the parking lot, Skylar couldn't see Orlov's ocular implant, which was more subtle than the flashy Chaser jewels. The control at his left temple was subcutaneous, a bump beneath his brown flesh, like a standard Casual. So Skylar didn't know he was being scanned, but there was no denying that Orlov was staring at us—at him in particular.

"I dunno," I lied. Skylar would confront Orlov if I told him what was happening. "Let's just get out of here."

During our next session, my suspicions were confirmed. Orlov, who had only loosely pursued the topic of Skylar in the past, had plenty of questions about my boyfriend and our relationship.

"How safe do you feel in your relationship?"

"Safe. Great, actually. Why the sudden interest in Skylar?"

"I'm interested in your well-being, and Skylar seems to be becoming an important part of your life. Have you met any of his friends yet?"

"Yeah, sure." It was a lie. Skylar and I were not dressed long enough to leave his apartment, let alone invite friends over.

Orlov nodded, scribbled a note on his tablet. "Do you find him to be controlling? Maybe limiting where you go or who you talk to?"

"No, not at all. Look, I know you scanned him last week. But whatever you saw must have been wrong. He's a great guy, and he's helping me a lot, okay?"

He nodded, setting his stylus down. "Be careful with him. Every person comes into a relationship with their own issues."

It was the first time Orlov mentioned Skylar's issues, but far from the last. Over the years, he continued to poke and prod at our relationship as if he was looking for some weak seam to unravel us.

○

I never asked what Orlov had seen in his scan. I had been certain he was wrong, whatever it was. But now I wonder. Did Orlov see this strange Skylar all those years ago? Did he know this would happen?

"You always knew Skylar was . . . I don't even know how to say it . . . that he was just using me?"

"I didn't know that." He folds his hands together and nods at my chair again. This time, I sink into it, my eyes glued to Orlov's unreadable face.

"But you scanned him."

"I never should have scanned him. It was wrong. Besides, my implant was so new then, the results can't be trusted."

Bullshit. "What did it say?"

"What Skylar is dealing with won't change the relationship you had with him. The things you went through with him will still exist even if you know the traumas that caused him to act the way he did."

"I just want it to make sense."

"It'll take time and space to make sense."

I give a heavy sigh. "Fine. That's not the most important thing right now. The thing is . . . I posted that."

He rubs his forehead with his meaty hand. "You aired Skylar's dirty laundry for the whole world to see?"

I bite my lip and shrug. My eyes sting. "I wasn't thinking."

"Valya, I'm not sure how much I can help you here. I think you might want to talk to a lawyer."

CHAPTER TWENTY-FIVE

A DAY LATER, Olivia calls me.

"We need to talk. Now." Her voice is terse, bordering on angry.

"What did—"

"Not over the phone," she cuts me off. "Meet me at the park."

I don't have to ask which park. With Olivia there is only the one we grew up on. Days down in the grass, nights up on the jungle gym. Crawling in the sandboxes, running through the sprinklers. I splash water on my face and pull on a fresh pair of leggings. A ripe stink comes from my armpits, but based on the tension in her words, I don't have time for a shower, so I cover it with a stick of deodorant and a spray of cheap perfume.

Only once I'm on the street do I realize I forgot my mask. Screw it. I don't need it. The air is fine and Janice worries too much. Besides, I'm the mother, it's my choice. I breathe deep, the scent of stale dirt filling me. I cough, but keep my head up and walk briskly towards the park.

Olivia waits on the corner, her face twisted somewhere between shock and anger.

"What?" I ask from ten feet away.

She shakes her head, once to the left, then back to center. I walk closer.

"What the hell are you doing?" she asks when I'm within arm's reach. She grabs my elbow, not hard, but firm enough to guide me into the park.

I let her lead me, stumbling along to match her irritated pace. "What do you mean?"

"What do I mean?" She snorts. "You're going after Skylar now. Are you insane?"

I stop and jerk my arm back. "I'm not going after him. I'm just sharing my story. Weren't you saying I should share about my pregnancy?"

"Yeah, yours. Not his." She has her mask on—a dark blue bit of silk that gives her eyes a shadow of mystery. It's only a fashion statement for her, probably doesn't even have a filter in it. My fingers itch to rip it off, so I can see her face.

"I'm pregnant with his baby. Some of his secrets are mine now."

"Yours to keep, not to share with the world. You know how powerful Skylar is. He can make your life hell. I don't even know what he'll do, but it's not going to be good."

She's right. Orlov said something similar during our session. I need to be careful about what I share. I hadn't meant to share my vlog, but the likes and shares felt so good that I craved more fodder for adoration. Now the thought of not pursuing it seems absurd. Irresponsible, even.

"It's a risk," I say. "But it's also a way to make money."

Like most parks, this one's filled with Chasers. I barely even notice them anymore. They're like moving benches or playground equipment. The teens, still too young for implants, play on their phones. Some more well-off kids have vibrating wearables—bracelets and glasses—that make the game easier. Proving Emersyn Enterprise's new crystal implants are safe for these kids would bust open a whole new market for them.

"He could take the baby."

My face goes numb. "You obviously didn't watch the whole thing. He wants nothing to do with her."

"Yeah, that was before you attacked him online."

"Why do you even care? It's not like you're even around these days."

Her eyes widen, then she looks down, her face limp with . . . guilt? Exhaustion? Hints of frustration?

"I understand. You've got kids and a wife. I don't expect you to be free all the time. We're growing up is all I meant. Going in different directions."

"No, you're right. I've been avoiding you. It's just hard watching you fade away all because of some guy. I love you, and thinking you would eventually go back to that asshole . . . It's more than I can take sometimes."

A young, lean Chaser runs around a tree in front of us. She has the same Chaser style as Lala—the shorts covered in chains, a gray tank top, an archaic gas mask, and black goggles. Her hair is cropped short and shaved on the implant side to reveal glowing burgundy jewels.

"You won't have to worry about that anymore. He's moved on." I try not to sound as miserable as I feel.

"And I hope you have too," she says. "He was no good for you, and he wouldn't have been any good for that baby."

"I have. Or I am. That's why I could finally vlog about him. I know there's no going back now." My eyes still follow the Chaser who is now bending low to the ground, sending her hands out in front of her with a fast, jerking motion. "I don't get how he's with a Chaser."

Olivia snorts, her eyes wide with disbelief at my naivety. "I can't believe he wasn't always with a Chaser. That man's all about control, and what's easier to control than an addict when his hypocritical money can supply their next fix?"

My attention shifts sharply back to Olivia. "But it wasn't about control with us."

Olivia rolls her eyes with the same tilt they always take when I defend Skylar. "Oh, honey. You still believe that?"

The past five years are crumbling in my mind. My memories burrow deep in my brain, like untrustworthy weasels with something to hide. Skylar helped me maintain balance and control. But maybe it was him controlling me, allowing me to believe he was empowering me. Like the way he stopped my night terrors. I'd wanted to give him that control. But what about when I wanted to take it back?

Now there's Lala, and she changes every one of those fights. Because if he didn't hate technology, then why didn't he want me to get Caz? Without Caz, I would have always needed him to read my moods and fix me before I fell off the edge. Even once I got it, the rough sex, no longer necessary, never stopped. If anything, it grew more aggressive as he tried to reach past my implant, into my soul.

I'm nauseated in a way I haven't been since the first trimester. I press a thumb hard into my wrist, trying to make the twisting, churning sensation go away.

"You okay, honey?" Olivia asks.

"I loved him. And he never loved me, did he?"

She wraps her long, thin arm around my shoulders, pulling me close to her.

"Five years. A baby. It's complicated, honey. But you're better off without him." She puts her hand on my stomach. "And she's better off without him."

"How didn't I see it?"

Her chest rises and falls against my arm and she kisses the top of my head. "Valya, there are so many things you choose not to see. I used to think you were pretending they didn't happen, but now, well, maybe that's the good part of your brain-issues. Maybe they're protecting you."

"What are you talking about?"

She sweeps a loose strand of hair behind my ear before returning her arm to my shoulders. "Nothing. I'm just talking nonsense."

I should press harder, ask again. But something stops my mouth from moving. Part of me doesn't want to know what she meant. Part of me thinks it might be better to let it go. I have enough to worry about between Skylar and the baby.

CHAPTER TWENTY-SIX

THAT EVENING, the tears come with no sign of stopping. I double over on myself, cradling my most sensitive parts, and collapse onto my bed, letting the hot drops flow. My grief must have a bottom. The human body's made of two-thirds water, so even if the tears take it all, a third of me will remain. Maybe it will wash away all the lies and leave only what's true—a dry twig of a girl who can see what's real.

My thoughts are like that stupid, beautiful sculpture Emersyn sent me. They reach out in slender tendrils, winding around whatever they can reach, clinging to ideas and following them out until my mind can't support them anymore. Orlov would ask me to interrupt the process. He would remind me how important it is for me to find a solid base of thinking when I feel out of control. But even he would realize I need to mourn the end of my love for Skylar. This, finally, is the end. The hope I held onto for the last eight months has been slaughtered. It's time to lay it to rest.

The tears alternate between sorrowful and cleansing. Cathartic. They wash away the final bits of our relationship. It doesn't matter if it was love or borderline abuse. There's no sense in rewriting it to either truth, because it's only history now.

The realization strikes me around three in the morning. The silence of my room closes in around me. The wall, warm against my back as I stare at the unmoving curtains, becomes real and hard. Everything is still. I hold my breath, waiting for inspiration.

Baby girl kicks hard against my bladder, setting the word in motion again. I inhale the sour air in my room. It isn't enough. I roll to the edge of my bed, stand, and open the window, not bothering to reach for my mask. The first tendrils of fall have broken the heat of summer. The tang of cut grass and water on sizzling concrete waft up to me. I close my eyes and take in the air.

CHAPTER TWENTY-SEVEN

MY HEART POUNDS strong and even in my chest, and lightness fills my body. But my eyes in the bathroom mirror tell the story of how I got here. No matter how many times I splash my face with water they stay red-rimmed, with puffy greenish bags under them.

I spend too much time trying to look like I haven't cried out the entirety of my soul and miss the bus. I wait at the stop for half an hour until the next one rolls up, and I'm late to my cohort. When I palm my way into the room, the rest of the girls are lined up on the spongy floor, completing deep breathing exercises.

I take a position two arm-lengths away from Brianne and sneak a glance at her while trying to follow Riker's instructions for stretching my neck.

She's looking back at me, no sneaking involved. Her eyebrows knit down with concern.

"You okay?" she mouths.

I nod, but the worry doesn't leave her eyes as she turns to listen to Riker.

I sneak glances at her as we stretch. Her belly hangs low like a teardrop, creating a perfect slope along her body. Mine pokes out like a basketball beneath my tunic, and I sometimes wonder if people on the street think I'm faking my pregnancy. No stomach should protrude like mine. They should grow out of the natural landscape of the body, like Brianne's.

I try to concentrate on the blond girl telling us about her fear of giving birth.

"Don't worry so much," Riker assures her. "You'll be using the Casual birthing program. Your brain will divert the pain into more pleasant sensations."

Brianne raises her hand and waits for Riker to call on her. "What about those of us without Casual?"

"Ah yes, you two." Riker wrinkles her nose as if we smell. If Brianne didn't look so serious, I'd burst with laughter over Riker's obvious disdain for us. "Well, I suppose there are more traditional methods for pain management. Positioning. Breathing. Massage. TENS machines. There's even an epidural, although none of these are as effective as Casual."

"Can we go over some breathing techniques?" Brianne presses.

Riker's face clouds over. "I'm afraid I have a schedule for the course, and I don't want to waste time on techniques most of your cohort won't use. You can find plenty of information online. I think the cohorts in Old Sofia still teach those techniques, if you want a demonstration."

Two pink spots grow on Brianne's cheekbones as she nods. Riker has already moved on.

After class I squeeze through the other women to catch up with Brianne and almost bump into her in the hall. "You waited for me?"

She offers a half shrug. "I'm sorry about the other day. It was unfair of me. We had never even talked about . . . well, you know."

"What do you mean?" I wrinkle my brows at her.

She sighs and looks away. "It doesn't matter now. I saw your latest vlog. It's okay. I get it. We can still be friends."

I snort with laughter and have to lean against the wall to catch my breath. "Everyone else who saw that vlog is mad at me because they think I'll piss off Skylar. You think it means that I'm back together with him?"

A small smile creeps into the corners of her mouth. "You're not?"

"No, I'm not. I told Skylar about the baby. You were right. It was something I had to do. I was holding back because it scared me. But now I'm free to live my life the way I want to, without him hanging over me." I don't go as far as saying the life I want is one with her.

"I'm proud of you." She reaches out and takes my hand in hers, offering me a warm squeeze of support. She doesn't let go as we walk down the hall.

"What was that about? The breathing stuff?" I ask.

Brianne runs the fingertips of her other hand over a crystal wall, making tiny oscillations with her fingertips while we walk. "How are your Braxton Hicks?"

"I dunno, normal, I guess. I feel a slight tightening sometimes. That's them, right?"

"Mine are painful. Like, stop what I'm doing kind of painful."

"But Braxton Hicks aren't supposed to be painful. Are you sure that's what they are? Maybe you should get it checked out."

"I've gone into the hospital twice. They hooked me up, monitored me. They're sure they're Braxton Hicks. They say they don't know why I'm in pain. I can't help but wonder if these aren't supposed to hurt, how will I make it through actual labor?"

"There's no sense worrying. We can't imagine what birth will feel like. Maybe these stronger contractions will make actual birth a piece of cake."

She glares at me and my brain burns with the stupidity of my comment.

"It's times like these I wish I could handle a Casual. I wonder what's wrong with my brain and if I'll pass it on to my baby. Am I setting him up for a lifetime of unnecessary pain? Should I even have a kid if my brain architecture is so . . . un-evolved?"

I stop in the middle of the hall, pulling her hand to make her face me. Her dimpled chin quivers and I pull her tight against me. Her heart pounds against my chest. Her baby kicks out at mine.

"There's nothing wrong with your brain. Nothing." I cup her face in my hands. My lips graze her soft, moist cheeks, our noses brush. Then my lips fall on hers, pressing, waiting for her to react.

For two breaths she does nothing. But eventually her lips move against mine, parting as she wraps her arms around my sides, resting her hands on my hips. She pulls me into her, and we stumble, the wall catching us as our tongues seek out the wetness of each other.

My fingers entwine in the straight, fine hair at the base of her neck. The kiss slows. Stops.

Brianne pulls back. Her brown eyes flit over my face as if it is a book. I lean towards her again, but she remains stiff.

"Do you want to go to my apartment?" she whispers.

My heart flutters, my stomach tightens. Yes, I want to go to her apartment. But my lips don't get the message. They say, "I don't think I'm ready . . . "

She takes my hand from her head and swings it in the space that's grown between our bumps.

"We don't have to . . . " She nods at my body. "We can look up those breathing exercises Riker was talking about. Practice them together."

"Yeah, that sounds good," I agree. "I bet she doesn't even know them. That's why she wouldn't go over them."

Not letting go of my hand, Brianne leads me down the hallway, around the edge of the atrium, and into a translucent elevator. With her guiding me I don't have to count hallways and doors. I'm able to see the crystal city for what it is: gorgeous.

The impermeable smoothness of the walls creates a dual impression of strength and delicacy. Each room is a soundproofed cell with internal acoustics designed for the area. The atrium muffles voices, keeping them close and intimate. The hallways do the same. A man and woman pass us, and their conversation is nothing but shards of indiscernible sound until they're within five feet. Suddenly, their voices come into focus.

"It's not like I knew," the woman says.

The man grimaces. "But you did it. That's what matters."

Another two steps and I can't hear their conversation. "The acoustics down here are amazing!"

"Of course they are. You didn't think the little ridges and lines in the walls were imperfections, did you?"

I had. Or maybe artistry.

My free hand stretches out and caresses the wall the way Brianne had. An appreciation for each divot grows in me. I close my eyes, safe between Brianne and the walls, and let myself exist only in touch.

Brianne's hand is damp with sweat. The pressure of her thumb on the back of my hand sends an electric excitement up my arm.

Opening my eyes, my warm giddiness freezes. Three doors down, Emersyn approaches us. She floats, maintaining a gait between efficient and graceful. But the way her eyes lock onto my face can only be described as a hunter stalking her prey. I drop Brianne's hand.

"Valya, I wouldn't expect to run into you down here." She slows to a stop in front of us. "Maybe New Sofia is growing on you."

It's a lie. She knew I was here and came to intercept me. She must be tracking my location. My Caz is turned off, but I bet she still has my GPS signal. Skylar always complained about the way implants invade our privacy even when disabled.

My stomach turns at the thought of him and I ball my hand into a fist. I force out a "Hello," but my tone is far from polite.

A flicker of emotion crosses Emersyn's face too quickly for me to read it.

"I talked to Skylar. He's signing away his rights. Wants nothing to do with my baby. So you may as well stop trying."

"Skylar?" Emersyn laughs, the sound not reaching her steely eyes. "I wouldn't expect him to be on my side in this, dear. Wherever did you get the idea he would be?"

She winks at me, as if we share some grand secret, but I have no idea what it might be. She turns to Brianne, pauses, stares at Brianne's face, and after a beat says, "Brianne? Nice to meet you. I'm Emersyn."

There must be dozens of Emersyns in New Sofia, but authority drips through this one's voice, making it obvious who she is. Brianne doesn't say a word as she pumps Emersyn's waiting hand.

"I see you're showing our little Valya around. Maybe you can make her more comfortable with New Sofia, convince her to move here. I've been trying to, but she doesn't even respond to my emails." Her voice is light, as if she's joking, but there's a hint of an icy threat beneath it.

"Uh, I," Brianne stammers, and I can't believe I ever thought she was working with Emersyn.

Emersyn continues as if Brianne said something intelligible. "You must take her down to E-level. I'm afraid she doesn't believe me when I say how comfortable she would be there." She turns to me. "I'm busy, so I mustn't linger. But I hope you're considering our offer. When you're ready to discuss it further, I will make time for you."

Emersyn continues past us, and Brianne whirls on me.

"E-level? She's crazy. I don't have access to that."

"If Emersyn suggested you take me there, she's arranged access."

"Oh man, we have to go. It has its own atrium and spa center, like an entire sub-city for the rich. I hear it's gorgeous."

"I wouldn't give her the satisfaction," I huff. "That woman is insufferable. She says she'd never try to bribe me, then sends me all sorts of gifts and offers me the best apartments in the city. Sorry, baby-girl isn't for sale."

A dark cloud of disappointment flickers over Brianne's cheerful features. She hides it and takes my hand again. "I see what you mean about her. She's an intense woman."

For the next week, I spend my days deep underground in Brianne's cozy one-bedroom apartment. We practice he-he-he and ho-ing between fits of giggles. Brianne's mother, who lives two doors down, home-cooks delicious lunches, and sometimes we take breaks to just lie together. The breaks are the best part. We sit on her couch and our legs tangle while our lips find new areas of face and neck and ear to explore. Then she pulls back and smiles this warm, pleased smile, as if I'm—we're—something fantastic.

At night I return to my shabby apartment. Brianne's crystal walls don't collect dust or grime. She changes their colors to suit her mood and even taught me to fiddle with the control panel. Orange or green or the same caramel as her eyes, the walls always gleam. It makes the spots of grease on mine even more noticeable. But I don't have time to clean. I take the urge to scrub—building deep in my belly, nearly undeniable at this point—and direct it at my tablet and new camera.

I've stopped vlogging about Skylar, at least in an obvious way. My rants have taken a more musing tone, and I've started exploring his ideas rather than him as a person. Did I have a reason to hate New Sofia or did I catch his disdain? When did I become anti-tech? Was the village as beautiful as I remember it? Do I actually want to travel? The only way to know for sure is to strip away the things he taught me. The problem is I'm not the person I was before I met him. That girl's gone, and a stranger has taken her place.

The rigid tip of the stylus scritches on the glossy surface of my tablet, and I imagine it chipping away at the person I grew into with him. I use the fine point to pick at my scabs, tearing away the ideas he covered me in. The more I write and talk, the more clearly I see the scabs he dressed me in. The way they stick to my soul fascinates me. I wonder what I am beneath them. When I press against them, I feel the liquid of my vitality. I'm still there.

I'm not afraid of a little blood.

Each night I try to peel deeper. Past the pain. They need to come off.

Sometimes I tell secrets to my camera until the sun comes up. I catch a few hours of sleep before heading back to Brianne. I'm exhausted, but as long as I don't sleep, my thoughts stay under my control.

CHAPTER TWENTY-EIGHT

BRIANNE WAITS FOR me at the sweet shop in the atrium where she took me the day we met. She greets me with a lingering kiss and hooks her hands on my hips.

"The way you greet someone sets the tone for the whole interaction, don't you think?" she asks when she releases me. "That's why, when people used to travel, greetings at airports and bus stations and train stations were so important. The moment they saw each other after being separated, the feelings they showed, that is what they would base the rest of their interaction on."

She's not wrong. When I was a kid, my dad would come home from work at six or seven in the evening. What greeting did we share? I looked up from the television or whatever constructor set I was playing with long enough to say, "Oh, hey Dad." His response? A nod with at most a grunt. For the rest of the night, we ignored each other, floating around the apartment as if each of us was alone with a ghost.

How different would have our life been if seven-year-old me had gotten off the couch and flung her arms around him? Would he have become real? Would our evenings had turned into the family affairs they showed on television?

With Skylar, it was like meeting a different person each time, and I never knew who to expect. Sometimes he was like my dad. He'd come home after a week in the village and drop his bag on the floor to announce his arrival. When canvas hitting hardwood was the first thing I heard, there was no point in rushing to his arms.

"Hey." A single syllable, gruff, not exactly cold, but without the warmth I craved. Then his boots, still on, would trek mud from the front door to the bathroom. After he closed himself away, I'd get out the mop and wipe the prints while he washed the dirt from his body.

When he greeted me like that, a few days would need to pass before his soul caught up with his body. We hovered around each other, but didn't speak. Didn't touch.

Other times, the door would slide open a crack and, before his sun-kissed face appeared, his voice floated into the room. He didn't talk fast, but words flowed without stop, as if he had to talk about all the things he had seen or they'd disappear.

These times, his voice hit my ears before I saw him, so I couldn't ramp up to the same volume quick enough to jump in. Those greetings resulted in at least an evening of listening on my part. By the time we went to bed, my neck ached from the nodding. Even then, he kept talking. Thoughts. Ideas. A spoken treatise on the world, unedited.

At the time, I felt special. Everyone read Skylar or watched his documentaries. They looked to him to tell them what to think about the possibility of re-settling the villages. But all they got were his carefully pruned ideas. They got pretty packages designed for them. I got his raw thoughts. They never felt like lies. They still don't. But maybe he didn't know his own truth as well as I trusted him to.

The greetings I yearned for—the ones that predicted a wonderful week together—were physical. The door flung open, hitting the cabinet behind it with a resounding thud. The hollow echo of that thud stopped my heart. It was surprising, but not angry. That thud was intentional, calling out to me wherever I was in the apartment. My lover was home.

He didn't say a word as he stood there, door hanging open, bag on his shoulder, smile draped lazy over his lips.

Our eyes would lock, his boring into me with fizzing hunger like acid threatening to devour me. I would try to return his gaze. It was a battle neither of us ever won, at least not to my knowledge. We fell into motion at the same moment, rushing to collide into each other.

Those greetings were all hands and mouths and the sweet ache of urgent sex. They were devouring lust wrapped in tissue layers of love. Sure, we tore open and discarded the love, but it made the present of our bodies beautiful.

Brianne's right, greetings are important. I let my eyelids close and seek the warmth of her face with my own. Our noses collide first, the tip of mine caressing down to her cheek. Then my lips find hers to return her kiss.

My kiss sets her ablaze. Her cheeks glow pink, her eyes hold fire. "I got you something."

"Me?"

She fumbles in a pouch strapped to her waist and pulls out a small ball of tissue paper. She kisses the tip of my nose and puts the light package in my hand. "You."

"I didn't get . . . what's it for?"

"Because I think you'll like it. And don't worry. I don't expect anything in return."

The hunger in her eyes doesn't match her words. I look down and carefully peel back layer after layer of the protective tissue. Beneath the final layer I catch a glimpse of muted red. I pick off the translucent covering to reveal a tiny red fox.

"It's perfect," I whisper.

"I thought, even though you don't have your game, you can still have your fox."

Words refuse to come to my lips, so instead I press my mouth against hers in a heated thank you. She matches the heat and kicks it up a notch, her hand wrapping around my neck and pulling me closer to her.

When we break apart, I notice the people surrounding us, watching two pregnant women make out like teenagers.

"To my apartment?" Brianne asks.

Something tells me he-he-he-ing and ho-ing won't satisfy her today. She wants more. So do I. But something holds me back. It's too soon after Skylar. Or . . . there's something else I can't quite put my finger on, whispering, "no, no, don't do it."

"No," my mouth echoes the whisper clamoring behind my ribs.

Brianne's eyes dim. She pulls back.

"You know where I want to go today?"

"Where?" she asks.

"E-level."

She practically squeals with excitement and throws her arms around my neck. Her kiss on my cheek is large and wet, with none of the tension of the moment before.

"Yes! Let's go before you change your mind."

It's hard for me to catch Brianne's excitement. New Sofia is clean, temperature controlled, and designed to enhance visual pleasure. The people float along in therms of various cuts and colors, going to or from actual jobs. The canteens have real chefs who work with real food, and yet people still cook at home for the pleasure. There's always a quiet hush, like the entire city is satisfied, except when the occasional Chaser buzzes through, breaking the serenity. Besides having a ban on Chasers, I don't see how E-level could be better unless it's made of diamonds and people drink molten gold during the winter.

The elevator dings on E-level, but the doors don't open. Brianne and I share a glance. Maybe the infallible city has broken down. A subtle pulsing near the elevator door catches my attention. A palm pad has appeared where there had only been wall before. I shrug and press my palm to the scanner.

"Welcome, Valya." The eerily human voice comes from the crystal as the door slides open.

At first glance, E-level isn't at all what I expected. It's too normal, almost like Old Sofia might have looked when it was first built, before it crumbled and a layer of smog settled over it. My feet take thirty seconds to get the message that the door has opened. Even then, they are hesitant to cross the threshold into the world before me.

"Wow." Brianne grabs my elbow and tugs me out of the elevator as the door starts to slide shut again.

The ground beneath my shoes is soft and springy. I look down. Grass. Real grass, growing in real dirt. Two columns of tall trees line either side of a dirt path. The wilderness on E-level is groomed, but not as sterile as the rest of New Sofia.

We follow the path forward. Between the trees and bushes, wooden doors, with old brass and iron knockers, are set into crystal walls cut and textured to look like brick.

"It's gorgeous." Brianne spins around to take it all in.

"Whoever would have thought? What the elite want most is what the poor have too much of."

Brianne lifts one eyebrow, waiting for me to explain myself.

"Dirt. Wilderness. They want to go beyond the sanitary back to the natural."

We wander along the path. There's a different kind of muted silence around us, provided by the silver-green leaves and smooth bark.

The path opens into a large park. It's like the atrium in size and function, but it's planted with real plants and decorated with wooden benches instead of the multi-functional crystal furniture. Two other wide corridors spin off the atrium, but across from us is the facade of a large building, complete with steps and ten towering columns.

I lean toward Brianne. "What's that?"

Her brow crinkles. "The community center?"

A community center. Something peppered throughout the rest of New Sofia collected in one place.

"It's like being on the surface," Brianne whispers.

"Yeah, if the surface was perfect and free of pollution," I grumble.

"Oh my god! Is that a garden?" She takes off across the E-level atrium toward a wide patch of dirt with green vines winding up chest-high sticks. There's nothing to do but follow her. By the time I catch up, she's dropped to her knees and is reaching out to stroke a dark green cucumber.

"Maybe you shouldn't touch it."

"You don't understand. There are hydroponic stations in New Sofia, but they're heavily restricted. This, growing out in the middle of everything? It's amazing."

"It is," I agree. Almost as amazing as the real thing.

It hits me that this is where Skylar was from. Not just New Sofia, but E-level. This manicured garden, made for the most elite, is the place he resented. When I imagined his childhood closed within the hard crystal walls, I had sympathy for his disdain. But now I can't imagine what made him run away from E-level. All the way to the villages.

My mind reaches for a memory of him. He took me to the village once. It was hot and sticky, surrounded by a jungle of green—

No.

I shake the ghosts from my mind. His problems aren't mine anymore, and he can't live in my mind.

"You can eat it, if you want," a voice breaks into my thoughts.

"Really?" Brianne asks.

The voice belongs to a young girl, maybe nineteen, sitting a few rows away. She wears cream therms stained with dirt on her thighs, butt, and knees, betraying each of her favorite gardening positions.

"Yeah, that's what they're here for. It's a community garden." She nods to a small metal compartment with a shiny touchscreen at the head of the first row. "You can request utensils there."

I move to the screen and look down. Pictures of plates, bowls, cups, forks, knives, and spoons fill the small screen. I press the icon of a plate and a knife. There is the subtle clink as a lock slides shut near the handle on the metal cover. Thirty seconds later, a beep lets me know to open the compartment. Inside rests a crystal plate and knife. I take them out, pick two cucumbers from a vine, and slice them against the matte-finish plate with the sharp knife.

"This is weird," I mouth, hoping the young gardener doesn't hear me. "Are these disposable?"

"Recyclable," the girl chirps from behind a pea plant. "Put them in and press the recycle button when you're done."

"Thanks. We're not from here," Brianne says.

"Yeah, I know. I have an ocular. You're Brianne, and you're Valya." She nods at each of us as she says our names. "Says here that you're thinking about moving here."

I laugh despite myself. Emersyn is thorough. "Not quite. Just checking the place out."

"Well, it's a great place to live," the girl notes. "You'd be hard-pressed to find somewhere better."

"You know, I'm thinking you may be right," I agree with her, biting into the crispy cucumber. It tastes almost as good as the ones from Skylar's village garden. But not quite. There's something missing.

I remember the one time he took me out of the city and showed me his garden. The heat was unbearable, the air wet from the greenery around us. The tomato and cucumber he fed me had tasted of sunshine.

Here, they're sterile.

Maybe that is what drove Skylar from E-level—it's so close to natural but not quite. My head spins as I try to pin down the reality of the room, whether it's crystal or greenery, manmade or natural.

CASUAL

It's hard to enjoy the treat with the girl's eyes on us. So we speed through our salad and fifteen minutes later, Brianne and I are back in the elevator, moving up to floors we're more comfortable on.

"Were you serious when you told that girl you would move there?" Brianne whispers, as if the elevator might be listening.

"I didn't say that. I said it seemed like it'd be hard to find a better place to live."

"And you have the chance."

The elevator stops and we exit onto C-level.

"I'm thinking E doesn't stand for elite. Maybe it was meant to be Eden-level, like the garden of Eden," I muse, avoiding her question.

When Emersyn first offered me an apartment in New Sofia, I couldn't imagine living within these cold, hard walls. But living in a place where real plants grow and the air isn't orange with pollution? Where I don't have to wonder whether I need a mask or not? It's more natural than Old Sofia, as pure as the villages. It would be the perfect place to raise a baby.

"Would you put a Casual in your baby if it meant you could live there?" I ask.

Brianne palms into her apartment and leads me to her purple couch, which looks shabby compared to the perfection of E-level.

"They couldn't put one in him since they can't put one in me." She won't look at me, and I think I know what the answer would be, if she had the choice.

"Yeah, but if you could, you would, wouldn't you?"

She picks up my hand, kisses it, snakes a leg over mine. We maneuver into our regular cuddling position without thought.

"They wouldn't have to offer me an apartment down there," she admits. "I would have one put in, if they thought it was safe."

"Even after this?" I touch the scar at the back of her head. "Wouldn't you be afraid he would reject it?"

"I'll always be afraid of that." She takes my hand away from her scar. "Not only because it hurt like hell and put my life at risk. But because if he rejects, he will be isolated. You don't understand how lonely it gets. I don't want him to feel alone, like I do."

I stroke her cheek and lean over to kiss her forehead. "You're not alone."

CHAPTER TWENTY-NINE

I **CAN'T KEEP** putting off sex with trips to E-level or conversations about philosophy. The weight of our swollen bodies draws me and Brianne to each other with a gravity so strong it's impossible to ignore. More importantly, I don't want to ignore it.

Brianne and I take the four steps from her couch to her bed. We settle back against the pillows, and the down gives way beneath my weight. I'm sinking.

"I need to come up for air." I pull away from her even though my skin screams like a spoiled brat for her tender touch.

Her hand remains tangled in my hair, her eyes searching my face. Beneath her worry, an ember of hunger burns, threatening to consume us. Her breath comes fast. With our babies pressing up against our diaphragms, the littlest bit of exertion makes us pant.

"We can stop," her lips say. But the way her fingertips stroke the back of my neck, lazily fiddling with the bump of my dormant Caz tells me differently. She's ready. Anticipating. Hell, so am I.

I reach out and tug on the metal zipper of her cream therms. The fabric peels apart, revealing her swollen breasts and stomach. My fingers dance along her collar bone and strip the therms down her shoulders, off her arms.

"We're doing this, then?" She doesn't wait for an answer. Her lips are back on mine as she pulls at my tunic.

Our eagerness is too much for our heavy bodies. Our desire demands we tumble and cling, straddle and pin. But our abdomens and low blood pressure slows everything down. We maneuver carefully. Scooting. Rolling. Cleverly positioning pillows.

As much as our bodies slow us down, they also contribute to the rushing need building between us. The months of aches turn into sensitive tingles beneath her touch. She brushes my nipple with her fingernail and an almost sparkling satisfaction races through me. Her breath on my moist skin makes me shudder, and when her tongue flicks out to pick up that moisture, the shuddering grows warm.

"Everything feels so intense," I murmur as she kisses down my belly, her black hair disappearing beneath the horizon of my bump.

It's too much. My hormones swelling from her undivided attention threaten to overwhelm me, and I feel like I might be sick.

As if sensing my panic, she slows, covering my inner thighs with delicate kisses. She lays her head on my hip and traces my hair with her fingertips. I haven't shaved in months.

"You okay?" she asks.

"It's a lot. My skin is vibrating," I admit, trying to slow my racing heart.

"Should I stop?" Even as she asks, her fingertip is pressing deeper, revealing to myself how ready I am.

"Just go slow . . ."

"Mmm hmm." The final syllable of her agreement buzzes against me.

I close my eyes and fall into pleasure. There's no turning back. But now it doesn't seem so scary. Relaxing warmth. Building pressure, but no tension.

Before I peak, my eyes flutter open and catch a movement in the corner.

It's nothing, but my eyes won't close. The peak is gone, replaced with tightness.

There it is again, in the opposite corner. When I try to focus on it, there's nothing there.

There's nothing there. Focus on Brianne. The slow swirling of her tongue.

There's nothing crawling towards us. There's only wet and pressure and . . . a face. A familiar face that shouldn't be here when I'm awake.

He's impossible, but that doesn't stop him from towering over us in our naked vulnerability.

I scream and scramble to the head of the bed, my pelvis jamming sharply against Brianne's teeth before I can get away. Brianne jumps, holding her hand to her mouth, her eyes darting around the room.

There's nothing for her to see, though.

"What the fuck, Valya?" She lowers herself onto the far edge of her bed.

I shake my head and choke out, "I'm sorry," but nothing more.

She inches closer, rests her hand on mine, waits.

My fear melts away beneath her reassuring touch. "I thought I saw . . . it was a man who used to be in my nightmares. It was so clear, like he was here."

I point to the end of the bed where the white man had stared at me with hollow eyes and sharp cheekbones. He hadn't said anything, hadn't attacked or threatened. His mere presence was enough to send me into shivers.

"You fell asleep? That doesn't say much for my skills."

I give a weak laugh at her attempt at a joke. I can't bring my eyes to meet hers, but I lean into her touch. "No, I was awake."

She wants me to call Orlov, tell him I had a hallucination, and have him fix me. But I can't tell Orlov. He'll think I'm crazy. Crazier. Different crazy. The dangerous kind of crazy. I need to be alone and figure out what happened.

I shrug off Brianne's offers to take me home and make sure I'm safe. Her voice is tender, her eyes dark with concern, but I can't let myself relax into her concern. I promise to call Orlov and head to my apartment alone.

Once inside, I lock the door and slide down the wall, sinking onto the grimy tile floor in my kitchen.

It couldn't have been a hallucination. Anxiety doesn't cause hallucinations. The hard tile and concrete building, once indestructible, no longer seem solid enough to hold me. I'm slipping deeper than I've ever gone, losing my sense of reality.

That on its own would be enough to terrify me, but there's still the matter of what I saw. I can't shake the feeling of being watched. Around any corner that face could pop up again. Even being awake doesn't keep me safe. I keep seeing flutters of movement out the corner of my eye. I jerk my head, sending my cortisol skyrocketing, only to find an empty room. Just the play of shadows.

Noises become amplified, take on a life of their own. I know the flowing sensation of movement next to me is the water rushing to my neighbor's taps or the scraping of their dining room furniture as they finish their meal. But my mind creates more ominous possibilities, always coming back to the White Man.

Deep breaths. There's nothing there. Nothing can hurt me. Deep breaths. In. Out. I calm myself, and the flickering shadows shed their animosity. I run my fingers through my hair, tugging at my scalp, pulling my head back against the solidness of the wall.

Brianne's right. I shouldn't be alone.

Orlov says nothing but tilts his head as I tell him, as clearly as I can, what happened. When I finish, he opens his mouth, closes it again, and finally says, "It sounds like a frightening experience."

"Does this mean I'm getting worse? Like I'm psychotic or something?"

He smiles that warm, reassuring half-smile and shakes his head. "No, Valya. Hallucinations, on their own, do not change your diagnosis. Many people who experience anxiety also experience hallucinations during more stressful periods."

"Really? How come I've never heard of it?" I shift back and forth in my seat, unable to get comfortable.

"It's one of the less talked about symptoms. Anxiety, in today's world, is acceptable. It's logical. People can empathize with anxiety. Everyone has been anxious even if they can't understand the pervasiveness of clinical anxiety. But hallucinations?" He shrugs, letting his hands flutter to complete his sentence.

"People will think I'm really, finally crazy."

"Unfortunately, the stigma is still there. Most people experience lighter, less obvious hallucinations, maybe auditory or olfactory. Often, they aren't even aware they are hallucinations. Full visual hallucinations are rarer. But with everything you're going through, I'm not surprised."

"You mean with Skylar?"

He folds his hands in front of him and holds me in a steady gaze. "I hope you recognize this is about more than Skylar. Your pregnancy puts stress on your body and brain. You're preparing for a big change, so your subconscious is dealing with that."

He shifts his knees away from me and stares at his desk, his voice falling into a gentle rumble. "Your understanding of your position in the world is shifting, and you're having to rebuild. That would give anyone mental health challenges. Over the years, your anxiety had created a groove in your consciousness, so your first reaction to these stressors is anxiety. And when they get to be too much for you to handle with your usual anxiety? Your brain compensates in other ways."

"Hence the scary dude from my nightmares."

"He seems to be a significant figure for you. Does he remind you of anything?"

I hesitate. His sunken face reminds me of something. It tickles the front of my brain like a sneeze that won't come. Maybe I saw a costume like that at Carnival one year, but if I did, I can't force the memory forward. "No. Nothing."

"I would usually encourage you to reflect on it, to try to understand the meaning you've assigned it. But right now, the most important thing is getting you through these final weeks of pregnancy. So instead, I will recommend you lower your stress. Maybe consider moving in with someone you feel safe with, or have someone stay with you for a while. Someone who can be there for you if you have more nightmares or hallucinations. Olivia?"

What he doesn't have to say is it should be someone who can call him if I go off the deep end. And here I thought I was already swimming in waters deep enough to drown me. "No, I couldn't impose on her family with this. It's impossible. Can't you give me some tranqs or something?"

He hums, taps on his tablet, and shakes his head. "Not this late in your pregnancy. The risk is too high. Janice would never sign off on it. If you reconsidered the trial, we could turn back on your Casual. Things would balance out fairly quickly."

The steely reserve that has fueled me for the past two months falters. Balancing out sounds good. Better than good. It sounds like finally being able to relax after weeks of being on edge. "No."

"I know you think this is too risky for your baby, but I think it's time for you to reconsider those risks. How safe is your baby going to be if you're hallucinating?" He gestures to the bags under my eyes, my tousled hair, and my wrinkled clothes.

"There's got to be another way," I snap.

"Well, I suppose there is LOFES."

"LOFES?" I perk up at the hope of a solution, even though the letters mean nothing to me.

"Low-frequency electrical stimulation. It's an outdated method of stimulating the brain with a low, patterned current of electricity.

Based off Deep Brain Stimulation, it was the precursor to Casual. You already have the architecture set up with your implant. We would just have to program an appropriate stimulation pattern for you."

"How's that any different from Casual?"

"It's not interactive. Once we get the right patterning, you won't even be aware of it, so it won't distract you from caring for your baby. But it's not as good as Casual. Casual's interactivity allows your brain to manage your stimulation according to your exact needs. LOFES is relatively crude. It will control your anxiety at a similar rate to SSRIs, on which you still experienced night terrors."

"But it won't affect the baby?"

"It shouldn't." Not it won't, just it shouldn't. Nothing is without risk, and I will probably spend the rest of my motherhood doing this: making the best choice for baby-girl from a series of options that will never be completely safe. With the dexiety, the choice between my health and hers will continue to plague me, maybe for the rest of my life.

"Let's do it," I say.

"It sounds sketchy. You're sure it's safe?" Olivia fills every half-second gap with questions about the LOFES.

"I don't have a lot of other choices. It's pretty much this or have the grim reaper move in with me." I turn my little crystal fox over in my hand. My fist closes around it and its sharp edges dig into my palm, the slight pain staving off any chance of hallucination.

"The grim reaper?" She snorts, trying to hide her amusement at what she thinks is melodrama.

As I explain my vivid hallucination, her amusement melts off her face. Her eyes cloud over, and she reaches out for my hand. But her touch is like the zap of static electricity, and I jerk away.

"Sorry," I say. "Orlov turned it on, and things feel weird. Pins and needles, you know?"

She brushes away my comment, her eyebrows still furrowed and her mouth set in a small line. Deep in her jaw, a muscle twitches.

"It's not the grim reaper," she says, her voice low and strangely even, like a machine.

"I know that, but it's the best way I have to describe him. His face is so sunken and weird. It's like it's glowing, almost. Glowing bones in a halo of black. I'm sorry, it's a shitty description, but you just can't imagine it."

"I don't have to imagine it. You really don't remember, do you? All these years, I thought you were pretending—just ignoring what happened—but you don't remember."

A thick nausea settles in my stomach. They must have adjusted the pattern again. With the nausea comes a heavy dread, and the intense need to stop Olivia from saying anything else. She needs to shut up or I'll vomit. I cover my mouth, my shoulders already pulsing, ready to heave forward and release.

"It was the mask," she continues, unaware of how her words twist up my insides.

Hot, metallic liquid rushes up my esophagus, but I choke it down.

I stand, my wrought-iron chair scrapping against the stones. Our cups clatter on the glass table top. My fox jumps from my hand and lands on the concrete, a chip flying under the table.

"Are you okay?" Olivia stands with me. Her hand reaches out to steady me, but I jerk away and bend down to retrieve the fox and hide the tears taking over.

"I think it's the LOFES. Something's not right." My hand hovers over my mouth as if it could prevent vomit flying in all directions if my stomach lets loose. I would clamp down with my muscles, hold it all in, but everything is stretched so tight that there's nothing left to clamp. "I should go home."

"Do you need me to come with you?"

Yes! I need her strength and comfort. My best friend should be able to ground me, make everything better. But I can't look at her without my nausea threatening to double me over.

"No," I tell the cloudless sky behind her. "I need to be alone."

As soon as I leave the cafe, my stomach settles and my skin stops tingling. Whatever frequency or pattern they were testing, they must have realized it wasn't working. If it can get that intense so quickly, it's best if I stay at home.

But at home, every time I think back to my conversation with Olivia, nausea overpowers my thoughts, doubling me up with something between physical pain and confusion. Even with the familiarity of my apartment, I'm afraid every shadow will turn into a hallucination, or every time I brush my skin against a piece of furniture, the point of contact will send tingles into my stomach, turning it against me again. At this point, the treatment and the illness are neck and neck in the race for which is worse.

I flop into bed, careful to fall on my side. They just need to get the right frequency and my paranoia will fade. Until then, I'll sleep it off.

I tug my pink kitten pillow towards me and lay my head on it. The worn fabric caresses my cheek, and I close my eyes.

It's not a hallucination, because my eyes are closed. But the picture in my mind is so vivid it makes my body go rigid with the same fear that gripped me when the White Man lingered at the edge of Brianne's bed.

I'm looking down on a little girl, four, maybe five years old. My pink kitten shirt hangs on her scrawny body. She's unbelievably small. The sleeves fall almost to her elbows, and the hem hangs halfway down her naked thighs. No underwear. I can't see, but I know they're not there. Her empty eyes fix on my face, and she cocks her head as if she's waiting for me to say or do something.

Behind the girl, a figure approaches. Also naked from the waist down, he wears a cheap Carnival mask over his face. The black fabric with the outline of a skull painted in white covers his face. I'm too far away to smell him, but somehow I know his mix of sour body odor covered with cheap cologne—wet wood and citrus.

My stomach turns at the scent, and my eyes fly open. I lurch from my bed and my stomach empties on my carpet. My body heaves until there's nothing left, then keeps going, pushing tears out with each lift and fall.

Orlov. Olivia. Brianne. I go through my list over and over again. I need to call someone. But none of them can make me unsee what I saw because it wasn't a hallucination. It was the stripping away of a hallucination I've laced throughout my life. It was me as an innocent girl, before I started lying to myself, saying it never happened. Before I forgot.

A low sound, somewhere between a scream and a growl, grows in my chest. It erupts with a burst, filling my bedroom, echoing against the concrete walls.

I don't know how long the wail goes on, but an angry tapping from my neighbor lets me know it's time to stop. My throat aches. My muscles ache. My heart aches. I don't even have the strength to hurl the grotesque pillow—my macabre shrine to a forgotten offense—away from me. It lies on my bed at eye level, mocking me with its truth.

My phone rattles against my desk, breaking the spell holding me. I reach for it, clicking accept on the call without looking at the screen.

"Hello?" My voice sounds hollow and far away, as if someone else is speaking through me.

"Valya? Oh, god, Valya . . . " Brianne moans into the phone. It's a primal pain, and I wonder how she can feel what happened to me. "The contractions. They've started, and oh my god, this sucks. I'm at the New Sofia hospital. Come help me through this."

Brianne's distress gives me something to focus on. Bus schedules, getting to New Sofia hospital, helping my friend breathe, putting firm pressure on her lower back. These are all things I can do. Basic, one-foot-in-front-of-the-other-type accomplishments.

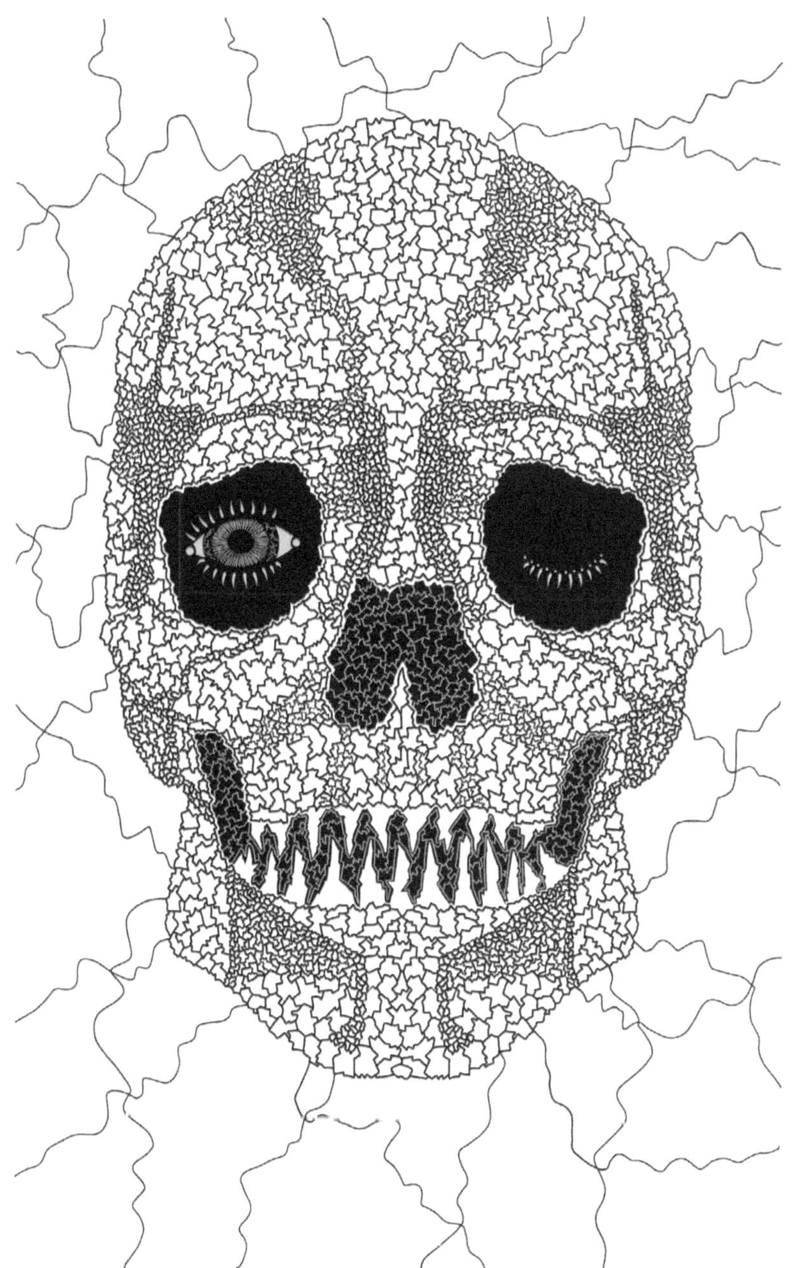

CHAPTER THIRTY

I FINALLY UNDERSTAND why Skylar craved personal transportation. I always thought of it as an indulgence our ancestors abused that we pay for. But when a hurting friend calls out for help, waiting on the corner for a slow bus to trundle down the street is absurd. I could get to the tunnel quicker with a bike if I could find one. But my sense of balance is so bad these days, I'd most likely tip over. So I wait.

The bus comes ten minutes late.

On my way, I message Brianne. She doesn't answer, and I wonder how many contractions she's had in the half an hour it took for me to catch a bus, and how many more she will have before I get to her. At least she has Tony. A pain shoots through my heart. Jealousy? Probably just reflux from my adrenalin.

The hospital is three floors up from the central atrium, and when the elevator door slides open, I'm hit with memories of being seventeen, strapped to a bed, waiting for my psych evaluation. Of my father picking me up. The father who never spoke to me. Never touched me. I shake the memories off and ask the woman behind the desk where maternity is.

Like everyone in New Sofia, she nods to the palm scanner on the desk before speaking. I roll my eyes and press my hand to the device. Sweat makes my hand slip, but it still beeps to accept my print.

"Valya, who are you here to see?"

"Brianne. She's in labor, called me about an hour ago."

"Right. Well, there's a Brianne here, but you're not on her list of companions."

"She isn't due for another week. You can ask her about it."

The woman's eyes scan the screen again, and she shakes her head.

"I wish I could. Our patients' desires are our highest priority. But she's already in active labor."

"Which is why she needs me there," I growl.

The woman looks me up and down, like I'm another screen. Her eyes rest on my belly as if she's afraid my anger will send me into labor.

"I'll see what I can do."

I pace the small waiting room until she returns, her face expressionless.

"Can I go back now?" I ask before she reaches her desk.

"I'm afraid not."

I clench my hands into fists. "I'm her girlfriend. She wants me there."

"You don't understand. I shouldn't tell you this, but she's in emergency surgery."

"Emergency surgery?" My rage melts to soft concern.

"There were complications."

A surge of fear leaps in me like a hot fire. My knees go weak and I grip the smooth edge of the reception desk. "Is she . . . will she be okay?"

A white face, hovering over the woman's shoulder, mocks me, whispering that she won't be okay. I close my eyes, try to breathe.

"Maybe you should sit down. I can bring you a bottle of water."

"Will she be okay?" I whisper through clenched teeth.

"It's a good team working with her. I'll let you know as soon as she's out of surgery."

I sink into one of the hard chairs and put my head on my palms, breathing deep until the spinning slows. I can no longer tell what is from the LOFES and what is from my mind, scrambling for some sense of normalcy. I sip cold gulps from the water that appears in my hand and wait, trying to think only of Brianne and her baby.

The woman clears her throat, and I look up at her, my hope hanging in front of me like a baby bird, fragile and exposed.

"Brianne is recovering. Both she and the baby will be just fine."

I spring to my feet. "Can I see her?"

She shakes her head. "She can't have visitors just yet. In another two or three hours, when she's moved to her room, she can request to see you."

I'm certain she'll want to see me, so I move back to my chair to wait.

"Maybe you should take a walk. Clear your head," the woman suggests. She just wants me and my scattered energy out of the room. I don't blame her.

The main atrium is too crowded for me. I take out my phone and search for somewhere quiet but nearby. The map reveals a small children's park near the hospital. While baby-girl may still be in me, I can't see any harm in visiting a park and imagining what she might grow into.

A few climbing structures make up most of the park, with spongy flooring beneath them to protect reckless falls. Two mothers sit on a bench, empty strollers next to them. Three children climb the structures, giggling and calling to each other. The youngest child crawls around the bottom and mewls up at its companions.

Off to one corner, a tall sculpture stretches up, almost brushing the ceiling. The thin crystal ropes, humming with energy, strike a chord of familiarity. I close my eyes. The sculpture Emersyn sent me. This looks just like a giant version of it. Could she be introducing the tech to the parents of New Sofia? Getting them ready to have these squirming tendrils placed in their babies?

The baby crawls towards the sculpture, looks up with its round eyes and chubby cheeks, and gurgles at it as one rope bends down, almost too slow to see the movement, and begins wrapping around the child's wrists, winding up its arms. The baby hesitates, its face somewhere between shock and amazement. I lean forward, waiting for laughter or tears. Neither of the women on the bench notice.

The tendrils keep winding, higher up, around its neck, over its back. The baby makes a decision and lets out a high-pitched, thrilled giggle.

My breath comes fast. I can't stop my mind from picturing the child strangled. Injured. Crushed. My heart pounds. I clear my throat and one of the women looks over at me. Then down at the child.

"Jimmy!" She stands and rushes to the baby, grabbing it away from the interactive sculpture. The sculpture lets go, standing at attention just like its smaller counterpart in my apartment.

But the mother is near tears, fussing over the baby. The baby wails and the mother looks for an injury that clearly isn't there. The two older kids approach, tentatively reaching their arms out to the statue and giggling as it wraps around their wrists.

"Sarah, Arthur, come away!" the second mother shouts. The two kids back away, the sculpture receding with a reluctance that mimics their own.

The mothers pack up and leave, eying the sculpture with suspicion.

I gaze up at it for a long time, watching its quivering tentacles react to every current in the air. I step forward and offer my scarred wrists. It snakes toward me and wraps around my skin, brushing the tiny hairs on my forearms.

I step closer to the base, and the ropes continue to wind around me, over my exposed collarbone, down my back. I shudder as they reach the thickness of my belly, but I don't back down.

They stop moving. I'm fully enclosed in a crisscrossing of flexible crystals. A deep breath moves my chest up, into the cage surrounding me.

The firm contact brings forward memories of being held by rough hands from behind. The arms had wrapped around me. Pinned me. Squeezed me to a body. Bodies.

With my exhale, the pressure eases and it becomes nothing more than a crystal sculpture, buzzing an atom's distance away from me.

Another breath brings the White Man in front of me. His face is no longer mystical. He's not a being from the beyond but a man in a dirty, old mask. The white bones are scratched. Peeling. Faded. The black abyss between the bones is actually a faded grayish color.

I exhale and step back. Tears sting my eyes. But the images of the White Man fade as I retreat. There's a buzzing in my head. I glance around for a trashcan to be sick in, but find nothing. So I swallow down the acidic taste and take deep breaths until the feeling passes.

I can't bring the White Man into Brianne's room, in front of her baby, but I want to make sure she's okay. I pace the hallway in front of the hospital for several minutes before taking a deep breath and entering the waiting room again.

This time, the receptionist smiles at me. "She's asked for you."

Relief floods me. She wants me there.

The woman leads me back to Brianne's room and palms the lock, gesturing for me to enter.

Brianne lies on a bed, a rope ladder near her head. Her black hair is matted, and she stinks of sweat.

"Sorry, I'm disgusting." She offers me a weak smile.

"Where's your baby?" I ask softly, entering her room and moving closer to her bed.

"Tony took Jackson for his examination. Thought he'd give me time to rest."

"Jackson. That's a great name." The scent around her bed is a strong mix of acid and body odor. "Should I leave you alone?"

"No, I wanted to talk to you. Before they come back." She tries to sit up but groans. She grabs the rope ladder and pulls herself upright, rung after rung, and then scoots back against her pillows.

"Was it . . . I dunno, am I even supposed to ask?"

She laughs, focusing on me again. "No, you're not. But who cares about what you're supposed to do? Yeah. It was terrible. The pain was unimaginable, then Jackson went into distress, and things moved so quickly."

"I wish I was here for you." I touch the sleeve of her gown, the backs of my fingers grazing her skin. She flinches away from me, and I jerk my hand back.

"We need to talk about the other day."

I swallow, lowering myself into the chair beside her. "Now?"

"I'll be stuck here for a week, and I'm not going to be able to rest and enjoy Jackson until we talk. So, yeah, now."

"Okay." She feels too far away, like I've already lost her.

"We need to slow things way down. End the romantic part, at least."

The statement should hit me in the gut. I should cling and scream and refuse. But instead, warm relief floods through me.

"You're going through more than I realized. I want to be there for you, but throwing two new babies into the mix, we can't be romantically involved. It's just too much."

The silence between us is thick. She's waiting for me to speak. I ache to tell her the reason for my recent freak-out, but I don't want to worry her. "Can we still see each other? As friends?"

She lets her gaze wander to the door, as if she's anxious for Jackson to return. "Yes, I think so. I can separate things out, if you can."

"Yeah, I can." I fight the urge to lean over and kiss her eyebrow. "Friends."

"Are you okay? I mean, the other day you were pretty out of it."

"You shouldn't worry about me right now. You have enough to handle."

"I'll feel better knowing you're okay," she insists.

"I'm better. Not fully better, but I'll get there. I'm talking to my psycher about everything. You were right the other day. I shouldn't have been alone."

"I don't want you to think that I'm abandoning you." She frowns with concern.

"Not at all. I get it."

She reaches out and squeezes my hand. The pressure reminds me of the wrapping tendrils of the sculpture. "I hope so. Maybe I'm just exhausted and making things up, but birth changes everything. You'll see."

She's right. I'll see in a couple of weeks. Maybe baby-girl will come early and I'll see how she changes things in a matter of days. My stomach flutters and that sickness fills me again. I've got to get the LOFES turned off. Or I've got to get baby-girl out of me. Or something else altogether.

The door slides open, and a short man with darker skin but lighter eyes than Brianne's stands at the entrance, holding a small bundle to his chest. "Am I interrupting?"

"No." The exhaustion sagging Brianne's face disappears, and she beams at the man, or maybe the bundle. "Valya, this is Tony. Tony, Valya. And that little guy is Jackson."

Tony gives me a nod and crosses to Brianne's side. He helps settle Jackson, nearly asleep, next to Brianne's chest. Her eyes go soft as she gazes down at him. Even I feel a bit of my worry and fear melting away.

"He's beautiful." I reach my hand out to stroke his tiny fingers, but pause before I reach his skin. "Can I?"

Even after she nods, I hesitate to touch him. His skin is so perfect, nearly translucent, and his entire hand is shorter than my finger. I'm like a giant next to him. Like some sort of monster. My finger falls against his moist skin, soft as tissue paper, and a grin pushes out my uncertainty. "He's perfect." Perfect and helpless.

"I know, right?" Brianne grins.

I retract my hand, but Brianne grabs it and gives it a tight squeeze.

Outside, I rest against the wall and hold my hand tight against my stomach. Baby-girl will be out of me soon, and she'll be just as vulnerable as Jackson. She'll have tiny hands and tiny fingernails and sleepy eyes. I have to protect her.

Instead of heading for the bus, I circle back at the atrium and take an elevator to Emersyn's lab.

My hands sweat when I knock on the door. I couldn't palm in if I needed to. But she's there and calls the door open. My legs twitch, as if they might run back down the hall without my consent. I grab the edge of the wall and pull myself into the room.

"Valya. What a delightful surprise. You don't look well. Are you okay?"

"I have questions to ask you about your trial."

Her hand flutters to her neckline as she steps towards me. Her fingers play over the hem of her therms like cockroaches racing for cover, and she clears her throat. I take a small pleasure in her surprise.

"Yes, of course. I'm happy to answer your questions."

"The tandem. Would I be able to know what's happening to my baby when she isn't with me?"

She motions to two chairs at her small table as she considers. We both sink into them, our gazes stuck on each other. "To an extent, but not in the way you might imagine. In the mid-twenty-first century, there was an experiment that allowed parents to see what their children were seeing."

"Ocular implants?"

"Crude versions of what we offer now, but yes."

"And?"

"They canceled the program. Turned out it wrecked havoc on the social and emotional development of the children. It also caused increased anxiety and guilt in parents. Privacy, especially in the age of connection, needs to be protected." Emersyn doesn't believe in privacy, not with the way she's constantly hunting me down.I wonder what happened to those kids that would be serious enough for a person like her to stop a project.

I rest my hand on my belly. Baby-girl presses out against the weight of me, and I smile through my fear. She's strong.

"But the point of the infant Casual is to help parents tune into the needs of their children. You'll know when she's hungry, when she's tired, and when she's in distress. As she grows, she'll gain more control over the device, and she'll choose what she shares with you. At that point, there won't be parental overrides. But for the initial years, you'll be able to detect when something is wrong."

I chew on my bottom lip, letting her explanation settle around me and baby-girl. Emersyn must sense my hesitation because she pries into the opening she created and presses on. "I'm not saying an infant Casual is without risk. You know it has risks. We don't know the social ramifications. But we're building on over a hundred years of research and experimentation. This project is well-thought-out, and it will improve the quality of life for young children and their parents." Her eyes soften. I want to believe her, but I'm shitty at picking people to trust.

"I was molested as a child." I state the fact as if I've known it my whole life, as if it's not a revelation, and as if it doesn't sting my heart to say out loud. But my voice quivers on the last syllables. As a child. A child. It echoes through me, and a sea of emotion rises, threatening to burst.

Emersyn's perfect makeup shows a flicker of confusion. "I'm sorry."

"I want to make sure that doesn't happen to my daughter."

"Of course you do." Her voice is soothing, like a swinging hammock I could fall into. I'm too exhausted not to trust it.

"Can you promise me that?"

She lifts her hand, holds it over my bare arm close enough for me to feel the heat and moisture within her. But she lets it fall back to her lap before making contact. Her head tilts forward, and she stares at my bump instead of my eyes. "I can't. There are no promises against that."

A tear sneaks out of the corner of my eye, rolls down my cheek to the fold between my jaw and neck. As it rolls, its heat leaves, and it settles into a salty chill.

"But if it happened. I would be more likely to know about it? To intervene? To stop it from happening again and again?"

"In theory."

Everything about the Infant Casual is theoretic. No answers. No promises, but possibilities.

I square my face to Emersyn's. Her usual composure has fallen and her pale face is drawn. She waits, not pushing me.

"I'll do it," I say.

She has won, but she doesn't even smile. She nods, her lips pinched together, her eyes glossy.

"I want to be clear, though. I don't like you, and I don't trust you. I'm not doing this for you. I'm doing this to keep my baby safe."

A hint of Emersyn's usual strength returns to her face. "Of course."

On the way home, I can't decide what to do first. I need to send those papers to Skylar, make sure Olivia and Brianne can get into the birthing room with me, make appointments with Orlov, Janice, Emersyn—the list goes on.

But as the bus leaves the darkness of the tunnel and enters the hazy Old Sofia sunshine, my mind plays tricks on me again.

I see him from the window. He's standing on the side of the road, as if he's waiting for the bus. But this time, holding his bony hand is a little girl in a faded pink t-shirt. I shut my eyes as the bus flies by them.

"They're not there," I mutter.

But when I open my eyes, they're still there. Well, not there, but here—on the bus with me. He's walking towards me, dragging the little girl with those wide, innocent eyes.

I close my eyes again, but they're in my mind. I can't escape them. I'm spinning, falling into a fizzing hole. My skin feels far away, as if I'm trapped in a wide, dark space with no form. They move closer. Closer.

"Not there, not there," I mutter repeatedly.

The man sitting near me gets up and moves to the empty seat behind the driver. The driver eyes me in the mirror.

I get off at the next stop. I'll walk.

The White Man and the little girl don't follow me. I waddle as quickly as my condition allows, trying to keep ahead of my mind.

I don't stop to message Orlov, just hope he's in his office.

I knock, sweaty and out of breath. There's a rustling behind his door and he opens it a crack.

"Valya, I'm with another patient." He looks closer at my face. "Wait here."

A few minutes later, a woman leaves his office, eying me suspiciously, and Orlov calls me in. The seat the woman vacated—my seat—is still warm.

"Sorry to interrupt your session."

"You look unwell. What's going on?"

I open my mouth, but no words come out. I don't know where to start. It's all too important and yet none of it is significant enough. Finally, my throat presses out, "You knew I was molested, didn't you?"

It's less of an accusation and more of a statement, but there's still enough fury behind it to make him lower his head.

"I suspected. But there is no way I could know what you yourself didn't know. Do you want to tell me about it?"

I shake my head, my hair flying around my face, creating a safe cocoon for a second. "No. I'm not ready to deal with this."

He sighs his old-man-sigh that shows his patience is wearing. "Valya, you don't always get to decide when you will deal with your emotional problems. It's come up now, and you can't ignore it anymore. You have to find a way to deal with it."

"I want my Casual turned back on."

"You know I can't do that."

"You can," I insist. "I talked to Emersyn today. I'm doing the study."

"Really?" He pushes his chair back and cocks his head to the side. A soft pain I've never seen laces his consideration. "I think it's the right choice for you and your baby, but I fear you may not be in the best state of mind to be making such drastic decisions."

"But it's my choice to make. Isn't it? So, you'll turn on my Casual and stop this LOFES shit?"

He hesitates, then nods. "Right away. But I have to say I don't think the LOFES is causing your symptoms. They are likey—"

"Just shut it off."

A light silence fills the room as if a buzzing I hadn't even noticed stops. I exhale and a tension falls away from my shoulders.

"I've stopped the LOFES, and I'll start up your Casual at the end of our session."

"Session? That's all I need. Just the Casual."

"Valya, you have to talk about this—process it—or it will eat away at you."

"Do you think I can forget this?" I snap at him. "Do you think I'm capable of pushing it back down and forgetting it again? Because I'm not. It's there, always and forever. But I can't handle it right now. You think I'm strong or ready—you think I need this. Why can't you believe me when I tell you it's too much right now? The things I'm seeing need to go away. I need more time."

Orlov waits for me to finish my rant, to come back to a level of logic he can work with. The smug way he folds his hands, bows his head, and makes space for my outburst makes me want to yell and scream until I get a reaction from him. But I've tried that before, and it's useless.

I take a deep breath and try to calm down. "I need time."

"And you've found a way to get time. You've come a long way over the years, to know what you need and get it."

"I have." It's a statement, not a question. I don't need his approval. I need Casual. But then something else comes to mind. "I'll most likely move to New Sofia for the study. Will you still be my therapist?"

"Of course. I support this study, and I support you. I'll be available to you, as I've been until now."

A weight lifts from my chest. Right or wrong, I couldn't do this without Orlov.

"In fact, I'll be the lead psycher on the project."

My tongue falls numb in my mouth. It takes all my concentration to force out a single word. "What?"

"Emersyn wants someone you trust making sure you're okay throughout the project."

My eyes narrow. "I thought you said there was nothing in it for you."

He seems confused by my anger, but he's a good actor. For years, I thought he had my best interest in mind. "I thought you'd be happy I'll be there for you."

"This whole time, you've been pushing me towards this, not because it's best for me, but because you'd get some cushy job out of it?"

"Valya, it's not like that." His hands are up, palms towards me, pushing my fury away from him.

I stand up, sick to my stomach, baby girl kicking like mad. I rest my hand on her thumping. "Just turn it back on."

CHAPTER THIRTY-ONE

'M UNSTEADY. I need something solid and, finally, I've got a rock to anchor myself to. Outside Orlov's office, I collapse onto the nearest bench and dig around behind my ear until my Casual starts up. I don't even bother pulling out my phone to create the illusion of something more cultured than my digital fix. If the almighty Skylar can date a Chaser, the world can get over my need to capture digital foxes.

It takes longer than usual. Most likely needs to hard boot or something, to access my history. How well the device knows me soothes me as I wait. I wiggle my toes with anticipation, my loose ankles popping from the movement.

A rust red fox appears in front of my closed eyes. Its tongue hangs out, tugging up and down with each rapid breath it takes. It snaps its jaws closed, raises its nose to sniff, and turns to run. A puff of white—the end of its bushy tail—fills my vision. The fox disappears, replaced by two dark trees, no leaves, deep in the snow, with a field of dots between them.

Returning to the game is like dropping into a warm bath. I know the game is in me, contained between the neurons firing in my brain. Each fragment of sight and sound hitches a ride across my synapses on neurotransmitters I've produced. Yet the way it plays on all my senses—how I can almost touch the crystalline snow and smell the wet winter air—it feels like I'm the one inside the game. Trying to figure out whether I'm creating the game or the game is recreating me is like trying to identify the beginning of a Möbius strip.

I force my mind away from the mechanics of the game and into the play. Selecting a rose-colored dot near the top of the field lights up a path along the perimeter of the dots. I walk the box, activating rosebuds and cream dots the same shade Brianne was wearing when we . . . Keep concentrating on the game.

I'm stuck on this passive perimeter level for what seems like forever. There's no excitement or action. There's no risk, no way to lose. Apparently, a month without using the device has demolished my chemical balance. The device takes it slow, activating lazy neurons, setting my neurotransmitters in action, forcing my body to produce more of what it's forgotten to make.

I want to be frustrated by the simplicity of my level, but the program knows what I need. After repeating the level again, my mind clears and a warm sense of satisfaction relaxes my muscles. The relaxation extends deeper, as if the repetitive task has calmed my cells, leaving no room for tension.

A dissonant horn wails in the background—a high note that sends shivers down the sides of my neck and into my spine—and the fox shows itself again. It races out from behind a tree, snow flying beneath its paws as it collects the dots I've marked. The dots it touches change color until they've all faded to shades of gray. There's another cry of horns, and the fox lopes out of view.

The scene fades. First the dots, then the trees and snow, disappear. All that's left is the blackness behind my closed eyelids and a stillness I haven't felt in weeks.

I blink against the gray-orange sky as if coming out of a deep sleep. I even yawn and stretch, more rested than I've been since they shut my device off.

Footsteps thud on the grass behind me, breaking my peace. One—two—hands on the bench, near my shoulder, and a whooshing of air as a girl jumps the bench, landing in a crouch on the ground at my feet. I can't get a good look at her before she's off and running again, a blur of black clothes and brown skin.

The Chaser startles me, but I'm so relaxed that once my heart stops racing, I laugh. No sense being frustrated with Chasers since they will be around as long as their game is. I can see why they love their game. It might be different from Casual, and not prescribed by a professional, but I couldn't deny someone the bliss and calm that comes from immersive technology. Not now that I realize how much I need it. Seeing the Chaser tuck behind the next building doesn't even bring up my anger at Skylar.

The way Olivia said he needed control—the twisting of her lips in disgust, the furrowing of her eyebrows with judgment—had me hating him as much as she did. But what if his control over people—over me—was his form of Casual?

I stare at the spot where the Chaser disappeared. She's like the fox in my game, unaware of the surrounding people, playing her own game, chasing her own high. It was real. Skylar was as lost in his own head as I am in mine, and he scrambles for control the only way he knows how. Meds didn't work on me, but Caz does. Chasing solves that girl's problems, even if it creates new ones. Skylar has his own game that gives him a sense of control.

The hate that's been bubbling up in me since I saw Lala standing possessively next to Skylar dissipates in a rush of empathy. I can't be his fox anymore, and he's found a new one. The poor girl. But maybe she wants to be a fox. The Chasers love to run.

At home I run a search for Dissolution of Genetic Rights papers. The search returns quickly, and when the forms appear, my information is already filled in. Name. Date of birth. Address. Due date. It's all there, correct. At the bottom of the form, an empty rectangle outlined in a thin crimson stroke asks for the second genetic parent's name.

"You know everything about me," I mutter to the screen. "You know where I'm from and where I'm going. You're telling me you don't know this?"

I type S, K, and Skylar's profile link-pops up.

"That's what I thought." I tap on the link and click send. No extra message, just the standard request to relinquish rights.

The screen returns to my homepage after the request sends. I stare at the picture of a distant mountain, shrouded in fog, briefly wondering where in the world it is. Then I turn from my tablet and push myself out of the chair. A gentle chime tells me I have a message, so I sink back down against the hard wood. I glance at the subject: New Status, Dissolution of Genetic Rights: Request signed by recipient.

He left a message on the file. *Just in time.*

Just in time for what? My heart does a slight leap into the slippery realm of possibility. It's a secret. An admission. A final chance at intimacy.

But he took less than a minute to sign and return the papers. It's time to be honest. Beneath whatever game he's playing, he wants nothing to do with this child. I expect to be overwhelmed with sorrow or relief. Something. Anything. But no emotion rises in me. It's simply over.

Half an hour before bed I spin up Casual. It rewards me with a more intricate level than the mush it offered yesterday. The field turns three-dimensional. When I tap on one of the colored discs, it turns into a deep, bending cylinder I can slide through. It isn't exhilarating, but it has enough risk that my adrenaline spikes and I get a satisfied buzz before the game turns off.

Optimal Sleep State Achieved it flashes in cream lettering before shutting down. It leaves a clean void in my mind that hasn't been around in weeks. I agree, it is the optimal sleep state. With a yawn, I snuggle under my thin cotton sheet to fall asleep. The White Man doesn't come tonight—not to my room and not to my dreams. I'm not afraid he'll show up. My fox keeps him at bay. I glance at the crystal figurine on my bedside table. Even chipped, it's beautiful. My protector.

Before I fall asleep, my mind wanders to the little girl wearing my favorite pink kitten t-shirt. She's not frightening or surprising anymore. All alone, clutching her arms across her chest and staring up with those trusting eyes, she's just sad. I want to wrap my arms around her and rock her, to sing her a lullaby. I want to go back in time and let her know I'm okay. She'll be okay.

CHAPTER THIRTY-TWO

DESPITE GETTING UP to pee four times during the night, my inability to get comfortable on either side, and the nausea that comes when I lie on my back, I have the most restful night of sleep I've had this entire trimester.

The sun streaming through my curtains wakes me up. I think about getting blackout curtains again, but then remember I won't be in this apartment much longer. Deep down on E-level, I can control the sunshine with a button. Curtains won't be necessary. I lay in bed, stretching like a lazy cat. Brianne's still in the hospital, and besides an appointment with Janice—my last one before my due date—the day is mine. For the first time during my pregnancy, things are falling into place, and I feel ready for whatever comes next.

At the automat, I splurge on breakfast and order a meal with synthetic sausage and real eggs. It isn't pregnancy approved, so I pay the full price. But if I'm moving into a rent-free apartment for the next year, I can afford to splurge. I let my mind think about toys. A stroller. The things I'll be able to buy for baby-girl now.

Real eggs need cooking, and I'm no good at it, but I dig out a dust-coated frying pan and wipe it with a damp cloth. Skimming the instructions on the package, I open the sachet of oil, put it in a pan, and scramble the eggs. Not as good as Skylar's. They turn out a little too runny, but still more delicious than the powder I usually buy. The sausage is a burst of spices over a thick, meaty texture, filled with pockets of juice that squirt around my mouth as I chew. Baby-girl kicks at my stomach as I hum with pleasure.

I leave for the Old Sofia hospital early, taking my time. The first hints of autumn nip the air. The leaves on the trees lining the narrow hospital road have the slightest hints of brown and red on their edges and a breeze suppresses the end-of-summer heat, making the day pleasant instead of overbearing.

I meander, the steep hill stealing my breath and sucking away my energy. As I approach Janice's door, another girl leaves. Her white cheeks flush pink. Her shy excitement, bowed head and quick eyes make me guess she just confirmed her pregnancy. I grin at her in solidarity, but she doesn't notice me.

Janice waves me into her office, shutting the door behind us as I walk around her partition. I head to the ultrasound table, but she nods at the wide chair with the stirrups.

"We're about there. I want to get a look at your cervix."

I strip from the waist down, fold my stretchy leggings and place them on a chair near the wall. Stepping up to the table is awkward, and I almost lose my balance as I turn around and maneuver into it. Janice waits until my feet are against the cold, metal stirrups before she approaches me.

She pulls a white glove over her hand and waves me closer to her. "Scoot down to the edge, please."

I scoot until my butt's three-quarters of the way off the pleather, taking the crinkling paper down with me. I'm afraid I might fall as my legs split apart, exposing me to Janice.

"There you go." Janice stops me with a hand on my knee. "Nice deep breath, this can be uncomfortable."

Uncomfortable is an understatement. Without the slightest hint of delicacy, she jams her fingers into me. A metallic pain—sharp and throbbing—runs from my pelvis up to my throat. I clamp my jaw shut to keep from crying out, but a tiny whimper escapes.

I close my eyes against the pain and exhale quick and deep, the way Brianne and I practiced. On the inhale, a familiar face surfaces. Just his cheekbones, his nose, part of his jaw, all bone white.

My eyes fly open, and I squirm away from Janice's probing fingers. She withdraws them and the pain subsides to a dull ache. Dark red blood coats the fingers of her glove.

"All done." She throws the soiled glove in a wastebasket and pats my knee again. "I noticed some solid breathing techniques. Have you been practicing?"

I nod, pull my feet from the stirrups, push up on my elbows, and plunk down from the table.

"Is everything okay?" I gesture to the wastebasket, now holding my blood.

"Don't worry about the blood. It's normal. You might have a little cramping or spotting for the next day. If you get a heavy flow or any significant pain, you can call me or the nurse's line. But your baby is in an excellent position, your cervix is about two centimeters dilated and thirty percent effaced."

Relieved, I wiggle back into my pants. "Does that mean I'll go into labor soon?"

"Not necessarily. What it means is that when your water breaks, you should come to the hospital sooner rather than later so we can monitor you. You can labor at home if you're just having contractions, but as soon as your water breaks, come on in." She sits behind her desk and types on her keyboard.

"Okay. Oh, about coming to the hospital—I will give birth in New Sofia."

She stops typing and turns a neutral face to me. "Why is that?"

It's like admitting to my primary teacher I forgot my homework. My voice fails me, and I squeak out, "I'm enrolling in the Casual trial."

Her eyes bulge. "No, Valya. Tell me you didn't."

I pat my belly. "I had to. I know there's some risk, but you don't understand how bad things got these past few months."

Her eyes narrow, and the warmth I've come to count on leaves her face. "I don't think you understand the risk. They will insert an untested device in your daughter's brain. Even if she doesn't die or become permanently injured, this can change her personality, her development, her very being. You may never get to know your actual daughter. The lovely being growing in you. She'll be gone."

My heart pounds. My nausea rises. She's right. My poor baby isn't born yet, and I'm a monster of a mother. I made the wrong choice. I could have been stronger for her. I could have found another way . . .

"No!" I stop my spiraling thoughts. "I'm giving her a chance to know her mother instead of a shell of a woman. I'm putting myself in a position where I can be there for her, protect her."

I'm telling myself as much as I'm explaining to Janice.

She nods sharply and turns back to her computer as if I'm no longer in her office. "It's good you're transferring to New Sofia, because I could not, in good conscience, be part of this. I'll transfer your records. Do you have a new doctor who I should direct them to?"

Her abrupt coldness unsettles me, and I don't know how to respond. For the past nine months, I thought she would be with me, coaxing me through the most difficult part of my pregnancy. Now, with one decision, she washes her hands of me.

"I'll send them to the hospital, then. I guess that's all." She gestures to her door, not bothering to stand with me.

My face burns and my eyes swell with unshed tears as I turn to leave.

Janice came highly recommended. People raved about her. She was intuitive, nice but professional, and had saved countless women from losing their babies. Supposedly. It's hard to tell how much of the hype about her was true and how much was the women basking in the afterglow of childbirth. Either way, since I was pregnant in Old Sofia, Janice was the obstetrician to go to.

Booking my first appointment was easy. She had a free slot less than a week after Orlov told me I was pregnant. I snapped up the slot and waited five days with a mix of glee and dread to meet the woman who would deliver my baby.

Women with swollen bellies, along with their partners, waited in chairs lining the hall as I approached Janice's office. I knocked on the door, and one woman glared at me.

"Are you waiting for Janice?" I asked, the saliva sticking in my mouth making it difficult to apologize for cutting in line.

"Of course I'm waiting," she snapped. "We're all waiting."

"I have an appointment for ten o'clock," I said, as if an appointment meant something.

She blushed and didn't say anything else, but shot daggers through me with her steel eyes.

Another woman, a bump barely showing, left the office and the woman waiting on the chair tried to corner her way past me, but I held the handle and poked my head in.

"Janice?" I asked the woman sitting behind the desk.

"Come in, come in." Her voice was cheerful for the number of women demanding her attention. "You must be Valya."

"Yes. There are women waiting, should I wait?"

She waved away my question. "There are always women waiting here. One day, you'll be one of them, too. Some of them forget to book their appointments and come in hoping I'll squeeze them in. Other times, there's a birth, and I get backed up. Things happen. People wait. Pregnancy and birth, it's a lot of waiting."

I walked the few steps past her wall of baby photos to her desk. She motioned to the gray canvas chair across from her.

"So, let's talk about you, Valya. You're pregnant?"

With those simple words, the women in the hall and the babies on the wall faded. It was just me and her in her office, and the warmth and care she had for me nearly knocked me back. It was like a mothering love—warm, overpowering, and somewhat harsh on the surface while soft and accepting the deeper we went.

Before I knew what was happening, my whole story was tumbling out of my mouth. I told her about Skylar, how I had never wanted children until I met him, how he had left me and didn't know I was pregnant. By the end of my explanation, I was crying those silent, wistful tears that come with new vulnerability.

"It's okay. You're a strong woman, I can tell, and many women have had babies on their own. Besides, I'll be with you through the whole thing. We'll take good care of you."

It was a promise I had never second guessed. I hadn't imagined her ever turning her back on me. But now disgust coats her voice. It's still like the love of a mother, but on the day she disowns her child. When she leaves for Paris and never comes back.

"Valya," she calls when my hand twists the doorknob. "It's not too late to change your mind."

But it is. "You say you're looking out for my baby. But I think you're just as set in your ideas as everyone else. They think their trials are best. You think no tech is best. And none of you believe I can decide for her. Well, I can."

I push through the door and am met with Janice's chaotic cork board. Baby-girl definitely won't go up there now. A pain shoots through my heart. She belongs with those babies. She's one of them. Or maybe it's just heartburn.

The romantic atmosphere of impending fall has disappeared,

replaced by impending sickness, as if the trees are dying instead of shedding their leaves. The air closes in like a wet woolen blanket I can't shake off. I need to get away from the weight of the day, and there's only one place I can think of where the air will be thin and pure.

I catch the next bus into New Sofia.

I settle deep into the bucket seat and set my destination in my phone so it will buzz for my stop. Then I switch my Casual on. I don't need it right now—my mood hasn't dropped very far. But it's a good idea to use it every day, to keep my balance.

The game recognizes my mood as playful and adventurous. Sociable, even. It sets me on a difficult, interactive level, pitting me against my little fox friend. We take quick turns stealing apples from a tree-stump, collecting matching colors in various bins. It's a game of balance and skill. Several times my bins fall over, and I laugh out loud. The other people on the bus are probably staring at me, but I've stopped caring.

Once I'm underground, my mood lightens even more.

I stop in the atrium, not sure where I'm going. Before, unless I was with Brianne, I rushed through the atrium. It was like I didn't belong here and had to get through before someone realized how out of place I was. But if I'm going to move to New Sofia, this space will belong to me. I slow down. Stop. Take it in as mine.

It's not busy today. Near one entrance, a group of teens lounge on a raised mat. Heads in each other's laps. Hands idly stroking hair. None of them are old enough for an implant so they chat and touch each other, fulfilling their animal need for contact. I loved that stage, when touch was easy. Olivia and I groomed one another endlessly during our teen years.

At the sweet shop, two men in matching black therms share a table. They take turns talking, but the vacancy of their eyes betrays at least a third companion in their conversation, somewhere on a Connect.

Off to one side, I notice another of Emersyn's sculptures, newly constructed. Several strands of crystal, as thick as a shoelace, grow out of a platform to a height twice as tall as me. I approach it cautiously, raising a hand towards it. It springs to life. Two strands snake up my arm, winding around me, slithering a millimeter above my skin. Two other strands bend, searching out more of me to encapsulate. One finds my ankle and starts up under my pants. I squeal and press my legs together. It retreats. Harmless.

"Be careful," an amused voice calls from behind me. "They've got a mind of their own." I don't bother to turn. Emersyn's voice has become familiar, and this time I half expected her to show up.

I hold still, only my breath moving my chest in and out. One translucent tentacle rests its tip against my chest and taps out a fast, lopsided rhythm, echoing my heartbeat.

"I saw one the other day, in a park," I say. "They're good. Almost alive." I don't tell her how frightened the mother had been. She probably already knows.

She puts out both arms, and two strands capture her wrists. She oscillates her arms like hummingbird wings to encourage the strands to wrap around her wrists in tight, even bracelets.

"There's a whole movement of artists who believe that."

"The singers . . . " I drop my arms and step back. The strands retract from me and return to their original positions. "I wondered how long it would take you to notice I was here."

Emersyn flicks the strands off her wrists and turns to face me. "You can't blame me for wanting to keep close tabs on you. Your participation is vital to this study. Once you move into your new apartment, we'll see each other regularly. You'll have weekly check-ins with me. Then I won't be so desperate to hunt you down, so you'll be able to stop worrying about seeing me every time you turn a corner, and I'll be able to get back to my lab. We all win."

"Speaking of check-ins. What about Orlov? Do I have to see him?"

Her lips curl into a smirk. "I thought you'd be put off by that. Told him he should tell you."

I don't believe her, but I bite my tongue.

"He's leading the trial. I guess that doesn't make you feel better. But the truth is, that since you agreed, he's the best option we have. He knows you. He will spot any problems a new psycher might miss. We have a responsibility to keep you safe. Which means we hire Orlov."

I bow my head so she won't see the tears stinging my eyes. He's a good psycher. Or was. I shake the confusion from my mind. "What if I refuse?"

"It's part of the trial. You would back out of the trial now?" Her voice is even, not threatening for once. She knows I can't back out. They are the only thing offering safety for baby-girl.

"Emersyn, you think I need you, and you're right. I do. But I know you need me, too. You need me participating fully. I can't do that with him. I won't. Too many men have betrayed me."

She raises an eyebrow and considers. Then she gives a slow nod. "Okay. We'll look for another psycher for you. A woman."

I exhale, relief flooding in. He's a good psycher, maybe, but I don't need him.

"Do you want to see your apartment? It should be ready."

Emersyn leads me to the elevators and presses the button for E-level. She palms in and the door slides open.

My breath catches as the perfect yellow sunlight glistens off the waxy leaves. Down here, fall may never come—the leaves are green without a hint of the brittleness on the surface. Emersyn's gaze doesn't wander as she starts down the narrow, tree-lined path. It wouldn't awe her, living here every day. Maybe someday I'll pass through the manicured green hall without gaping at it.

"I'm surprised it's so wild down here."

"My dear, E-level is anything but wild. It's curated nature."

"I guess I meant natural, then. I didn't expect it to be so natural."

We've made it to the open atrium, which looks like any park on the surface, except cleaner. There's a thickness to the greenery we don't have in Old Sofia. She gestures around the entire room, her fluttery fingers directing my attention to benches and trees. "The poor live in nature because they have to, and it makes them miserable. They view nature as harsh because it is. The slightly better off spend their time and money escaping nature, trying to find comfort by eradicating the wilderness. But the rich . . . we control nature."

"You sound like someone I used to know."

"Yes, well, my nephew and I agree on the importance of nature, but I'm not about to turn my back on our recent advances to eek out a miserable life in an abandoned village."

My new apartment isn't far from the lower atrium. Emersyn leads me down another wooded path, and we take a smaller branch that leads to two crystal doors set in a wall textured to look like stucco. Emersyn palms into the left door, assuring me they'll key it to me once I move in.

The apartment is too luxurious and big for me. Across from the entryway is a large, open kitchen with crystal counters set to a slate gray, the floor a pinkish, swirling marble. The living room, connected to the kitchen, is carpeted with a thick beige shag. The heavy coffee table is real wood, the couches are buttery leather. The bathroom has a deep crystal tub and a shower behind a frosted partition. Then there are three bedrooms—two with double beds, one with a crib. Even with baby-girl to help me fill the space, it'll be too big.

Emersyn misinterprets my frown. "The crystal's high quality and extremely adaptable down here. We programmed it to suit your needs, but it can accommodate most structural and visual changes if something isn't to your liking. If the furniture is not your style, Emersyn Enterprises has a cataloged collection you can requisition from."

"It's beautiful." I let my hand fall on the soft back of the couch. "It's so big, though. We don't need this much space."

"I'm sure you'll be happy for the space. You wouldn't want to share a room with the technician."

I tear my eyes away from the oak dining table. "Technician?"

"Even though you should be in complete control with the tandem, the law still requires someone not under the influence of Casual to be available to the baby until the results of our study prove it's unnecessary."

Emersyn will most likely be monitoring us through the walls. But the thought of living with one of her people crosses a line. "But it doesn't have to be an actual technician, does it? I mean, I could ask a friend?"

"You're going to fight us every step of the way, aren't you?"

"Probably." I spin slowly around, taking the room in again. "I will always be her mother, which means I make the final choices."

She shrugs, as if bored by my questions. "It would have to be someone without an active implant."

When I enter her room, Brianne sits up on the bed without the electronic assist or the ladder, but her smile is worn—half as wide as the one she usually offers me.

"Where's Jackson?" I lower my voice, expecting to see him

suckling. She nods to his bassinet. His tiny eyelids are closed, his tongue sticks out from between his tiny lips. My heart pounds. He's too little to be on his own. Even an arm's length away is too far. But my fear settles before it can take off fully. I sigh with relief and turn back to Brianne.

"He's a great baby. Eats, sleeps, poops, just like they're supposed to."

I laugh and move closer to her bed. "And you?"

"Everything's sore." A glare escapes her as if there could be no other answer and my asking is almost offensive. I refuse to let my mind latch onto her tone. It's about her, not me. This time I'm almost sure.

I sit on the edge of her bed. "I've got a proposition for you. How would you and Jackson feel about moving down to E-level?"

Her tired eyebrows knit together as if she can't understand the meaning behind my words. "You're doing the trial?"

"I am."

"What changed your mind?"

I glance over at sleeping Jackson. "You. Jackson. I've realized I've got a lot of stuff to work on, and I can't do that without Caz. It's not something to talk about here and now. But I promise, I'll tell you when you're out of the hospital. Especially if we're roommates."

She reaches for my hand. Her cold fingers play against mine. "I meant what I said the other day. It's not the right time."

I squeeze her hand, stop her fingers. "I know. There's too much new in our lives for romance. This isn't about that. It's about two friends looking out for each other in a to-die for apartment on E-level. I need a roommate as part of the trial, and I'd rather it be you than some tech I don't know."

"You're sure?" She searches my face. Whatever she finds, or doesn't find, appeases her. "Okay, then."

"Okay?"

She breaks into a tired but genuine smile. "I mean, E-level. How could I say no?"

CHAPTER THIRTY-THREE

PACKING SHOULDN'T TAKE LONG, but the task looms over me. After showing me the apartment, Emersyn sent a self-driving pallet to transport my belongings. A low, flat chassis, about a square meter, waits for me to fill it and press the preset "home" button on its metal frame so its continuous track all-terrain wheels can carry my belongings to the train station. All I have to do is throw my clothes in a few boxes and press the button—everything will be set in motion. But I let the pallet block the hall in my building. My neighbors curse as they maneuver around it, their voices carrying more clearly through the thin walls every time they pass it. They're ready for the pallet—and me—to leave, but I'm not.

It's not a problem with my energy. Between Casual stabilizing my mood and the nesting drive of late pregnancy, I could be ready to push that button in less than two hours. But instead of packing I lie in my bed, staring at my grimy, off-white ceiling. Part of me grows nostalgic at the thought of leaving my little hole of a home, and I can't figure out why. I've only been here nine months, and they've been some of the darkest of my life. I should be eager for the synthetic sunshine of E-level. But my body refuses to push itself upright.

Once I find the motivation to stand, the thought of staying in my tiny apartment needles under my skin, pushing me out my front door. My big toe rams the edge of the pallet, and I echo the cursing of my neighbors. But there's nothing to do except side-step the machine and continue to the elevator.

Outside, the neighborhood feels too still. Quiet. As if abandoned. Down a side-street, the screech of a child pierces the heavy silence, but its uncomplicated joy is muted by the weight of the day. I pull out my phone to check the date. The older kids are already back in school. No wonder the streets feel empty.

I stretch my mask across my nose and mouth, clip it to my hair, and let my feet wander where they wish. They point into the heart of Padalo, past the park with the toddler and its mother, towards the roundabout the neighborhood radiates from. They carry me to my old block apartment, curved around the roundabout as if it's too tired to hold itself straight. The falling insulation hasn't changed since my childhood. I can still see the men leaving to work in the grow houses, the women returning from cleaning the steps of other buildings around the city. My father and uncles still live here. Gregor probably comes home at night to whoever he settled down with—because everyone in Padalo settles down, even Gregor. My neck cranes back, exposing my throat to show me the roof we used to drink and smoke on. Does he still get high up there?

I lower my gaze back to the front door—cheap white aluminum with a rusty mail slot from years ago when mail carriers still slid letters and packages through a door and let the residents sort them for themselves. Everything how I left it.

The day I left, my door, like every other door in the building, was unlocked. No one had anything worth stealing, and everything could be borrowed without asking. Even a daughter, apparently.

"You're really going?" Olivia nodded to the large backpack near my front door as I filled a canvas tote bag with a few old books I had found at the market. The backpack, an extravagance I had saved six months for, was stuffed with my clothes, makeup, toiletries, and a rolled-up blanket.

"Why wouldn't I? More space and privacy in the dorms."

Olivia followed me into my tiny bedroom and sat on the edge of the bare, stained mattress. My desk and dresser were already empty, and I turned around, forgetting why I had bothered returning to my room.

"More of a future, too, huh?" she said.

I sank down next to her and threw my arms around her slumped shoulders. She didn't respond, so I pressed into her. "It's not too late. You could still apply and get in."

She shrugged me off and turned away, picking up the only thing left in my room: a ragged, hand sewn pillow made from an old pink t-shirt. I couldn't believe I had almost forgotten it.

"I don't want to go to university. I'm just going to miss you. But it's good. You should get away while you can. "

"There's no way you'll stay here forever, either. We're not like them, Olivia."

"Not like Gregor?"

I flushed, my breath taken away by his name. Things with Gregor were complicated. He hadn't grown to resent me yet, and I was realizing I loved him, in whatever way I was capable of loving.

"Hand me that pillow."

She tossed it up, and it came back to her hands heavily. "You should burn it. Get a new one."

"I can't afford a new one." I grabbed for it in mid-air. "Besides, I need something to remind me of home, right?"

She raised one eyebrow as if she wasn't sure if I was joking. But when I didn't laugh, she shrugged, handed over the pillow.

"When does your dad get home?"

"I dunno." I shoved the pillow into the bag, maybe harder than necessary.

"Are you going to wait for him?"

"Nah, I want to get settled in before dinner, maybe meet my roommate."

She pounced at me, crushing me in a tight hug. I nuzzled into the soft, familiar space at her neck.

"I won't blame you if you never come back."

I never did. Olivia and I met at the park or the cafe. She came to my dormitory. We went to the market together. But I didn't go back into the apartment building we grew up in, and I never ran across my father. As far as I know, he didn't bother trying to find me, either.

Looking at the front door now, I half expect him to come out and greet me with his usual disinterested nod, as if he never realized I left. My eyes flit up to what was once my living room window. The curtains are pulled open, but I can't see into the room from the street.

Olivia's phone rings four times before she picks up.

"Was the White Man my father?" I ask low, my voice barely carrying to the device in front of my lips.

I can almost hear her disinterested shrug, as if it doesn't matter anymore. As if it never mattered. As if the little girls we were never mattered.

"One of them, sure."

The silence of the day hangs between us.

"Are they still . . . "

A memory surfaces. I came home from school, maybe first grade. My father sat in his chair, staring at the television that wasn't on. His face was all sorts of fantastic colors. Purple and red and green. That was the first time he gave me his classic disinterested nod. He'd never touched me after that. I'm certain of that much.

"Look, Valya, you were lucky. You forgot for all these years. I didn't. Trust me. Keep forgetting. Don't go chasing ghosts."

A shadow on the stairs comes towards the door. Whatever face comes out, I'll recognize. There's not a stranger in that building. I turn on my heel and stride away.

I waste three hours on Casual, trying to forget my surfacing memories. Nothing more than a few flashes have come, and it's enough. I don't need the details. Not now, and maybe never.

My head's far from clear when the system boots me back into reality. I have to remind myself that Casual isn't a miracle, just another medicine. It can't cure me of what happened, only distract me from the paths my psyche wants to cut through my brain.

I'm still not ready to pack, so I tap my tablet awake and look over my notes from the past few weeks. Page after page about Skylar and the lies he told me. But the more I read my words, the more I realize it's not Skylar's lies that took away my stability. I've been waiting to be knocked down since I was a child. The lies I built to protect myself were dissolving.

I create a new folder on my tablet.

Name:

My stylus hesitates above the screen. I tap cancel, exit out of my writing program to my workspace and tap through to the administration section of my vlog.

My profile hasn't changed in years. It's as if I'm still a senior in university, optimistic for the future and foolishly in love with a man I just met. I scroll down the menu on the left: Editing, updating, upload pictures, create a video. There's the command at the bottom.

Create New Vlog
I tap the words and a form fills the screen.
Title: Casual Tandem
Subtitle: Parenting In An Era of New Technology
For the main picture, I select a snapshot from my four-dimensional ultrasound—the one that shows baby-girl's perky nose and fatty cheeks in pinks and oranges. I hesitate over the description box, and the stylus moves without my thoughts pushing it.

Description: From the beginning of time, parents have had to make difficult decisions for their children. What do we feed them? Where do we raise them? We decide what they wear and who they spend time with, hoping we're making the right decisions. For mothers, these decisions start before their child is born. The foods we eat and the medicine we take will affect them.

With advancements in neuro-technology, we will face more choices about which pieces to give our children and when. Not a hundred years ago, the argument was over, "screen time." Tomorrow's argument? When to introduce our children to Casual and its counterparts.

For select mothers, tomorrow's choice is available today. I am one of a handful of mothers enrolled in the Casual Tandem Infant trails with Emersyn Enterprises. I have a prescribed Casual that manages my dexiety (depression and anxiety). Instead of shutting down my medical device, I have opted to share the experience with my soon-to-be-born daughter. She will have the next level in Casual devices implanted days after her birth.

The decision was difficult, and only the future will tell if I made the right choice. But I have determined that at least one good thing will come from this situation: other parents will be able to make more informed choices for their children. Because of that, I want to share my experiences, as they occur, with you.

I read over the description twice before tapping, "publish."

I turn off my tablet, unplug it from the wall outlet, and put it in a large purse along with my phone and its charger. Four large cardboard boxes lean against my bedroom wall, waiting for me to put them together and fill them. I pick up the first one, pop its flatness into a cube, and look around my room. Clothes. I'll have to splurge on some therms if I want to fit in on E-level. The bed sheets won't fit my new bed, and no sense bringing the blankets or pillows, either. I wrap up my crystal sculptures in a few shirts, then move to the bathroom. Toothbrush. Razer. Dry brush. Wet brush. Flip flops. Half-empty shampoo, full conditioner, the end of a tube of toothpaste.

The second box is for the kitchen. Most of it isn't mine. A jacket hanging in the entryway, an umbrella I won't need in New Sofia. The pots and pans came with the apartment, but some dishes are mine. I put them in the box along with the interactive sculpture Emersyn sent me. That's it. Two boxes. I probably didn't need the pallet.

I open my door, put both boxes on the pallet, and leave my door open to make sure they stay there while I go through my small apartment one more time.

On the floor next to my bed is a worn, pink pillow. I squat, my stomach turning as I grab it. It's weight, the softness of the cotton fabric, the raised lines of paint . . . its familiarity confuses me. Hate should course through me with disgust hot on its tail. But instead I'm overcome with nostalgia. Wistfulness for a simpler time.

I crush the pillow in my hands, bite my lower lip until the tang of blood trickles into my mouth. Tears fall on my cheeks, and I don't brush them away. I take the pillow into my bathroom, set it above the drain and pull the shower head down, just in case. In the kitchen, there's a pack of matches left over from someone who smoked or celebrated birthdays or was a pyromaniac. We all have our issues.

The match head slides smoothly over the gritty strip on the box. Too smoothly. Nothing happens. I try again, pressing harder. A flicker. The third time the match springs to life. I throw it on the pillow, but it goes out before it reaches the cotton surface. A deep breath and try again. I squat down, close to the pillow, and when the match catches, I lay it on its surface.

The flame almost dies, falls down into the pillow, hesitates, and then springs to life, consuming the small item. Years of my skin and oils from my body. I've never washed it. Not once in twenty years. It still has the filth of those days. I let it all burn away.

It burns clean, leaving nothing but dry ash and a room full of smoke behind. I turn on the ventilator and spray the hot ashes down the drain.

When I turn off the water and leave the apartment, I don't look back.

CHAPTER THIRTY-FOUR

I **SEND THE** pallet ahead of me. It knows the train schedule, and no one will mess with the device while it's active. Its live camera feeds and state-of-the-art face recognition tech protect it from tampering. I have a few more goodbyes to deliver before I descend to my new home.

"Order anything you like, it's my treat," I tell Olivia when we sit at the riverside cafe.

"Your financial priorities seem to have changed," she muses, taking a seat next to me.

"I'm moving to New Sofia."

"I know."

"I'm doing the tandem trial."

"I know."

"Is there anything you don't know?"

She laughs. "Well, you haven't told me the details about the new vlog you started."

"You saw it?"

"Valya, you still have dedicated followers. When you posted that new vlog announcement, it went out to all of us. We're waiting to hear what you have to say about it."

I order a fresh salad, one with real honey vinaigrette over dark, garden-grown greens. Olivia orders actual grilled chicken, not the lab-grown stuff.

"I'm proud of you," she says when the waitress leaves.

I pick up the heavy fork, twist it around, and set it back down. "Do you hate me?"

"How could I hate you?"

"I'm leaving you behind, again."

Her smile falls, her face serious. "I'm in a good place now. I have my wife and kids. I'm out of that hell. If I was still in Padalo, maybe I'd be mad. No, not even then. I would always be happy you got out."

"Why didn't you tell me? All these years, you lived with it on your own."

"You seemed happy. Or, as close to happy as you could be. I didn't want to be responsible for making you go through it all again."

The waitress brings our plates. Olivia's chicken sizzles, a sweet, meaty scent floating from it. My stomach growls and my salad seems like it might not be enough.

"Will you come visit me in New Sofia?"

Taking a small bite, she lets out a pleased moan. "Delicious. I'll give New Sofia a try, sure. And I've got to meet that baby of yours. But, you know, you don't have to get trapped in there. You're from Old Sofia. You can come visit us."

"Of course." As I agree I tilt forward, my stomach cramping.

"You okay?"

"Sure." The sensation passes. "I think the honey might be too rich for me. My stomach's sensitive these days."

"Right. Those final days everything hurts."

I wash my salad down with a cold drink of bubbly soda. My extreme thirst surprises me, and I empty half the bottle in three long gulps.

"You know," I say, "I want this to be the end. I leave behind Padalo and Old Sofia and start over. But it's not the end, is it? It's just the beginning."

"I'm afraid so, sweetie. It's taken me twenty years to put it behind me. You're going to have to work through a lot over these next few months."

"Insane amounts of work," I grumble.

"It'll be worth it," Olivia assures me.

"You sound like Orlov."

We continue chatting, aware it's the end of an era for us. Both of us will have kids, live in two separate cities. As little as we see each other now, we'll see each other even less once I board that bus and leave behind the concrete city for its crystal sister.

Ten minutes later, my stomach cramp returns, this time with a tightening around my belly. It stretches out for half a minute, and then the tightening loosens.

"Oh, fuck," I interrupt Olivia as she tells me about her daughter's preschool art exhibition. "I think they're contractions."

"Are you sure?"

I shrug. "Not really. But what else could they be?"

"Braxton Hicks?"

"They hurt more. Like a sharp little pin prick. Is that how it was for you?"

She frowns. "Honestly, I only remember the end, not the beginning. I have no idea."

We both burst out laughing. How can two women, one of them with two kids and the other nine months pregnant, not know how contractions feel? But they don't hurt, and if they are contractions, they aren't close together. We order dessert. A chocolate mousse to split.

I take one bite and the tightening returns, this time my whole stomach turns hard, and the cramping has a hint of pain. I breathe into it and exhale long and slow.

"Definitely contractions."

"Let's get you to the hospital."

"Let's finish dessert," I insist.

CHAPTER THIRTY-FIVE

LIVIA COMES WITH me to New Sofia. I haven't added her to my list of approved companions, so I don't let her leave my side. I refuse to let what happened to Brianne happen to me.

Admitting takes longer than I expect. The doctor comes down, listens to the tones of baby-girl, finds her heartbeat, measures her. A nurse takes my blood pressure, my weight, runs an allergy test by scraping needles over my forearm.

"Don't you have all of this information?" I moan between contractions. During the bus ride they started coming harder and faster, with only four minutes of rest between them. Olivia holds my hand, letting me squeeze against her when the pain comes.

The doctor is a short, heavy man. The bright light shines on his bald spot. He asks me to get in the stirrups, and I maneuver down into them. Without warning, he sticks his fingers into me as another contraction starts.

I forget to breathe, forget to relax. My eyes are open, but all I see is that face. Those bones. That white hardness.

I scream and wiggle away from the man. He withdraws his fingers and waits for the contraction to end. But even when the physical pain subsides, I'm still squirming away from him, moaning, "No, oh no, no," to Olivia.

"You're okay," she whispers, leaning down to my ear to shush me with a warm, soothing murmur.

"The White Man." I think I'm whispering, but the way the nurse and doctor stare at me, I'm probably louder than I realize. I don't care. "I saw him. I don't want him here. Not for this. He can't have this."

She shushes me again and turns to the doctor, keeping her voice low. "Is there any way we can get a female doctor?"

"Tilbo is the only doctor available," the nurse explains.

"She's been abused," Olivia whispers.

My chest tightens with shame, and I can feel tears rushing in front of another contraction.

The doctor clamps his jaw shut, and his eyes dart to the nurse.

"I can try calling one of our female doctors, but I'm not sure if she will get here in time."

"She's six centimeters," Dr. Tilbo says. "And it's looking like this will go fast."

"It's fine." I moan, another contraction starting. I curl up into it. The breathing lessons are gone. The pain has pushed them out.

Oliva presses though, always the protective friend. "Can a female nurse do most of the monitoring?"

"I'll monitor her myself," the nurse assures us, waving the doctor back a step. "Now, let's get you up to your room and get your Casual started, shall we?"

It's the best news I've heard for the past hour.

The nurse keys a few strokes into her tablet and informs me I've been approved to start the Casual Birthing program. I lay on my side, holding tight to Olivia's hand, refusing to let her go. She reaches behind my ear, smoothing my hair back. I'm a teenager again, looking up into the face of my best friend.

"It's time," she tells me. "Let's turn it on."

I nod, able to speak between contractions, but too anxious about the next one starting to say anything.

Her fingertip slides through the roots of my hair, searching for the button. She finds it and presses, too gently at first, then harder until it clicks.

The program starts with no wait. Maybe because it's generic, or maybe because it's considered an emergency program. Whatever the reason, I'm thrown into it immediately.

Instead of a field of vision, I have the distinct sensation of being in the middle of an enclosed space. The room is small, the walls just beyond reach. The light is dim, but I can see something soft and wet all around me. It pulses. In. Out. The walls rise and fall before me, creating a rippling effect through the material covering them.

The next contraction starts. But instead of rushing in with overwhelming pain, time slows enough for me to detect the tightening first. As my stomach tightens, the walls of my cozy cave crush in around me, hugging me. When I fear they can't get any tighter without hurting me, they explode out into a kaleidoscope of color. Bright white light swirls away from me, carrying effervescent bubbles of color along its streams. I race after the color, expanding in all directions as I try to catch the beauty of the moment.

There is only pleasure, and a deep, sweet longing. Then it fades.

I am back in my tiny room. Waiting with the breathing walls. I didn't even feel the pain of the contraction, and it's over.

As I adjust to the room, I hear Olivia's voice coming in through the walls. "Are you okay, sweetie?"

I think about nodding, not sure if my body obeys my command or not. "Great."

The next contraction is coming. The pulsing has been replaced by the squeezing. Time slows. Stops. I stretch against the moment, waiting for the burst of pleasure. It's wetter this time, as if warm rain is falling on me from above. The water feels fresh and wild. I'm clean and at peace as it sprinkles on every inch of my sensitive body.

Back to the room. Breathing walls.

Over and over, I'm returned to my room to wait. As soon as I realize where I am, something amazing distracts me. Beautiful bursts, moments of flow. It's almost too much pleasure to keep up with, and I'm vaguely aware I might be exhausted.

This time, returned to the room, something is different. There's another sensation, from beyond the program. From my body. An immense pressure, low in my stomach. Stretching. Baby girl is ready.

A final burst of pure white light, too bright to look at. I'm back in the hospital room, somehow on my back on the delivery table.

"That's it, your baby's coming," the nurse encourages me.

I'm pushing without realizing it. My chin folds down to my chest and my hand grips Olivia's. I squeeze, and I push, exhaling hard.

A moment of pain and burning, and I'm confused, looking around at the faces of the two nurses and Olivia. Then, the strangeness of something slithering between my legs. Wet and wriggly and satisfying. My labia pulses. My thighs shake.

"The head's out. One more good push," the nurse commands.

I hold my breath and push hard, and baby-girl's body follows her head, leaving me empty.

The nurse wraps baby-girl in a blanket and lays her on my chest.

Her skin is red and purple beneath a thin film of white goop. I lean down and kiss her head of dark hair. She smells amazing, and I let myself fall back, giddy with joy.

Baby-girl's already looking for my breast, wiggling against my somehow naked skin.

"Perfect," I breathe.

"Does she have a name?" one nurse asks.

"Lisa," I breathe out as her tiny mouth finds my nipple and tugs against it.

"Lisa," she murmurs back. "It's a beautiful name."

"It was the name of the fox in old folk tales. She's my little fox."

Lisa opens her bright blue eyes. She's a fox worth concentrating on. One worth catching.

○

My first two days with Lisa are the most amazing days of my life. I'm weak and exhausted, but there's no way for me to be anxious or depressed. Happy chemicals flood my brain every time I see her or hear her mewling cry from across the room. But they are nothing compared to the wave of emotions that takes over when I hold her tiny, warm body in my arms.

I can't believe she's getting enough milk, from how little her mouth is and how short her feeding sessions are. But the consultant tells me she's a strong eater and will do fine. Her encouragement puts me at ease in a way words haven't been able to soothe me throughout my life. It helps that the nurses weigh her twice a day, take her vitals both morning and evening, and assure me everything about Lisa is perfect.

During those first days, time stops. Or rather, it continues to flow but ceases to matter. I only know it's morning because the orderly brings eggs or oatmeal instead of soup and salad. In the afternoon, the nurses offer to take Lisa and let me get some sleep, but I decline. She sleeps in little bursts. An hour here, two hours there. But it's enough for me, for now.

The first day I keep her bassinet next to my bed so I can pick her up the second she cries. Of course, there's the careful maneuvering first, getting myself upright, propping pillows behind me. I only leave the bed to pee and change my pad, soaked with blood, every two hours. Towards the evening Olivia comes back, holds little Lisa while I take a long, hot shower.

The stink of my effort runs down the drain, and I gather strength from the heat of the water. The aching of my shrinking uterus takes a break, and I manage to sit up and coo over Lisa with Olivia.

"She's lighter than you." She's careful not to say Lisa looks like Skylar, but I know she does. Despite her thick, dark hair, her skin is light and her eyes are as pale as his.

"They say eye color can change during the first two years, so I bet they will get darker." Wasn't there something about darker colors being more dominant? Surely she'll get my muddy green eyes. But so far it doesn't matter. I don't see Skylar when I look at her, only her miraculous beauty.

"When does she get her little addition?"

"On the third day, they think. They have to run more tests, do a scan, make sure her architecture will be receptive to the implant."

"How are you holding up? Still going to go through with it?"

She hands Lisa back and without thinking, I drop the shoulder of my nightgown and put her to my breast. She barely wakes up before curling into me, drinking little sips.

"Of course. I mean, I've had her. I could shut off my implant and not give her one. But think about it. How good of a mother would I be if I start hallucinating again? Besides, with the implant I can make sure she doesn't go through what we went through."

She reaches out and smooths Lisa's hair, which is sticking up in all directions now that it's been washed and dried.

"Our mothers didn't need to be in our head. They just needed to be around."

"Are you saying you don't think I should do it? Because I don't think I could handle one more person against this decision right now."

She runs her finger down Lisa's cheek. She has fallen asleep and is sucking air. I put my nipple away, but don't set Lisa back in her crib.

"No. You should do it. I'm just saying that no matter what choices you make, you're a good mother, because you care. You want to be here for her. There's nothing more important than that."

If there is nothing more important than my desire to be there for my baby, then why does my heart feel like a stone in my chest? Why do I feel like I'm betraying this innocent little creature?

They take her away for tests and my room is large and empty without her. It feels a degree or two colder without her skin seeking mine.

I try to distract myself while I wait. Olivia brought my tablet so I can craft a vlog. But I can't bring myself to write, let alone film myself.

I scroll through an online store, pick out a few infant therms for home. A soft green and yellow one and a bright purple one. They both look cozy, with plenty of room for Lisa to kick and wiggle. I order them so they'll be waiting for us when we arrive.

Despite the shopping, my mind keeps coming back to Janice. She warned me that I was basically killing my child, giving her no time to develop her natural personality. But who is allowed to develop their personality? The outside world impacts everyone. We have parents who love us, parents who don't care about us, early trauma, a safe home . . . everything we go through shapes us. This is nothing different. Except it's my conscious choice. Janice tells me it's the wrong one. Emersyn tells me it's the right one. I don't trust any of them. I'm the only one left to trust.

I scroll through the blogs I'm following until something catches my eye. A picture of Skylar. It's an older one, taken before we were together. His chiseled face stares into the middle distance with youthful optimism. Quiet, sure strength radiates from him. *Radical Blogger Realizes Dream, Opens a Private Village.*

That must have been what he was talking about when he wrote that I was just in time. I scan the article. He's north of Sofia, using an old hydro station to power a small village. No statement has been given, and the village is protected by a hemisphere force-field. No one knows who else is involved or where the tech for the force field came from. But I have an idea. Lala, so weak and innocent, who I thought of as a little girl who liked being chased. It has to be. A half smile grows on my lips, as much from my secret as from happiness for Skylar. He got what he wanted. And signing baby-girl over to me, it wasn't because he didn't care. He was protecting her from a woman who might be more of a technical wizard than Emersyn. At least, I hope that's what he was doing.

It doesn't matter what his reasons were, though. He signed the document. Baby-girl is all mine.

The nurse wheels in Lisa's bassinet and I take a deep gulp of air, as if I've been holding my breath. I stand and take her from her bassinet before the nurse has set the locks on the wheels. Emersyn is a step behind, but I don't give her more than a nod. Instead, I snuggle my baby to me.

"Everything is set," Emersyn informs me.

"Set?" My finger swipes behind her ear, but there's nothing there.

"The scans went well. She has a strong, healthy architecture. We can place the device this evening."

I stare down at Lisa's face. Her eyes are half open, and she stares back at me even though she can't focus on my face yet. My heart melts for her, and I want to wrap her in the goo I'm turning into.

"You're sure it's safe."

"All of our tests say it's safe. The chance of something negative happening are negligible."

"And you're doing the placement yourself?"

"Yes."

"How long will it take?"

Emersyn considers, looking down at my tiny baby. "Set up will take about twenty minutes. The actual placement will take seconds. But then there will be calibrations and tests. We will need to take her for two hours, at least."

"What if she gets hungry?"

"She won't get hungry."

As if to answer, Lisa roots for my nipple. She's always hungry.

"I want to be there."

"You don't need to be—"

"I don't care. I want to be there in case anything happens. Or in case nothing happens. I want to share this with her."

Emersyn presses her lips together and doesn't argue. She's starting to understand how insistent I'm going to be about everything concerning Lisa.

CASUAL

The nurse comes for us after dinner. The empty tray waits for an orderly, and the nurse ignores it as she wheels Lisa out of the room. I struggle to keep up with her.

"You're brave," she tells me. But her tone tells me I'm idiotic.

"They say it's safe."

She smiles down at Lisa. "No matter what, you will be an important part of the future. You and Lisa."

I don't care about any future but ours, but I don't say that to the nurse.

We arrive at the operating room. It's crowded. Besides Emersyn and our nurse, two other nurses and a cluster of people I can only assume are scientists working on the project gather. They stare at us as we enter, our nurse wheeling Lisa to the center of the room. I stand on one side, across from Emersyn, and reach down to stroke Lisa's plump fingers.

"Okay, let's get started," Emersyn says, more to the cluster of people than to me. "This is Valya from Padalo and her daughter, Lisa. Lisa is seventy hours old and will receive the latest Casual implant, CC-202." She holds up the tiny crystal grain for the crowd to see. "CC-202 utilizes new crystal technology to allow the implant to move in response to neural changes and growth in the brain. Once the device is placed, it will sit dormant for twenty-four hours, after which limited tandem access will be given to the mother."

Emersyn loads the implant into an injection gun while one of Emersyn's nurses applies a heart rate monitor to Lisa's chest and several diodes to her forehead below her hairline. The nurse turns to a machine, reads the screen for thirty seconds, then turns back to Emersyn.

"Monitoring heart rate and brain activity. Recording session."

Emersyn nods to another nurse who turns Lisa on her side. I hope she'll stay asleep, but the movement makes her stir. Her eyelids lift, heavy, then fall again. The nurse pins Lisa's fragile shoulders with one hand, her fingers snaking to the bottom of her neck. With her other hand, she secures Lisa's head. Lisa lets out a faint whimper in her sleep and there's a joint inhale around the room. The nurse nods to Emersyn.

Emersyn places the gun behind Lisa's ear.

I can't watch, but I can't look away either. My eyes track away from Lisa and back to her sweet face.

"Inserting," Emersyn murmurs, and pulls the trigger.

A soft hiss of air, and Lisa stirs, crying this time. Several lines on the screen jump, and I reach out for my crying baby, but the nurse puts a hand out to block me.

"It's okay, let her," Emersyn says, and the nurse lowers her arm.

I scoop Lisa with all her wires into my arms. Her head falls against the soft part of my chest, and I sway back and forth, shushing her and whispering.

"There there, that was it. A little sting, and it's all over."

At least I hope it's over. She seems to be calming down. She doesn't fall asleep, but her whimper-wail has stopped.

Emersyn is studying the monitor and flipping through results on her tablet.

"Successful implantation," she says. "The device is growing. Over the next five minutes it should reach its final placement. Vitals?"

"Well within range," the nurse answers. "Heart rhythm is steady. Brain function is normal."

I ignore all twenty people in the room, half who are staring at us, and the other half who watch Emersyn intently. I snuggle Lisa closer, cooing to her.

After two hours of monitoring, Emersyn releases us. The nurse removes the wires, and I push Lisa's bassinet back to our room. Exhausted, I pull her into bed to sleep next to me. We both doze, half awake and half asleep, well into the next morning.

After breakfast, she has her first bowel movement—a sticky black tar I would rather leave for the nurses than clean myself. But I hold her butt under the faucet and rinse away the poop. It's what a good mother would do, and I'm determined to be a good mother.

All day I'm waiting for something bad to happen. But nothing happens until after dinner when Emersyn comes in. This time she has a team of four people trailing her.

"You ready to turn your tandem on?"

I want to say I'm not. What if it's too much and Lisa can't handle it? What if it's a mistake?

I nod.

She taps a few buttons on her tablet, then looks up at me with a twinkle in her eye. "Valya, I'd like you to meet Lisa."

The familiar white screen as my Casual pushes the room out of my sight. For a second, even Lisa is gone. Then, the game starts.

ABOUT THE CONTRIBUTORS

A born drifter with plenty of dark stories, childbirth is the closest thing to eldritch **Koji A. Dae** has experienced. Now she finds herself strangely settled in Bulgaria with two kids, a cat, and a whole lot of responsibility. She writes about things mothers see from the corner of their hearts and all varieties of human relationships—with each other, with technology, and with the greater universe.

Cristina Bencina is an award winning artist & illustrator living in Aurora, Colorado. Born on Long Island, New York, she studied illustration and received her BFA at the School of Visual Arts in New York City. Cristina currently spends her days with her husband Stephen and two dogs—a cattledog mix named Freya and a tweenie dachshund named Corvo.

Helen Whistberry (they/them) is the pen name for an indie author and artist who began writing after retiring from a long career working in libraries. Their whimsical digital artwork often focuses on the natural world.

CONTENT WARNINGS

Being a work of mature Horror, a degree of violence, gore, sex and/or death is to be expected.

Casual contains scenes of:

Child Sexual Abuse (off-page)

Pregnancy & Medical Procedures

Vivid Anxiety & Depression

Abusive Relationships

Please be advised.

More information at
www.tenebrouspress.com

Grab another Tenebrous title!

Grab another Tenebrous title!

TENEBROUS PRESS

aims to drag speculative fiction into newer, Weirder territory with stories that are incisive, provocative and intelligent; delivered by voices diverse and unsung.

FIND OUT MORE:
www.tenebrouspress.com

@TenebrousPress on social media

HAIL NEW WEIRD LIT.

HAIL THE TENEBROUS CULT.